BAHAMA BURNOUT

BAHAMA BURNOUT

A NOVEL

DON BRUNS

Oceanview Publishing

IPSWICH, MASSACHUSETTS

ISBN 978-1-933515-20-5 (hc)

Published in the United States by Oceanview Publishing,
Ipswich, Massachusetts
www.oceanviewpub.com

2   4   6   8   10   9   7   5   3   1

PRINTED IN THE UNITED STATES OF AMERICA

I dedicate this book to the
Benedictine nuns at St. Martin's Convent.
I admire your hard work and dedication
to the children of the island.

ACKNOWLEDGMENTS

A toast to my traveling partner, Bill Lodermeier, who walked away a winner. Thank you to the Benedictine Nuns at St. Martin's Convent in Nassau, and especially to Sisters Anne and Cecilia. You do great work. Thanks to Sherrie and Terry Manning from Compass Point Studios in Nassau, the greatest studio in the world that doesn't have an "Abbey" in its name. To Justin Bell, I look forward to working with you, and to my family and extended family, especially my wife who is the first editor of everything. I thank you for your support. To the flight attendants on Delta, you're wonderful, and finally thanks to the friendly bartenders, cabdrivers, and Caribbean folk who feed me wonderful food, drink, and stories. I couldn't do it without you.

BAHAMA BURNOUT

1/2 ounce apricot brandy
1/2 ounce banana liqueur
1/2 ounce coconut rum
1 ounce dark rum
1/2 ounce lemon juice
1/4 ounce honey
1 ounce orange juice
1 ounce pineapple juice
1/4 ounce grenadine

Combine all ingredients except dark rum in a blender with 2-3 ice cubes. Pour into a wide-mouth glass. Put rum in brandy snifter, and lay snifter horizontally over wide mouth glass. Light rum with a long match or torch, slowly rotating snifter as volcano of flaming rum pours into wide-mouth glass.

BAHAMA BURNOUT

CHAPTER ONE

The smell of burning rubber hung in the air as the thin black man surveyed the dimly lit room. The twenty-foot long mixing board with its glowing slides and meters gave off an eerie greenish-gold hue, and just beyond the board he could see the glass-enclosed recording studio. He used to mix sound that came from that room. On this very board. Now, they used Pro-Tools and you could get about as much sound off a personal computer as you could from this expensive piece of electronic wizardry.

He'd shut the vacuum cleaner off five minutes ago, and still the odor lingered. Damned rubber drive belt. The smell was even stronger now. He gave the room one more glance. There was a time when he ruled this room. When his ears and his style with the board were in great demand. There was a time, several years ago, when he would tweak the sound, punch the percussion, compress the throbbing guitars, and Highland Recording Studios would release a song, a song he'd engineered, that was already destined to be a monster hit. Times had changed. Music had changed. The bands were engineering their own music now, and he didn't understand the new music anyway. It wasn't music anymore. Not even rock and roll. Just percussive madness that was peppered with grotesque lyrics and repetitive electronic rhythms.

He leaned down and smelled the sweeper. He'd been wrong. The vacuum wasn't the cause of the odor. He'd been relegated to cleaning up other people's messes. On a larger scale, that had been his job as an engineer, cleaning up the sound. Now, they asked him to clean up the studio. On a part-time basis, and the engineering jobs were infrequent at best.

He'd produced the album for the band Johnny Run. Just recently. It was the last project they'd given him, and the album wasn't doing well at all. Deep in his gut, he knew that the project wasn't up to par.

If it wasn't the rubber belt overheating on the sweeper, it must be coming from another part of the building. Or maybe kids, burning old tires or rags back in the alley. Highland Point, a small rise of land about four miles west of Cable Beach, sat directly across from the water. Like a lot of Nassau, it fronted out beautifully, but fell apart behind the scenes. An alley filled with trash and rotting garbage ran behind the old building that housed Highland Recording Studios, and kids were always causing trouble back there.

The man took another whiff and tried to identify the location. He'd blame it on one of his cheap cigars or a bad joint that he'd lit up, but to the best of his recollection, he hadn't smoked anything tonight. Probably the kids. Kids who lived in the cheap stucco homes behind the light blue pastel-colored studio. Kids who stole tires off cars in the village, who stole sea grapes, mangos, oranges, and kanips to sell and buy drugs with their profits.

He shoved the vacuum down a long hallway lined with gold records. Some of them he'd worked on. Robert Palmer, George Thorogood, Rick Ramone, Kid Rock, Jimmy Buffett . . . He didn't bother to look. It was a long time ago, and the plaques just made him sad.

The flash outside the lobby window startled him as he came to the end of the hall. Maybe a car's headlights from the road. But more like a flare, with a fiery brilliance. Then he saw it again for just an instant, a reflection from behind him. At the same time he heard a deep thundering rumble at the rear of the building. He spun around, his chest tight, and he gasped, his breathing raspy. An orange ball of fire had filled the hall he had just stepped out of, and it raced toward him, the oppressive heat sucking oxygen from the air. A mind-numbing explosion drowned out everything around him as he saw a young black man, running full speed, just ahead of the flame. The last thing he remembered was the sharp, intense pain as the window glass shattered and shards hurled from their frames, burying themselves in his body like dozens of knives as the flames consumed his clothes.

CHAPTER TWO

A rusty sixties Cadillac sat up on blocks at the house next door, its wheels bare of tires. "Elvis owned that car." Jonah Britt smiled, his eyes lingering on the eyesore.

"Somehow I find that hard to believe." Mick Sever sipped his Kalick Beer, sitting on a wicker chair on the crushed stone patio outside the studio.

"Lady over there who owns it keeps telling me that. Wants to sell it for ten thousand dollars. Of course, she can't produce the papers. The son who lives with her is a burnout, but he's got stories about that car." Britt rolled his eyes. He reached down by his chair and scratched the ears of a small gray cat. The feline rippled with delight, then walked away.

"Elvis always had General Motors put a small plastic plaque on the dash with the Cadillac logo and his name. I bought one of those plaques for a friend a couple of years ago. The car belonged to his girlfriend, Linda Thompson, after Elvis died."

Britt nodded. "I heard he owned at least twenty Caddies and gave away a bunch more." He flipped his cigarette ash into the colorful landscaping with its frangipani and croton trees and squeezed a lime into his mug, the golden beer shimmering in the bright sunlight.

"So, you like the new place?"

Sever nodded his head.

"It's great."

"Of course it lacks the charm of the old building." There seemed to be a sadness in the deep green eyes. Britt rubbed a spot on his receding hairline. Sever remembered when hair hung down in his eyes. Several years ago. "You know, Mick, the old building had its time and place. This is so much more efficient."

"The gold records?"

"Lost most of them. Just melted down to blobs. We've got a company trying to replicate some of them, and we asked some of the record companies to replace the rest but—" He let the words drift off. Both men were silent for a moment. "There was a lot of history here."

Sever looked back from the wicker chair and table, surveying the new, state-of-the-art studio. "Won't be the same."

"Nothing is, Mick. Christ, the kids today, they can do everything we do here in their bedrooms at home. I mean, the software gets more sophisticated every day. It's hard for us to keep up."

Next door, maybe forty feet away, a dark-skinned, shirtless man in his early twenties stepped out onto a small concrete patio, looked around with a glazed expression, then spotted Sever and Britt, both watching him. He stared at them for a good thirty seconds with that blank look on his face.

Britt finally lifted his arm and waved at the man. "Bernard, the lady's kid. He's got a twin brother who now lives with his father."

He waved back, recognition dawning on his face, then walked toward the two men.

"Did you show your friend the Cadillac, Mr. Britt? He can sit inside if he wants to. It's for sale, you know."

Britt smiled. "I did, Bernard. Told him who owned it and how much you want." He motioned to Sever, putting the reporter on the spot.

Sever gave him a look, then covered with the kid. "Haven't got that kind of money right now, man. And I was never a big Elvis fan." It was a lie, but the kid didn't have to know. Sever had been a huge Elvis fan. One of his biggest regrets was that he'd never interviewed the singer. "Sorry." He shrugged his shoulders.

"Don't tell Etta May that." The young man pointed his finger at Sever. "She loved Elvis. Says he was the first and last really good rocker. A good Christian boy."

Sever glanced at Britt. "Etta May?"

"Bernard's mom."

"Ah. Sorry, Bernard, no sale today."

The young man frowned. "You think about it. If you change your mind, you let me and Etta May know." He walked to the car and brushed some imaginary dirt from the rusted body, then headed back inside his small concrete-block house. He turned just before going in. "I can make you a really good deal."

"Can't swing it, man."

He nodded and walked back into the small house.

"Mom and the kid." Britt laughed. "They're a pair."

"Elvis, a good Christian boy?"

"Should have bought the car, Mick."

"If it had been Elvis's car, I'd have considered it."

Sever drained the rest of his beer as the French doors leading into the studio swung open.

"Jonah, the guys need you in Studio C. They're having a crisis over whether to add strings or just go naked." The forty-year-old woman with shorts, bare feet, and a T-shirt smiled at Mick. The shirt had a two-wheeled bike printed on the chest. The slogan was simple. *Put Some Excitement Between Your Legs. Billy B's Bikes, Nassau.*

"Let me get these guys settled down, Mick. You've got nothing but time, right?"

"Yeah. Nothing but."

Britt pushed himself out of the chair, took a moment to straighten up, and walked into the building as the girl walked out.

"So, Mick, you're doing a story for —?"

"Real mainstream, Rita. *Newsweek*. Stodgy old magazine trying to attract a younger crowd."

She sat down and took a swallow of Britt's beer. "And they want to do a story on our little studio, huh?"

"Highland Recording. It's where the action is."

She studied him, squinting her eyes to avoid the brilliant late-morning sun. "Was, Mick. Not so much anymore." She crossed her tanned legs, and Sever let his eyes drop for just a second. She noticed.

"I'm going to do a little bit of history about the old place, then write about your plans for the new place. Maybe throw in a little bit about home studios, too."

"What about the body?"

Sever paused. "The body?"

"The one they call the 'ghost.'"

"The remains of the person that they found after the fire — they call that person the 'ghost'?"

"They do."

"I hadn't heard him referred to as a ghost. Kind of an eerie tone to the story. Who started it?"

"The locals . . ." She hesitated. "It's an island of superstition, Mick. The Bahamians are superstitious people. Ghosts and things that go bump in the night."

"I've read stories. Christianity mixed with ancient African myths?"

"Oh, yeah. There's Molly Bay, a drowned African slave who haunts Little Exuma Island. There are stories about creatures called "chickcharnies." Three-toed sprites with red eyes who hang upside down from trees on the island of Andros and can turn a person's head around to face backward. It's amazing that in today's world people can still believe these things."

Sever nodded. "The story about the body has been in all the papers back in the States. As I understand it, they found the charred remains of a body. No one knows who it was, but the suspicion was that the ashes were the remains of the person who started the fire. I'm going to mention it in the story. It's what happened, right?"

"God, Mick. Why can't we just get back to business? As much as I want to get to the reason behind the fire, I do not want to revisit the fact that someone *died* in that fire. That was someone's child. It's tragic. And you've got to bring it up again? Can't you just leave it out of your report?"

"Come on Rita. It's already reached legendary status."

She gazed at him with watery eyes. "I suppose."

"So tell me this. Did anyone ever suggest doing tests to find DNA?"

"DNA?" She laughed out loud. "Do you think we have that technology here? This country is barely capable of delivering a newborn. They can't do a decent heart bypass, and you want DNA?"

"Well—"

"Mick, they have no idea who died in the fire. The body was burned beyond recognition. They think it was a young man, maybe fifteen to twenty, but they're not even sure about that. I don't think they will ever find out."

"Do you have any ideas?"

"We've talked about it a hundred times. There were a handful of musicians who had keys. A couple of part-time producers...a guy who did odd jobs around the place, but none of them were regulars, so we don't know who would be missing."

"If it was an outsider who started the fire—"

"Mick, I don't want to go there. Can we change the subject?"

"You pick the topic."

Rita took several deep breaths, looked away from Sever for a moment, then focused on him. "You're going to do a nice profile on Jonah?"

"You and Jonah. Yeah. That's the theme."

She nodded. "We could use the exposure." It was as if the subject of a dead body had been forgotten.

He gave her a broad smile. "You're all about exposure, Rita. Always have been."

"You're full of shit, Mick. And anyway, I've mellowed some since you saw me last."

Mellowed? He didn't think so. There was still a strong edge. "You still providing whatever the boys in the band want?"

She swung her head back in mock surprise. "Mr. Sever, everything but that."

They laughed. "So what's the latest strange request?"

"Not from the boys this time. From a lady singer, you know her ...not a virgin anymore. She's been around for a while, done some movies, she's one of the last ones who recorded in the old place. She and her band worked until about midnight, one o'clock, and Jonah was running the board. They finally gave up the ghost," she shuddered, obviously realizing she'd brought up the word ghost again, "and went across the street to the small hotel."

"And?"

"Nothing big, but I heard the phone at three a.m. I answered it and it's the girl. They're staying at the Compass Point Hotel across the street. Where you're staying. She wants a bikini wax and damn it, she wants it now."

"Wait a minute. You mean *you* gave her —"

"Hell no." She shook her head. "Close your mouth, Mick. I didn't give her anything."

Damn. Now that would have been an interesting story.

"But by God I found someone who would. Took me almost an hour. We had to wake this lady up, but the singer got the wax."

Sever gave her a big smile. "Rita, if you've got enough money, the world just opens up."

She stood. "And they all have the money, Mick. Come on, I want you to see something. I don't think Jonah showed you the latest addition."

They walked into the flat-roofed building, through the chrome-and-steel lobby with the swirling neon patterns on the wall. Past the long, glass-topped desk, the Andy Warhol original painting, and a charcoal sketch of Bob Marley. The insurance had covered some nice art.

"Down this hall." She took his hand and tugged as she picked up the pace. Sever noticed the gray cat following close behind. "Jonah moved his collection of guitars in here. It's like a hall of fame." They reached the door. "Now, before you walk in, remember some of the classics. The guitar that Jonah actually played on Black Medallions' *Lines In Faces*, a Pete Townsend guitar that Pete used on the *Tommy* album, and about thirty others. Take a look." She unlocked the door, pushed it open, reached around Sever, and flipped the light switch. Brightly colored electric guitars were displayed on the walls, hung by some invisible wires and highlighted with pin spot lights carefully placed in the ceiling. A handful of shimmering acoustic guitars were displayed on the floor, in matte-black stands, looking as if they were ready to be picked up and played by their owners in just minutes.

"Right here is one of Eric Clapton's Martin guitars." She reached out her right hand, motioning, but careful not to touch the instrument. "He used this on MTV's *Unplugged* show. And the one with the sunburst finish," she walked across the hardwood floor, pointing to the far wall, "it's a Paul Reed Smith. I think it may be Dicky Betts's guitar, from the Alman Brothers. And over there —" she stopped, the expression frozen on her face.

"Over there what?"

"Oh my God."

Then he saw it. The jumbo Gibson lay face down on the floor against the far wall. He recognized the body style, but it wasn't easy. The guitar was smashed as if someone had stepped on it with a large boot. The neck appeared to be snapped in half and splinters of spruce and mahogany spread from the center of the broken instrument. The small gray cat stalked the instrument, voicing a soft meow.

"Who? Who would, who could do something like this? My God. Who?" She was shaking, an ashen hue to her skin. Sever saw tears rolling down her cheeks.

He walked to the guitar and looked up at the wall. The small engraved plaque simply said *Sheryl Crow Gibson*. "Hey, settle down. It was heavy and maybe the mount didn't hold. Maybe it just fell." He gently knelt, his right leg slightly stiff.

Rita walked over and stared down at the crushed instrument. There was a tremor in her voice when she spoke. "No. It didn't fall. Damn it, Mick, it didn't fall. It's like —"

He waited. She tried to compose herself.

"It's like — someone or something is haunting this place."

"What? Like the ghost? The remains of the body?"

Rita's skin was pale and he realized that it wasn't a laughing matter. Not to her anyway. He'd almost laughed out loud. Almost. But he sensed she was taking this very seriously.

"Jonah won't tell you. He won't. He says there's an answer for all of this."

Sever looked her in the eyes, shining from the tears and the pin spots mounted in the ceiling. "All of this?"

"Every day. I swear, Mick, every day something new happens."

"Like what?"

"I shouldn't tell you."

"If you're worried about—"

"No. If Jonah wants you to know, he'll tell you."

Sever took a deep breath. "Rita, what's been going on?"

"It's just that—" She shuddered again. "That every day something comes up missing, something is disturbed, or—" She pointed at the guitar, lying in pieces on the floor. "Something is destroyed."

"So this isn't the first time."

"No."

"No idea who's doing it?"

"Who or what?"

"*What?*"

"You're going to laugh, Mick."

"Okay."

"I called an Obeah man."

"A what?"

"Obeah man. I know you'll think I'm crazy, but I wanted to see if he could give me any ideas. I mean, we lock this place up every night, Mick. We've got an alarm. And Jonah and I are the only two people with keys."

"Rita, what's an Obeah man?"

"He's an African, a spiritualist. He—" She paused, her eyes avoiding his. "He supposedly can put curses on people and take them off of people. And these Obeah men supposedly can communicate with spirits. I don't know, I am just very frustrated and not just a little scared."

Sever felt the need to lighten the mood. To assure her or at least smile. But the pleading look in her eyes told him to listen. Just listen. "So, what did this guy decide?"

"The Obeah man says there's a good chance the place has a spirit. Maybe it's the ghost, the person who died in the fire. But, maybe it's someone who haunted the old studio. Someone that we never met. Maybe that spirit feels displaced since the fire and is trying to voice its displeasure."

Sever nodded. "Rita, you're serious about this?"

"I don't know, Mick. All I know is, things are happening, and there's no explanation. Jonah thinks I'm crazy, but he doesn't have any answers either."

"So, what's the next step?"

"I can pay this guy to try to remove the spirit."

Sever put his hand on her shoulder. It finally was too much for him. "Rita, you can't be serious. This is the real world, sweetheart. Come on. Could it be enemies? People who would have a reason? There's got to be a real, logical explanation. Don't give me this ghost thing."

"That's what Jonah says."

"Maybe he's right."

"Mick, do you understand me? There's no sign of anyone coming in or leaving."

"If there's one thing I've learned in my years as a journalist, Mrs. Britt, it's that there's always a reason. There's always something behind everything that happens."

"Jonah just keeps saying 'take it easy. Things will work out. We'll figure out who's behind this eventually.'"

"And you will."

"Maybe." She took a deep breath and brushed at her eyes. She looked back at him with some degree of composure. Then she focused her gaze on the floor and the broken guitar. "But Mr. Calm, Cool, and Collected is not going to be happy when he sees this."

CHAPTER THREE

"It's not as bad as all that. You know Rita, she overreacts."

Sever knew Rita. She was somewhat prone to fancy. Still —

"You've been here, to the Compass Point Hotel before?"

"Never."

"Most of the acts stay here in the cottages. Your room?"

"Great. All kinds of African art. It's stuff I really have no appreciation for, but it's comfortable."

"Chris Blackwell started it. You know Chris, don't you?"

Sever nodded. Blackwell, the man who found Bob Marley. The man who started Island Records. He was a legend in the music industry. Sever'd met him once or twice. Hell, he'd met about everyone in the industry.

"Anyway, the pan-roasted grouper is really good. They have this fabulous Creole sauce and fried plantains."

"Sounds good," he said, closing the menu. Sever stared out over the pale blue water, wondering what the weather was like in Chicago. He instantly decided that he really didn't care.

"So," Britt closed his menu as well and took a swallow of iced tea, "you met Bahama Boize. Not much live, but they've got a studio sound that I really think can sell some records."

Sever was reminded of the last group from the island that went big time. The Baha Men. "Who Let the Dogs Out." Sometimes there was no accounting for musical taste. "Who busted up your guitar?"

Jonah Britt took his turn to look out at the water, drumming his fingers on the cloth-covered table. Finally, "We were shut down for almost a year. We had to let people go."

"And?"

"Obviously there was nothing we could do, Mick. It was hard on us, too, Rita and me, but some of these people —" He let it hang.

"What? They took it personally?"

"What I'm trying to say is, I don't know. We had a handful of employees who really had a bad time financially. It could be one of them. I laid people off. That was hard. Then there's always a musician or a band that isn't happy with our work. I mean, we don't hit one out of the park every time."

"But they've paid their money and they expect that hit."

"Yeah. You've been around it. The ego is so thick. I mean, we put out a damn fine product, Mick, but nothing's ever guaranteed. And believe me, we hear from some of those groups. If the song doesn't break the charts, it's our fault. I deal with it every day."

Sever watched the dark-skinned, curvy waitress approach the table, and she watched him watch her, giving him just a hint of an amused smile.

"And what will you two handsome gentlemen be having today?"

Britt ordered two grouper dinners.

"Mr. Britt, you must introduce me to your friend." She held Sever's eyes with her own.

"Tommie, this is Mick Sever. He's a journalist from the States and he's doing a story on the studio." The young, cocoa-skinned woman put her hand on top of Sever's and gave it a very gentle squeeze.

"Mr. Sever. Being that we're just across the street, I hope we'll see more of you." The hand lingered several seconds, then she walked away.

"Is she always that flirtatious?" Britt watched her too, her slender hips swinging as she turned a corner.

"No."

"Tommie?"

"Our own Tommie. Sort of a tomboy name."

"Real name?"

"Tommie. As far as I know."

Sever smiled. Interesting girl. A little young for him, but then again — "Rita said there were a lot of things happening."

"And I told you, she exaggerates." The sun played off the water, bouncing golden flashes on the blue surface.

"So it's not *a lot* of things?"

Britt let out a sigh.

"She's called a spiritualist? Some guy who removes spirits, puts hexes on people?"

"The Obeah man." Britt rolled his eyes. "There's something you have to understand, Mick, she's a little nuts about this."

"You think?"

Britt shook his head and closed his eyes for just a moment. "This guy tells her that there's a spirit living here who has been disturbed. This spirit could be the person who was killed in the fire, or he thinks it might be a lady who has seen and heard terrible things, and in order for either of them to be happy and at peace, they have to be destructive."

"Destructive?"

"I don't pretend to understand it."

"Then she told me that some people were buying into the 'ghost' that died in the fire."

"Makes no sense. The only thing I can come up with is that this guy was inside the building starting the fire."

"They don't have any clue as to who it is?"

"Body was charred. Destroyed. And this is the Bahamas. I mean, you don't get first-class forensics down here."

Sever smiled. He'd been here a very short time, but he sensed that the science was years behind that in the U.S.A. "You didn't have any employees working that night?"

"There were people who had access. Some producer might go in and do some late night mixing. A visiting musician might be there laying down a track. We had a guy — you might remember him,

Bobby Baron — Be-Bop. He did some part-time work for us. He had access. We had a secretary, Maddy, and she went in some nights when she wanted to get caught up —"

"Where are all these people?"

"We heard from some, not from others."

"You haven't heard from everyone?"

"I know, it sounds irresponsible, but we had a lot of keys out, Mick. The people we worked with, we trusted. I can't tell you how many people had access to the old studio."

"And you don't know who might have been there that night?"

Britt rubbed his forehead. "Don't think it doesn't go through my brain every day. It does. I guess we figured the police would sort it out, but I can't imagine the body is someone we knew."

"Still, it just seems you'd hear something."

"I didn't authorize anyone to work that night, Mick, but as I said, a number of employees, musicians, producers, and engineers had keys. And the combination to the security code. So like I said, I suppose that someone, somewhere could have been there."

"Lots of possibilities."

"Not anymore. Nobody's got keys and nobody has the security code."

"Tightened it up, huh?"

"That's what makes it so frustrating about the things going on. Rita and I are the only ones who know how to get in."

"This ghost thing. And the witch doctor?"

Britt rolled his eyes. "The Obeah man."

"Whatever. She won't seriously go through with that, will she?"

"Yeah. Well, that's what I told her. Back it off. But she says this guy told her the spirit, the 'ghost,' was being destructive. Trying to destroy sights and sounds."

"What?"

"Sights and sounds. Maybe people's visions, maybe the sound of music. I don't know."

"What else has happened?"

"No. I've said enough. You'll just use it in your story, and we don't need any more bad publicity."

He was right. They didn't. The fire had almost crippled the business, and they were trying to make a strong comeback. "Anything serious?"

"Tell me you won't print it."

"Off the record, Jonah. I promise you."

Britt swirled his straw in the glass. "The first session we did, two months ago, we were just getting the bugs out of the equipment."

"Okay."

"We worked from about noon to four a.m. It was a Nashville group that was looking for a certain sound they couldn't get there. The Thompson Brothers. We've got this steel drum guy on the island who really does create magic. So I brought him in and we mixed him with this country sound. I was starting to get really good vibes. We busted our asses, and everybody was really stoked, man. The sound was really fabulous, something you don't get every session. We'd play it back, and I'd touch it up a bit, and, man, it was just coming together so well. Sometimes it's magic, man. And this was one of those times. Anyway, as I said, about midnight we broke up. The band left for the hotel. Rita and I cleaned up and had a smoke before we went to bed."

Sever nodded. Jonah and Rita had built a bungalow at the rear of the new building, staying there when sessions were being produced. He'd just had a glimpse, but it was spacious, with two bedrooms, bath, kitchen, and den.

"We got up the next morning, fixed breakfast for the band about ten and went back to the studio." Britt paused. He stared hard into Sever's eyes. "You know how many years I've been doing this shtick? How many, Mick?"

"Twenty at least."

"Twenty-six. I know my way around a studio. Am I right?"

"Jonah, you've mixed some of the best. Your stamp is legendary. What are you getting at?"

"Here's exactly what I'm getting at. I know my way around a

studio better than anyone you know. So, I go into the studio to replay all the digital work from the day before, right?"

Sever nodded again.

"I set the volume — the levels had all been preset, and I turned on the speakers."

"And?"

"Remember what I said? About the spirit being destructive? Destroying sight and sound?"

"Yeah. Crazy stuff."

"You'd think."

"Jonah, just tell me what happened. I'm not going to write about it, okay?"

Britt took a deep breath. He avoided Sever's eyes and looked beyond, staring at something in the distance. "Mick, what happened is impossible. It had all been erased. Every note. Gone."

CHAPTER FOUR

The mail boat pulled up to Potter's Cay Dock, with its yachts, trawlers, haulers, and brawlers. The stooped black man with the long pants, long-sleeved shirt, sunglasses, and pulled-down cap waited his turn, then stepped off the boat. Many of the people from Norman's Cay had luggage, bags, or at least a sack in their hands, carrying some personal possessions. The man had nothing. He glanced at the fish shack, with its fresh catch-of-the-day displayed in ice-filled bins. He was hungry, but satisfying his appetite would have to wait. Paradise Island shimmered in the distance, the casino, restaurants, shops, and ships taunting him. Once, he'd been part of the scene.

He tugged on his cap, walking into Nassau. Norman's Cay would still be there when he returned. The deserted shack that he'd moved into, the sleepy little town and warm sandy beach that had been the playground for Carlos Lehder, the Columbian drug lord who owned the Cay back in the eighties. It would be there. The life of the very rich, the life of the very poor. You could have it anyway you wanted in the Bahamas. And Norman's Cay would still be waiting.

He had no one in the world. Pretty pathetic. To have lived this long and have no friends. To have no one who could understand his plight. To have to rely on this cabal, this group of controlling, aging *soeurs* as his last refuge. This was truly pathetic. High on their hill, they sat. Judging other people's worlds. But he would go there. Thank God they were still there. Thank God.

But damn the circumstances that brought him here. Damn them to hell. The joint he'd smoked several hours ago now was a dull headache, buried just behind his eyes. He was low on weed and down to his last pack of cigarettes. He hoped to rectify that soon.

A van's brakes squealed as the driver swerved to avoid him, and the man recovered from his reverie. He ducked his head and scurried across the street to the sidewalk.

"You should have been dead, asshole." The driver shouted from his vehicle as he stepped on the gas and sped away.

Bay Street was busy as the crowds of tourists moved from shop to shop, paying little attention to a man covered from head to toe. If they'd seen under the bill of the Greek fishing cap, they would have seen the large pair of sunglasses that hid his eyes. He looked up through the glasses only to see the sun-spackled mint green, faded avocado yellow, rose, and powder blue buildings. Merchants who catered to the rich Americans, the wealthy Europeans, the cheap Canadians, and the South Americans with their arrogant attitudes, stood behind counters and waited for the tourists, quietly begging them to part with their pocket change, their credit card limits, and the cash in their pouches securely attached to their belts.

Diamonds, rubies, watches, and souvenirs, the merchants offered them in abundance. He had no need, no desire. He walked toward the hill, with carefully measured paces, trying to avoid the traffic. The driver's shrill voice stayed with him. "You should have been dead, ass-hole." He should have been. Dead.

CHAPTER FIVE

Stretch stretched. And when a six-foot-five guy stretched, the physical mass easily turned into six foot seven, even if only for a couple of seconds. He stood up from the table, ducked as he went through the entranceway to the restrooms, and walked into the men's room. Two guys were just on their way out.

"Stretch?"

He looked. Always did. In their attitude, in the casual way they asked, Stretch? they seemed to know him in a more intimate way. He didn't recognize either of them. Two spike-haired twenty-somethings who wore cutoffs and T-shirts. One featured The Clash, the other was a Green Day shirt. Similar. Could be gay. He'd seen that all in a second.

"Man, this is the last place I thought I'd see you."

He looked down on the five-ten guys. "You *thought* you'd see me?" Sarcasm dripped from his words.

"Uh, no. I meant, if I *did* see you. I never expected to . . ." the young man was lost for words. "What I mean is, I love your music, man. I think between the two of us, we've got all your records."

Four. Four records in five years. Not a major accomplishment. Stretch said nothing, just warily watched the two guys, wondering how long this inquisition would take.

"You're, like, vacationing?"

There was no reason to tell them, but he did. "No. Recording."

The smaller of the men gasped. "No shit? Here? You guys have got another CD coming out?"

Don't go any further. Don't tell these two dweeb fans where he was recording, where he was staying, what he was doing. Just get beyond them. God, he needed a drink. Or a line of coke. Something to put this whole island out of his mind. To some people — the two idiots in front of him — this was a dream vacation. To him it was a means to an end. That was all. There was a fix back at the studio. Jonah would have something. Just get the food and get the hell out of this place.

"The whole band? You're all recording here?"

"Yeah." He really had to go.

"Where, man?"

"There's a studio. I can't say. Look, I've got to — you know?" Maybe the idea that he had to take a piss hadn't gotten through to these two dumb-asses. Deliver him from the mindless fans.

They both stood there, starstruck. Stretch moved to the urinals.

"Man, just like a regular —"

He heard them in the doorway. What the hell did they expect? Then the door opened and closed and without looking, he knew they'd left. For anybody in the band Johnny Run, being recognized was a blessing and a curse. You couldn't go anywhere. And maybe his six-foot-five frame added to the problem. Maybe.

He washed his hands and walked out into the crowded restaurant. He frowned as he walked by the tables. A six-five black guy got stares no matter who he was. Most people figured he was a basketball player, but the close observer recognized him from Johnny Run. Bass player, front man, for America's band. Well, last year's American band. This year, it was someone else. Yet they were back. Johnny Run was back at Highland Studios. Home of the last fiasco. It ate at him. He wanted a hit. His kingdom for a hit. It hadn't happened the last time, and it hurt. He wasn't sure why they'd given Highland Studios another chance, but management had made the decision. God, he needed a fix. A strong drink, anything. Where the hell was the food?

Should have been smarter than to pick the Hard Rock for

lunch, but truth be told, he didn't want fish and peas or watery Bahamian beer. That's what was usual fare over here. This place was American, but then with the greasy-faced tourists ogling him, he just wasn't in the mood. He'd ordered a burger, fries, and a beer to go, and when it arrived he would head back to the studio. There were places he'd rather be.

And then he saw it. He stared at it for the longest time, not sure it was real. Not sure it was one of his. But there it was. It certainly seemed to be one of his bass guitars, hanging on the wall right in front of him. He didn't remember donating it or selling it, or even signing it, but, of course, people had been hitting him up for the last several years and he'd sign just about anything put in front of him. The one time, a girl had typed up a love letter above his signature on a blank piece of paper that he'd signed. More than just a love letter, it was purported to be from him, apologizing for various sexual acts he was supposed to have committed with and on the female. He'd paid some serious money to an attorney and to that bitch to make that problem go away, and hell, it wasn't even his fault. Now, he was careful about who he signed for, and where.

But there it was, his Harley Benton five-string bass with his signature scrawled across the mahogany and maple finish. He studied it up close, trying to see if it really was one he'd played, or just his model. Couldn't tell. And was it his signature? He scrawled. You had to know it was his name, because you certainly couldn't read the handwriting. It looked like his, but he wasn't sure. Might have been forged. Stretch frowned. It was too coincidental. Normally he'd be pretty stoked that he was on display at the Hard Rock, Nassau. But not today.

She brought the burger and fries in a bag, a beer to go in a Styrofoam cup. Finally.

"Do you know where they get the guitars to hang on the walls?"

She shrugged her shoulders.

The Hard Rock Cafe probably had a company that solicited them. Maybe someone had contacted his record company, or maybe

Grant Davis, their former manager, was selling memorabilia just to make a quick buck and stay alive. Maybe. He'd never trusted the weasel.

"Is there anyone who would know?"

She shook her head. Probably didn't give a shit, either. She figured he'd stiff her on any tip since it was a carryout, so she just didn't care.

He handed her a fifty dollar bill just to mess with her mind and walked to the door as two shy teenage girls approached him, holding out napkins and a pen.

"Would you mind?"

He shouldn't. He just wanted to get back to the studio and get away from the people. But sighing, he put the food and drink on a tabletop and signed the proffered scraps of paper. He hated signing, but it was part of the job. At least these scraps weren't big enough for another love letter and lawsuit. He'd signed just about everything. Even body parts. White girls liked to have him sign their breasts for some reason. But you had to use a Sharpie. Regular ink pens were tough to sign on skin. He remembered one girl who had him sign right above her crotch. She'd pulled her jeans down, about as low as she could go without exposing everything, and he'd kneeled down and signed. No more of that shit. Stretch hadn't come this far for that. Signing a crotch, and hell, he hadn't even sampled it.

His rental was parked in the lot, and he set the burger and beer on the seat, started the engine, and pulled out. He crouched, the compact white car's roof a little too close to the top of his shaved head. Checking the rearview mirror, he caught a glimpse of the two young men from the restroom as they got into a rented Toyota and pulled out behind him.

The thought went through his head briefly. Were they stalking him? Did they want to find out where Highland Recording Studios was? He just as easily dismissed the idea. Nassau Paradise Island was a small place and you were bound to run into people on a regular basis.

Stretch drove back toward the studio, humming an AC/DC

song. *Dirty deeds, done dirt cheap.* Somebody had stolen his guitar, and possibly sold it to the Hard Rock Cafe. Damn. How the hell could that happen? It made no sense. Dirty deeds, done dirt cheap.

He took the main road, along the water, past crumbling stucco buildings and concrete piers, new condo complexes, rock caves, and the multicolored Compass Point Hotel.

He wasn't sure where, but he'd lost the two boys. They were no longer behind him. It was just his imagination, anyway. Just one more of the strange things that had happened on the island that were spooking him. Like the spaced-out kid next door to the studio who tried to get Stretch to share some of his grass. Begging him to sit in the old Cadillac and share a joint. And the kid's mother, standing on her porch every time he walked onto the property. She gave Stretch a stare that rattled him. Like a voodoo lady who was fixing him with a curse. The strange kid and his stranger mother definitely spooked him.

And like someone stealing one of his bass guitars. From a locked studio rehearsal room. And Jonah Britt telling him that it couldn't happen. Jonah, telling him it was impossible. There was no way anyone could enter the studio because no one else had a key except Rita. Well his guitar was gone. And now, he'd seen it hanging in a Nassau restaurant. *Dirty deeds, done dirt cheap.*

Stretch wanted to be back in L.A., back in New York, back somewhere where he could get a decent steak, see an American movie, or just hang out at his house. This island was the pits, and he'd about had all he could stand of the place. If the locals didn't drive you nuts, the American tourists would.

And finally, you couldn't trust the people in these little Caribbean countries. Couldn't trust them at all. Actually, it *was* just like back in the States.

CHAPTER SIX

The front door was unlocked. He pushed the handle and it swung open, directly into the white-tiled lobby. The front desk was empty, but if someone *had* been sitting in the rolling desk chair he had a perfectly good excuse to be there. He glanced down the hallway, back to the studios, the little guitar museum, and farther back where the Britts had a small apartment. He saw no one. Somewhere in the recesses of the building, he could hear music. Pieces of music. They were busy recording. He wondered where the ghost was now. Watching him? Sitting on the small couch to his right? You could never tell.

He walked to the reception desk and opened the drawer. In the right-hand corner was a folded twenty dollar bill. Reaching in, he palmed it, putting it in his pocket. Wouldn't they ever learn?

A framed print by singer/painter David Bowie, an expensive, scary, ghostly creature at the foot of a staircase, stared at him from the wall. A ghost. Like the ghost who now haunted Highland Studios. He didn't like ghosts. Especially not the one that now lived here. He'd hated the resident ghost, disliked him his entire life, even before he was a ghost. Envied him, loathed him, and, now that he was a ghost, feared him. Way too much attention when he was alive. And now that he was dead, the son of a bitch still was getting attention. For some reason this picture, this vile painting by Bowie, reminded him of that very ghost. Reaching up with his right hand, he grabbed the bottom of the frame and pulled. The print broke free from its wall hanger, crashing to the ground, the glass shattering on the tile.

His eyes stared down the hall, his ears tuned to pick up the slightest change in the sound. There was nothing. A semisoundproof studio kept the sounds out, and for that he was glad. He took a deep breath and surveyed the lobby one more time. He'd done enough damage for one day, and pocketed twenty bucks in the process. There was no reason to stay. As he turned toward the front door he heard a studio door open down the hall. A heavy door creaking on its hinges.

He dropped to the floor, hoping the quick motion went unnoticed. A shard of glass from the framed print dug into his right hand and he gently turned it over, seeing a thin cut on the fleshy part of his palm. A red rivulet of blood trickled off his skin, staining the white ceramic tile beneath him.

Footsteps clicked down the hallway, sounding closer and closer. Damn. Now it would be obvious that he was responsible for the damage. Abruptly the noise stopped. Now, whoever it was must be standing above him, probably watching and waiting for him to open his eyes and realize he'd been caught. He counted. Slowly. When he got to twenty he opened his eyes, feeling the perspiration on his face and in his hair. God, please, don't let there be anyone there.

His eyes snapped open and he moved them around the sockets, keeping the rest of his body still. Nothing. Not a sign of anyone. And then it hit him. The restroom. One door down the hall. That was it. Someone had simply gone to the bathroom. They hadn't noticed him at all. He let out a long breath he didn't realize he'd been holding and eased up from the floor. The bleeding was minimal and he wiped the hand on his pants. One more glance down the hall and he walked out of the studio, leaving the front door hanging wide open.

It was an old Bahamian superstition. If you leave your door open, an unwanted ghost may take the hint and leave. He'd always wondered why another unwanted ghost might not see this as an opportunity to enter the dwelling. Oh well, it was probably just that. A superstition. The ghost probably wouldn't leave anyway. The son of a bitch would stay forever and haunt him for the rest of his life, but you could always dream.

Hurrying down the walkway to the parking lot he glanced over his shoulder. Nobody was watching. Nobody was following. And he wondered what the apparition was doing right now. Had the spirit seen him? Had the ghost been in the lobby when he took the twenty and smashed the print?

Or was he busy, back haunting the studio? Was he wandering back into the Britts's apartment, looking for mischief? What was it spirits did in the places they haunted? Lost in thought, he turned and almost ran into the tall black man walking toward the studio.

"Hey, dude."

His eyes wide open, he simply nodded, stepped aside, and picked up the pace. He had to start using a little more caution. Someday he might make a big mistake and get himself in a whole lot of trouble.

CHAPTER SEVEN

Sever sat on a stool outside the glass. Behind the glass, the drummer, a white guy with long dreads, sat on his stool, wearing thick headphones, and methodically laid down a monotonous track. The bass player, a tall, thin black man with a bullet-shaved head, ran an intricate bass line to the rhythm.

Jonah stood behind a small mixing console, listening to the sound over two small monitor speakers mounted in the corners of the room. He played with some slides and would occasionally smile or frown, some sensor in his head either approving or disapproving of the sound.

"Can I make a suggestion?" Sever recognized Teddy Bartholomew, the band's new manager, as he walked into the control room.

"No." Jonah Britt never turned around.

"No?"

"When you walk in here, Bartholomew, you're walking into my domain. Sit down and shut up or leave."

The man opened his mouth, then shut it and walked out of the room.

"I don't need that son of a bitch telling me what to do." Britt moved some more levers, adjusting more settings.

Finally Britt spoke into a mounted microphone. "Okay. Let's do a take."

The musicians repeated the bouncy rhythm, and Jonah gave them a positive nod.

"They need a hit or two, Mick."

Sever kept his eyes on the boys behind the glass. "I hadn't been paying attention. They were hot a year or so ago, right?"

"Johnny Run? A couple of years ago, yes. But recently they had a couple of clunkers. Their last album had high expectations but fizzled early."

"They did it here?"

Jonah nodded his head. "Actually, yeah. It wasn't half-bad, but it laid an egg. Barely charted. But this is the first time I've had a chance to work with them. And they've got this washed up jerk of a manager looking over my shoulder every minute."

"I thought you said they did the other album here."

"They did. At the old studio. They wanted it done here, on the island. They saw the list of some of our clients and figured there was — some Bahama magic or whatever."

"And you didn't engineer the sessions?"

"No. Be-Bop did it."

"Be-Bop?"

"Be-Bop. Probably was a mistake, but I was tied up."

Sever raised his eyebrows. "This is the guy you said worked part time for you, right? I should know who he is."

"Nickname for Bobby Baron. An engineer who's been around for a long time. Guy goes back to the days of George Martin, Phil Spector, and Danny Murtz. He started when he was just a teen."

George Martin, the legendary producer of the Beatles. Phil Spector, who produced the Righteous Brothers and so many other groups in the sixties and seventies. And Danny Murtz, who'd been a successful producer but blew his brains out in St. Barts. Sever knew them well, and he respected their work.

Sever had started stringing for the *Chicago Tribune* when he was just a teen, writing articles about bands, concerts, records, and yes, producers and engineers. He knew their stories. And he knew the people who hadn't made the transition, hadn't kept up with the trends. This industry spit out old-timers every day. Old-timers like Be-Bop. If they couldn't keep up, they were on the outside.

"And why didn't you do the sessions?"

"I had another group. Timing issue."

"So, Be-Bop is pretty good on the boards?"

"Dated. You know. Grew up doing disco. Sessions with K.C., Donna Summer, Abba. Never embraced new technology, never embraced the new sound. So he gets a few gigs here and there, but—"

"You said he works for you?"

"He did. Produced for us once in a while and did some odd jobs. Probably was a mistake to put him on Johnny Run's last project. Not probably. It was a mistake. You know, sometimes things work out and sometimes they don't." Britt looked back at the board, studying it as if to ignore the other problems.

"They blame him for the record tanking?"

"Yeah. Maybe they blame me too."

"So why are they back?" Why would Johnny Run blame Britt and Highland Studios for their lack of success on the last CD and then come back? It didn't make any sense.

"Because I said I'd personally do the gig. The contract calls for me to do the entire project. From the mix to the final edit. A lot is riding on this, but it's going to be one hell of a sound. Really. As long as Teddy Bartholomew stays out of my way."

And because Jonah Britt cranked out hits, most of the time, it should put Johnny Run back on top. Sever knew what Britt was capable of. It was one of the main reasons he'd come over to do the story. There was a certain magic on a project when Jonah Britt was behind the board.

"Where is he now?"

"Who?"

"Be-Bop. Bobby Baron."

"When the studio burned down he disappeared. I figure he got another gig, maybe in the States. That's the other thing, man. He wasn't that reliable. You know, he'd show up for a week, then disappear for two. Right now I wouldn't have much work for him anyway."

"Man, I'd think with your reputation, you'd have groups beating down the doors."

"Reputation? Yeah, but as I said, Mick, with new technology, these guys can do a lot of it themselves. And save some money."

"But not get the sound you get."

"You might be right. Anyway, I'd like to think that I had *something* to do with it. If this band is going to have a hit, I'd like to think they came here because of me, but to be honest with you, a lot of it is just a chance to come over here when the weather's cold in the States. There's a lot of truth in that too."

"The big guy —"

"Marcus James, alias Stretch."

"I heard him grumbling to the drummer earlier about somebody stealing his base guitar."

Britt glanced up at the speakers and potted the sound down to where he could hear it without drowning in it. "You've got to get off this trip, Mick. Everything isn't sinister. He claims he's missing a guitar. Honestly, I doubt it. I don't think anyone broke in here and stole it. He's just not sure where he left it. But, we do have kids who live behind here, and vandalism is common in the neighborhood."

"You've got an alarm system, you and Rita live here when you've got a band you're working with. Seems to me it should be pretty safe. Instead, you've got a valuable guitar that is destroyed, tapes that are erased, and now, possibly a stolen bass."

"I told you —"

"Jonah. You've got somebody who is messing with you. These three things are —"

"Oh hell, there's more than that." The music stopped and Britt turned up his microphone, looking through the glass at the players. "Pick it up at the last bar. Right where Sonny plays the triplet on the snare."

Sever was impressed. Britt could hold a conversation, listen to his rhythm section, and not miss a beat. Literally, not miss a beat.

They counted four beats and started again, flawlessly.

"You already know that Rita thinks the place is haunted. But my guess is, it's drugs. These kids. They come in and steal some stuff to sell and buy drugs, or they come in because they're high and they cause some trouble. You know, it's upsetting, it's irritating, it's disruptive, but it's not ghosts and it's not someone out to get us, Mick. Believe me, we'll get through it. Really."

The small cat wandered into the room, rubbing his furry body against Britt's leg. The engineer ignored him, and the cat rubbed some more.

"We've been friends for a long time, man." Sever caught his gaze and held it.

"What?"

"You're having problems, Jonah. I really think someone is deliberately screwing around with you and Rita."

Sever heard the last three definitive beats. Bam, bam, bam.

"All right guys," Britt was talking into the mic again. "Let's do it one more time. We need about three of the same tracks to get one good one. Here come the clicks." He flipped a switch and the digital click track started. After eight beats the drummer slammed his set with the thick drumsticks and the repetitive rhythm started again, both of the musicians following the digital rhythm in their headsets.

"Well?"

"It's none of your damned business, Mick. I need to make this place a success. As big as it was twenty years ago. So can't we please just leave these minor inconveniences out of the story?"

Sever noticed the resignation in his expression and his tone of voice. "Tell me what else has happened."

"No. Nothing else happened. Forget it. We're cranking out some first-class shit here. That's the truth and that's the story."

The sound engineer spun around and focused on the two rhythm players. They played, stone-faced, the same rhythm tracks they'd played before. The stoic performance that gave the finished product a wild, uncontrollable sound on record. On stage, these guys would be beasts, prowling the boards, giving a raucous, lewd, crude show. In the studio, it was attention to detail. Perfection.

"Jonah. I want to write a story that reflects what's going on. The fire, the rebuilding, and the successes you've had. But, man, you've had some troubles. I think people are interested in those as well." Sever tried to engage the man's eyes. It was important to have him looking at him. Looking into his soul. "Rita thinks this place is haunted. There's something there, Jonah."

"Drop that shit! Mick, business is down fifty percent from two years ago. Fifty percent, man. It's all because of the fire. If you start going off on the petty problems we've experienced, it's just going to make matters worse, man. Can't you see that?" Britt held out his hands. "We're just getting the business back. We're rebuilding. Don't screw it up for us."

Sever was too old. Had been in the business too many years. Had too many friends in the business. A journalist could lose his integrity in this business, due to location, friends, and personal feelings. And if nothing else, Sever was a journalist. There were no favors in being a journalist. None. Well, maybe a couple here and there.

"All right, Jonah. I won't write it, I won't print it."

The rhythm section finished with the bam, bam, bam, and Britt flipped on the microphone. "Let's call it a wrap. I can work with those two sessions."

"So it's the kids out back?"

"Yeah. It's like a gang of them. And I think they may have caused the fire too. On purpose, by accident, no one's ever been able to prove it, but it would be my guess. It makes a hell of a lot more sense than the ghost theory."

"And the burned body may be —"

"One of the teenagers from back in the alley. I really don't want to keep going over this, Mick."

"But no one has reported a kid missing?"

Britt gave him an exasperated look, and Sever decided to drop it. For now.

"Why did you chose to rebuild *here*?"

"I own the land. I couldn't just walk away from it. And we're across from the water, so the location's really good."

Sever studied the man, his graying hair brushing his collar. The situation was wearing on Britt. Lines in his face, shadows under his eyes, and pale skin in the sun capital of the Caribbean. Hell, they were both too old to keep doing what they were doing. "So, it could be a disgruntled employee, a pissed off rock act, or the kids out back? I'd help if I could, Jonah."

"Look, just the fact that you're doing the story will help. A positive story, Mick. Positive. The word gets out that we've got a good location and put out a good product, we'll be fine. A couple of gold or platinum records on the wall, and we'll be back on top. My job right now," he paused and motioned to the two musicians coming out of the door to the glass-enclosed studio, "is to make Johnny Run's new CD a number-one hit. And that's the focus. That's for the record, Mick. You can quote me."

"You got a good take on that, Jonah?" Stretch came out from the glass room.

"I'm going to ask you to maybe do a little melody on a couple of lines on that song. Double bass kind of thing."

"I like that. We can synth it during the shows."

"Exactly what I had in mind, Stretch."

The big man nodded at Sever.

"Stretch, meet Mick Sever. He's doing a story on the new studio."

The bass player watched him for a moment, then tentatively reached out his beefy hand and Sever got ready for a squeeze. Instead the giant was almost tender with his shake. As if an apology was in order, he smiled at Sever. "I make a living with these hands, Mr. Sever. Got to protect them."

"I think all three of us use our hands in our work. I'm looking forward to hearing how your new material comes out."

"Not as much as we are. The last album didn't do so well." He shot a glance at Britt. "You probably know that already."

Sever nodded.

"I think we all learned a lesson. Go with someone who's got good ears."

Sever saw the look between Britt and Stretch. Just a recognition glance that showed each of them was aware of the situation.

"You're around the business a lot. Let me ask you something," the bass player looked down at him. "You got any idea where Hard Rock Cafe gets their guitars and memorabilia?" Stretch towered over Sever, a quizzical look on his face.

"I think a lot of it is donated. By the musicians, record companies, publishers, and they probably buy some of it."

"You think they've got documentation on that stuff?"

"Yeah, I'm sure they do."

Britt laughed out loud. "Maybe that's why they don't have Elvis's Cadillac in there. Bernard can't produce the documentation."

Stretch glanced at Britt. "Yeah, Elvis's Cadillac. The car next door. The two kids told me Elvis owned it, but I didn't believe them."

The engineer shrugged his shoulders. "I don't believe it either. But those kids and their mother swear it's true."

"They really believe that? Elvis owned it?"

"Ettta May and her kids seem to think so," Britt nodded.

Stretch agreed. "Etta May. She's the kids' old lady —"

"Yeah. They're twins. The other one, *the straight one*, he went to live with his old man about a year ago. She got stuck with the weird one."

"She scares me. I come over here and she's standing in the doorway, giving me a witch's eye. I don't think she likes me."

"She doesn't like anybody. Thinks that all of us are out to harm her strange son. And he's already around the bend."

"What the hell are *we* going to do to her kid?"

"It's a long story, Stretch. Over the years Etta May claims that the music, the lifestyle, the drugs have all had a negative influence on Bernard."

"Why don't they move?"

"She already shipped one of the kids out. And you know, if they got a lot of money for the car, she and Bernard would probably take off, too."

"How much for an Elvis car?"

Britt shrugged. "Just for kicks I looked up a couple one time.

Anywhere from $15,000 to $115,000. Like anything, it depends on the shape of the car."

Sever smiled. Stretch wasn't even born when Elvis died, but the legend of the King lived on. "Why do you want to know about the Hard Rock? Does Johnny Run want to donate some memorabilia?" Sever kept the conversation alive.

Stretch shook his head. "We apparently already did. My bass guitar, same model that was stolen from here, it's hanging on the wall with my signature on it."

"So why the question?"

"I'm missing a guitar. According to Jonah, there's no way in hell someone could break into a rehearsal room and steal it, but it's gone."

Jonah held up his hand. "I didn't say it was impossible. Improbable, yes. Rita and I are the only two who have keys to the new place."

"Well, it seems strange, Jonah. The guitar is gone. I'm not making that up. It's gone. And you know what? It's not the money. I mean, they're not cheap, but I can always buy another one. Hell, I travel with two already. But it's the rumors. That's what it is, Jonah."

"Rumors?"

"Rumors. That's what's bothering me. Rumors and stories that there are a lot of strange things happening at Highland Studios. Starting with the fire, a dead body, your creepy neighbors, and a lot of other things that you apparently can't explain. I just wondered if this is just one more of those things, Jonah."

Britt frowned. "I don't know where you got your information. Rumors in this business can be dangerous, so I'd be careful who you start telling that to. Whatever has happened doesn't involve you, your band, or the project we're working on. You'll still get the best damned record we're capable of." He was breathing faster and speaking louder. "But I can tell you this. Our insurance will cover your precious guitar. We'll get you all of your money back, Stretch, so get over it. Okay?"

Stretch nodded, a slow, methodical nod. He reached into his T-shirt pocket and pulled out a rolled joint. "Don't worry, Jonah, I know the rules. This is for outside. And, by the way, I'll get over it. But right now I'm trying to figure out one thing."

"And what's that?"

"A guitar, identical to mine, is hanging at the Hard Rock, with my signature on it."

"And what?"

Sever was surprised at the tension in the room. Minutes ago there was a team effort. An effort to put out the best sound possible. Now, a lot of friction over a missing guitar. He stood back, taking mental notes.

Britt asked again. "So you have a guitar at the Nassau Hard Rock. What's the problem with that? I've had groups in here who would die to get some memorabilia at the Hard Rock."

The big man stared at him for several seconds. "The problem with that, *Mr. Britt*, is that I don't remember ever signing a guitar, and I don't remember ever giving it to them."

CHAPTER EIGHT

Pulling his cap down low and adjusting the sunglasses on the bridge of his nose, he stood just down the road, glancing up as the bright Bahamian sun lit the big whitewashed building, casting long shadows into the courtyard. The structure stood tall and proud, with swaying palms gently waving above. The upper level was empty. That's what he'd heard. No longer occupied by anyone. Where there had been twenty scrappy, unruly kids, now there was no one. And there were only eleven of the women now living on the lower level. New recruits were hard to come by.

Dropping his cigarette on the ground and grinding it out with his heel, he once again tugged on the brim of his cap, wondering if they would recognize him. Knowing that they would have to accept him kept him walking. This was going to be tough.

To the front porch, just around from the circular driveway. The spotty grass grew in clumps between shady palms, and he could see the sweet corn in the garden. About knee high.

He hesitated. Right now he could walk away, back to the dock, and forget the whole thing. Right now he could step back and no one would know he'd ever been here. Or, he could take this one chance to right a wrong. He could take care of the business he'd threatened to do for the past year. Taking a deep breath, he glanced once again at the vacant second story, remembering it well.

He knocked. Gently, because it hurt his hands. The breeze through the trees whispered and occasionally he heard a car, but there was a peacefulness that he remembered. A sense that there was refuge here. He knocked again, and then a third time. His knuckles throbbed. Maybe no one was home. He'd tried. He'd made the journey, he'd made the effort. He could live with that. So they were out, shopping, doing whatever.

The door swung open, and the small black woman studied him. She studied as much as she could, as he stood there with his cap pulled low and his sunglasses hiding his face.

"Yes, can I help you?"

It was Sister Annie. Maybe seventy now? They'd all be in their late sixties or early seventies. And suddenly he started to cry. It hit him all at once. And he was at the same time embarrassed and grateful. Tears welled up behind the glasses and he took a deep breath, trying to stifle the emotional response, because that's all that it was. And there was no room for emotions. He was here on a mission.

"Sister Annie," choking back the sobs, "it's me." He hesitated, never comfortable at all with this part of the process. He'd avoided almost anyone who knew him for a long, long time. The man pulled his cap off, and removed the glasses, wiping the tears from his eyes.

She gasped and looked away for just a moment. He stiffened, knowing what she saw. The scars, the mottled skin, the disfigured ear, and the grafts that had never taken well. She looked again, a grim smile on her face.

"Do I know you?"

"It's Bobby, Sister. Bobby Baron."

She hesitated, just for a moment. He watched her clenched jaw slowly relax. Then, she put out her arms and stepped toward him, gently hugging the man. The first genuine physical contact with someone in almost two years.

"Bobby? Robert? My goodness."

And what more could she say? "A sight for sore eyes?" "You're looking well?"

They stood there like that for thirty seconds or more. Finally she stepped back, avoiding a stare. Sister Annie turned to the doorway and shouted. "Sister Estelle, Sister Mary, it's Robert. Bobby Baron, come to pay us a visit."

There was a rustling inside and the two sisters rushed out, both stopping short when they saw him.

"Robert." Sister Mary nodded. "You're back."

He returned her nod. A lot of tension, a lot of questioning looks as Sister Estelle came running to the doorway.

"Oh, Lord, it's Robert." Sister Estelle never gave a moment's hesitation. She gave him a wide smile. "Welcome, Robert. It's good to have you home."

"Robert?" Sister Alice stood back in the hall, warily watching him as she walked to the doorway. She studied him for a moment, and he detected a slight shudder. There was an awkward silence as she adjusted. He stood there, his scarred hands shoved into his pockets, and he wished he had kept the hat and glasses on.

"You didn't make your bed, young man." She gave him a stern look. God, he remembered those looks. He remembered the pointed finger that she now thrust toward him. He remembered the guilt, the confusion that he always felt.

Her stern look softened. She gave him a thin smile, disguising her shock. "Therefore, Robert, there will be no dessert for you tonight. Do you understand me?"

No dessert.

"Well?"

He knew the routine. Wasn't it strange? All these years, all the walls and barriers that had been put up and torn down. And now, here he was, face-to-face with what he and the others had called "the Mafia." The organizers, the tyrants, the Catholic mob who ran the convent. The ladies he'd despised, plotted against, hated, and agonized over. The ladies that he'd —

"Robert —"

— loved.

"Sister Alice, I've come to . . ." he felt the well of tears spring up again as he fought to hold them back.

Sister Alice reached out, her hands stretching. It was the invitation he'd dreamed of and he walked into her embrace.

CHAPTER NINE

Sever walked across the street, carefully checking the bending road for any speeding cars. Someone had tried to run him over on a street in downtown Chicago several months ago, just before he'd headed for St. Barts, and now he was a little more cautious than usual when he stepped onto a street or sidewalk.

He glanced up at the studio, noticing a Royal Bahamian Police Force car parked next to the rusty Cadillac. Everything seemed quiet and peaceful. Birds were chirping and, if you listened carefully, you could hear the faint sound of the surf on the Compass Point beach.

A cop car. That didn't look good. With all the trouble the Britts had been having, a cop car might spell more problems. Pausing for a moment, Sever once again surveyed the land and the studio, then walked past the front porch to the rear of the building. Another small porch with some chairs and a table, and an alley that ran behind were all that he saw. Several small houses and sheds, and a couple of beat-up compact cars littered the landscape. There was no one around.

Walking back to the front of the studio, he entered the reception area. No sign of Rita or Jonah. Strange. A cop car, the unlocked door, and nobody home. He slowly walked toward the hallway, glancing down to the room where Johnny Run had been working the night before. It had been less than twenty-four hours ago. Music was being made, an album was being produced, and tensions had mounted between Stretch and Jonah Britt over a stolen guitar. Lots of elements, but all of them real and palpable and yet now there was an eerie feeling about the place. It was too quiet. As if a supernatural presence was in the building, watching him, waiting for him to step just a little farther into the bowels of the studio.

Sever shook it off, embarrassed by the feeling. This idea of a ghost haunting the studio, and the Obeah man. It was crazy. "Jonah?" he called.

"Jonah?" he called again.

Nothing.

Again, the eerie silence. This was a building that was designed for noise, for music, for the celebration of sound. And there was nothing. Sever felt a brief chill.

The hollow sound of his own voice was the only noise. "Jonah?" This time a little louder. Finally he walked down the hall, his footsteps echoing off the empty walls as his shoes slapped the ceramic tile floor. Past the studio restroom door and six steps more he stepped into the doorway of the first studio. As he glanced around the empty room, another chill went through him. It was so unlike him. Sever could face about anything, any situation, and here he was letting the thought of this phantom throw him off. He was upset with himself.

The front door had been unlocked, and nobody seemed to be home. Safe? Secure? Hell, anybody could walk in and take whatever they wanted. *Do* whatever they wanted. And where was this cop?

He walked twenty feet down the hallway to the next studio. Hesitantly he leaned into the doorway and held his breath. There was the engineer, Jonah Britt, slumped in his seat, earphones on and his eyes closed. Sever froze for a second.

"Jonah?" He moved quickly, entering the room and walking up to the man. Maybe check his pulse — feel for a heartbeat? No movement. Jesus, let him be alive.

And then Sever saw the tiniest movement. The head moved ever so slightly. The movement was barely perceptible, but it was a steady rhythm. He put his hand on Britt's shoulder.

He spun around, startled. "Mick."

"Everything all right?"

He took the headphones off. "Can't hear a thing with the cans on."

That seemed to be a possible problem.

"Good sound, Mick." He pushed a lever, a couple of buttons, and eased himself from his chair.

"You scared the hell out of me. I thought you were passed out, or . . ."

"Dead?"

"Yeah. Maybe."

"I was just inside my head, man. Listening. Working out the music."

"The door is unlocked. Open."

Britt squinted and nodded his head. "Yeah. I should be more careful."

"You think? With all the problems you've been having?"

"No, you're right."

"You're crazy, Jonah. You're asking for someone to come in here and do whatever they want."

"You're dead-on, man. Okay. I've got to be a little more careful."

"And Jonah, what's with the cop car outside?"

"There's a cop outside?"

"Parked next to the Cadillac."

"Ah, yeah. Eric." Britt nodded.

"Eric."

"Yeah. He probably spends more time than he should over there."

"There being where? He's not here? I thought there was some sort of a problem. I mean, there's a cop car, the door's not locked, it looks like no one is home."

"Where is Etta May's place."

"Why is a cop at Etta May's?"

"As far as I can figure out, he's dating her."

"The cop is dating . . ."

"Etta May. Yeah. And the cop — he's our own Barney Fife. He was one of the guys who investigated the fire here, and he met the nosey neighbor. The two of them were around each other almost every day for a while. She'd have lunch packed for him, help him out, always at his side, kind of like she was watching out for him. I mean she was right there. Over his shoulder most of the time. And now they've become somewhat of an item."

Sever mentally pictured the matronly, plump woman. Not his type.

"Guy's name is Eric Evans. Nice man, but not too bright. Probably a good match for Etta May."

"Investigated the fire? For criminal charges?"

"Yeah. You know, he's trying to find out who burned the place down. And as far as I know, he's still working on the identity of the burned body. I told you, I was hoping they'd have an answer by now. Eric headed up the investigation, and I assume he's still putting pieces together. But he just putters around, and of course, he hasn't found anything yet. Probably never will. But now he's got a reason to hang around. Etta May." Britt rubbed at his temples with his index fingers.

"Strange bedfellows."

"It's not like back home. God, Mick, things move slowly down here. It could be years before they find an answer. But in the meantime," he paused, a slight smile on his face, "it's not all bad having him over there on a regular basis. He keeps an eye on our place."

Sever stared at him. "Keeps an eye on your place? My God, Jonah. How can you say that? From what you and Rita have been telling me about what happens here, Eric is apparently useless."

Britt took a deep breath and let it out. "Yeah. But if he wasn't over there, over at Etta May's, maybe it would be worse."

Worse? Sever shook his head. Optimism was one thing, but Britt took it just a little too far. Sever'd been involved with a lot of cops and he'd always felt that a useless cop was just that. Useless. "It was funny, and a little bit scary seeing the cop car and Elvis's Cadillac parked next to each other."

"I don't know. Rita likes the arrangement. She thinks the cop car is a deterrent. If whoever is breaking in sees that a cop is nearby, maybe they'll think twice."

"And how's that working out for you?"

"We're not quite sure. As you pointed out, the poltergeists still seem to show up. And, my guess is that Eric the cop may have been there when two of the incidents happened."

"So, having this cop next door is —"

"You're probably right, Mick. It's useless. I know it and you know it, but don't tell Rita. She's looking for anything that gives her hope."

"Have you told Eric? Made a police report?"

"Not everything. But we've called the department a couple of times, for all the good it does. The last two times they didn't bother to even come over and check it out." Jonah shook his head.

"Eric, huh?"

"What am I going to tell him? Somebody erased a session? I can't prove that. The other day a picture was smashed in the lobby. Could have fallen. The busted guitar? There's no evidence that someone smashed it. And I'm not sure that Stretch ever had a bass guitar in that room where he claims it was stolen. It's just the frustration of it, Mick. Just the frustration."

Sever was silent. Didn't want to burn the interview.

"Oh, and speaking of next door," Britt stood up, and walked to a wall shelf. He picked up a DVD case and handed it to Sever. "Check this out. Two hundred Cadillacs."

Sever took the DVD. "You're kidding. This is about Elvis? How many Cadillacs?" He stared at the cover of the video.

"Maybe two hundred. This guy did a video with interviews and pictures about the stuff Presley gave to people. Claims it might have been as many as two hundred of them." Britt sat back down and was pushing levers, watching the computer screen as the bar graphs climbed up and down.

"Two hundred Cadillacs that he *gave away*?"

"That's the story."

Not including the ones he kept? Sever tried to picture two hundred Cadillacs, lined up side by side. One hell of a lot of Cadillacs. General Motors must have been extremely upset when the King passed away. Sever stared at the DVD cover. A picture of the King and the fin of a Cadillac. Two hundred Cadillacs. In today's dollars — he didn't want to think about it.

"And speaking of Etta May, she stopped me this morning. Complained as usual."

"About what?"

"About the people going in and out at all hours of the night. About the possibility of people doing drugs and the loud noises. How it influences that basket-case kid of hers. Usual bullshit."

"I suppose she could call the cops."

Britt laughed. "If she didn't already have one there."

"If I were you, I think *I'd* complain about the rusty piece of crap in her front yard."

"Well, I mentioned that and that's when she told me that Elvis owned or bought two hundred Cadillacs. She walked into her house and brought the DVD out. Told me to watch it. Jesus, Mick. Two hundred. Do you believe that? And *she* wants me to buy that damned car, too. Just like her two kids did. They used to double-team me and half the recording acts that walked through the door. The twins would offer to give guided tours of the car. Since the one brother moved, Bernard is always trying to get me to make an offer."

"How much do they want?"

"Mick. It's not worth ten bucks. It's not Elvis's car, okay?"

"So they're just holding out for a couple of dollars?"

"Oh, I think Etta May believes it has value."

"She needs the money?"

"I think she envisions moving away from here. She says it will help pay for her son's medical expenses."

"Medical expenses?"

"Mom says he's got some psychological problems. Hell, I caught him the other night, out by the road, howling at the moon. Seriously."

Sever smiled. "I thought the kid was a little off."

"Oh, he's off all right. You know they're both off right away when he's trying to sell a junkyard dog for a Cadillac price. I've heard her ask for prices in the ten and fifteen thousand dollar range. Hell, it's obvious the thing won't run. You'd be lucky to get a junkyard to haul it away unless they charged *you*."

Sever laughed.

"Listen to this." Britt lifted a lever and lush music filled the room. A lead guitar faded in, as if appearing from nowhere, and there was the steel drum, fading in, fading out, giving the country song a Caribbean flavor. It was mystical, marvelous, and magical all at once. No vocal track. Not yet. But the track was hypnotizing, and Sever was enthralled.

Britt smiled at him. "Pretty special, isn't it?"

"It is."

"I'm laying in the vocals this afternoon."

"And what about Johnny Run?"

"Working on them this evening. They'll be in around five, and we'll work until maybe two o'clock. Maybe later."

Sever shook his head. "Do you ever keep regular hours?"

"Mick, those are regular hours."

Sever nodded. The older he got, the more he tired of the late nights. "Jonah, what was the deal with Stretch's bass guitar?"

"Deal?"

"What makes him think somebody actually stole it from a rehearsal room?"

Britt eyed him, pursing his lips and squinting. "Off the record?"

"You keep doing that, there won't be any record."

"Yeah. I'm sorry, but I want it off, Mick."

"Okay."

"Stretch had a bass in here last week. Different than the one he played today, but same make and model. He claims he left it in the room across the hall."

"Claims?"

"You can't quote me on this, Mick. The man has been known to do some blow, to smoke too much, and he's a legendary drinker. Also, you may have noticed, Stretch has a chip on his shoulder about this place. He's laid the blame for last year's record on my shoulders, and to be perfectly frank, I think he's looking to hang whatever he can on me."

"So he's —"

"Not the most trustworthy guy out there. Anyway, we lock all the studio doors with a key every night. If there's a break-in, I want it to be as difficult as possible for the intruder to walk away with anything."

"So what are you saying? It's possible the guitar was in the room?"

"The locked room? That room was still locked the next morning. There are only two keys, and Rita and I are the only ones who have them."

CHAPTER TEN

A Rolex. Solid gold band, the Presidential model. He stared long-ingly. It was on his wish list two years ago. But things hadn't gone well. And even at that time he knew he was close to being fired.

"Mr. Smith?"

He heard the voice, but paid no attention. Then he remembered. He *was* Mr. Smith. Not Grant Davis, but Mr. Smith. Certainly he could have been more original with his manufactured name, but what the hell. They'd told him to be discreet, so he'd made up the name.

"We can offer you a very attractive price on this watch."

Like that would work. With his financial situation. No way.

"Or, we have the stainless and gold band and—"

"No."

"Mr. Smith, we have an attractive finance package that would—"

"I said no."

Nothing left to say, he spun around and walked out. His life had been destroyed through absolutely no fault of his own. He slammed the door shut, hearing the glass rattle in the frame.

Davis stumbled down Bay Street, with its tourist shops and the Rum Cake Factory. He'd had a little too much to drink, a little too much to smoke. He was woozy, off his game. And he laughed out loud. He didn't even have a game. Hell, it was time to get off the island, back to New York or L.A., and find what was real in his world. *Almost* time to do that.

However there were a couple more jobs to do. A couple of things to accomplish. Talk to the band, and see if there was any chance of getting his job back. That wasn't likely, but they were all here. They were assembled, and he had a chance to at least approach the subject. Go to them and promise to get a little more control over the new project. Get them to fire the new guy and hire him back. Maybe they'd listen. Maybe.

And, he was here because the syndicate wanted him here. He'd lost a lot of money investing in Johnny Run's big fiasco last year, but not nearly what the syndicate had lost. They blamed him, and expected him to turn it around. Now how the hell was he going to do that when he didn't even work for the band?

Be in Nassau, and be discreet. Well, fuck them. He wasn't going to pussyfoot around anyone. Who the hell did they think they were, demanding that he take charge, and push this new project to the top? It wasn't even his project anymore.

Seven blocks to the cheap rooming house. He pushed the key into the slot and held the door handle for support. Very woozy. Very unsteady.

"Grant."

Scared the hell out of him. Somebody's booming voice. Like some scary movie or something. The room was pitch-black. The only light was in front of him through the slatted blinds, and he could make out the large silhouette of whoever was sitting across the small room. His heart doubled speed.

"There's a lot of money riding on you. And you're out looking at jewelry?"

"Jesus." Part prayer, part fear. His religion was based somewhat on fear.

The figure holstered what appeared to be a cell phone and stood up, towering above six feet. "We lost a lot of money. You. Me. Our associates."

"I understand." Had to be talking about the record.

"You were in a position to make suggestions. You were in a position to set the agenda."

He nodded. "But, as you know, the CD didn't do that well. I'm a good example of what happened. You may know I'm no longer their manager? I was fired." Well, of course, they knew. And they knew his prospects weren't very good. He needed this project to come in more than they did. His investment needed to pay off. "At the moment, I don't even have a job, so I understand, okay? I mean, *you* understand that the buying public can be fickle and . . ."

"Instead, you shrugged your shoulders, Grant. You gave the project a basic 'oh, what the hell.'"

Davis wasn't exactly sure what he was talking about. Maybe if he'd smoked a little less, had a couple fewer drinks —

"You were in a position to make millions. Millions of dollars for every partner in the group."

Davis nodded. "I did everything I could. I explained that on the phone. Look, I came here because somebody asked me to help, but I'm not sure —" his eyes adjusted to the dim light and he took three steps to the bed and sat on the edge. "And who the hell are you? How did you get in here?"

"But you didn't pay attention to business, did you? Did you, Grant?"

He shook his head. "Arc we talking about the same thing? Johnny Run's CD? I tried my best. Please, understand that. I lost as much as anyone." He was defending, big time. What else could you do with a six-foot-plus giant telling you off?

"So, we talked and the backers are willing to give you one more chance."

Now Davis was sure. The big guy was talking about the record. Johnny Run's last record. This guy was representing the syndicate. And it was only a record, for God's sake. A simple record. With the potential to earn a lot of money, of course, but a piece of vinyl nevertheless.

"What do you expect from me? I told you, I'm not employed at this time."

"You were the manager for five years. Five years, Grant. You have a lot of history, a lot of insight into what makes that band work."

"Maybe."

"Maybe? We think you do. That's why we asked you to be here while Johnny Run was recording. Because we believe you still have influence. If you don't have any, then get some. And if that sounds like a threat, so be it." He paused, letting his message sink in. "Grant, do you know how many records that Spears girl has sold?"

Davis closed his eyes. This guy was going to dazzle him with Britney Spears trivia?

"Over eighty-five million. Eighty-five million records for God's sake, Grant. All we asked was for you to give us one good album."

"Listen, I tried to . . ."

"U2, a hundred seventy million albums. Metallica, nine hundred million. I'm pretty sure we didn't come close to that with Johnny Run's last effort."

"It was one album. Not every album can . . ."

"Brian Johnson's debut with AC/DC, *Back In Black*, has sold almost forty-five million albums, Grant. Not bad, eh?"

Davis shook his head. "No, not bad."

"You convinced us that Nassau was the place to do the new project. You convinced us that the Bahamas was the answer. Then you set Johnny Run up with a has-been engineer/producer, Be-Bop Baron, and the album bombed."

Be-Bop. It had been a big mistake. He shook his head rapidly, trying to clear away the fog. "The critics —"

"Fuck the critics. The critics had nothing to do with the sales. Do you understand? The project was a piece of shit. That's what happened. And that's where it becomes your problem. *Back In Black*, Grant. Forty-five million. Do you know how much money you could make with forty-five million albums?"

If the album had been a big success, would they have given him all the credit? Doubtful. Yet when the album tanked, it was his problem. Exactly. And there was no mistaking what happened. The album tanked. But this was the way the game was played. You win some, you lose some. If this syndicate, this group of misguided investors thought that you hit a home run every time, they were sadly mistaken. Critics did have something to do with sales.

"Look, it's a crapshoot. One minute you're hot, the next you're not. Not every album is going to make millions. I don't think we have to get drastic on the next attempt. I think this next record will kick ass."

"But you're not sure."

"You can't be sure."

"So do you have another suggestion?"

"No. Yes. I mean, we've got a hot-shit producer on the project. *They've* got Jonah Britt. At the moment, nobody's better." *They* had Jonah Britt. It wasn't his band anymore.

"Finally? You should have had Jonah Britt on the last project, Grant. You know it, we know it."

Yes, he should have. But the band was hot. It's easy to be lulled by the sweet smell of success. It was easy to be fooled into believing you could do no wrong. Be-Bop had been a huge mistake. The washed up has-been really hadn't known what to do with the band.

But this time they *did* have legendary engineer/producer Jonah Britt. And Davis had had a lot of input in that decision. Sure, he'd been fired. But before he went, he tried to right the sinking ship. Surely these guys knew the story. They still had a huge investment in Johnny Run. "And I think we're going to knock one out of the park."

"The baseball analogy? Mr. Davis, you'd better hit *this* one out of the park, because there are some very unhappy investors in this group."

"And what am I supposed to do?" They'd financed promotion, they'd financed the tour. Now they wanted their payout. Davis wasn't certain that even the band knew how much money this group had put up. Johnny Run blindly recorded their records, paraded their show on stages around the country, got into their private jet and flew away, oblivious as to how the rock machine worked. Management signed checks, and Davis was convinced the band had no idea where the money went. As long as they got a cut, they didn't seem to care.

Meanwhile this syndicate of shady investors worked behind the scenes, not because they were aficionados of the rock and roll genre, but because they wanted to make a lot of money. And right now, they were all way behind the eight ball.

"Put the fear of God into the act and into the production."

Davis cleared his throat. Acid reflux reared it's ugly head.

The spokesman took two steps to him, and Davis could make out his face in the dim light. He didn't recognize him, but the message was clear.

"You either fix this problem or we'll fix you. That's exactly how everything will play out. And Mr. Davis, we *do* understand you are now playing from a less than effectual position."

No shit. He'd been fired by the band. Fired. They'd blamed him for the dismal results.

"Look, I understand that you —"

"It makes no difference what you understand. The only thing you need to do is find a way to turn this production into a money-maker. You still have a financial investment in this band, as do we."

He did. If the new album took off, Davis stood to make some good money. And if it didn't, it sounded like these guys were going to make it very rough on him.

"The pressure to tour, the pressure to promote, whatever it takes. You are going to find a way to make this project very profitable. Even from your lesser position. Do you understand?"

"I —"

"Do you understand?"

"I'll do what I can."

"Let's hope it's enough. Because my group is out for blood. And they'll get it one way or the other."

The tall man walked up to him, stared into his eyes for maybe fifteen seconds, then pulled his fist back and hit him hard on the mouth. Davis reeled, catching his balance as he tasted the metallic flavor of his own blood. The jagged edge of a tooth caught his tongue and his brain felt like it was swimming. He found a chair and leaned on it with his right arm, trying to shake the stars from his head.

"Grant. You are responsible for making the project fly. Bring attention to it," he was smiling, like a long-lost friend, glad to see him again, "and do anything at all to put it on the charts. We don't care how extreme the action. There are millions of dollars at stake and we need your attention."

Davis righted himself, wobbling as he pushed off the chair. The fist was faster this time, totally catching him off guard. It caught his temple, spinning him around and the next thing he was aware of, he was looking up from the ground.

"Grant. Grant. You've got to be quick." There was a smile in the voice. Through the pain, the throbbing pain, he could hear the smile. A condescending voice, but a smile nonetheless.

"What?"

"What, what?" The stranger asked the absurd question.

Davis watched the dark ceiling overhead, spinning, spinning, spinning.

"You've got to be quick, Grant."

"At what?"

"At figuring out what to do." The guy was eight feet tall at least. Staring straight up, Grant's eyes were floating outside his skull.

"Oh."

"You have one mission, Grant. Draw attention to Johnny Run. At whatever cost. Put this new record through the roof. And don't get caught, because no matter how bad the authorities treat you, we'll treat you worse. Got it?"

Authorities? What did this guy want him to do? Whatever cost? He was afraid the cost could be his life. Davis looked up with his watery eyes. He gasped as the pointed boot caught him in the ribs.

"I asked you a question? *Now* do you understand? Do you understand how serious we are?"

He couldn't talk. The air was gone from his chest and he was gasping, afraid he'd already drawn his last breath.

The tall man opened the door and walked out of his apartment. Grant Davis lay on the ground, bent into a fetal position. He finally caught a lungful of air and drew it in deeply. His chest heaved as he gulped in oxygen, all the time feeling as if he was having a heart attack. What the hell did that mean? Put the fear of God into the act and into the production? Draw attention to Johnny Run. Right now, Davis was the one who needed attention.

But deep inside he knew what it meant. Put some fear, some excitement, into the situation. Let the band, the producer, and even the critics understand that they needed to be held accountable. But he was accountable too. His life was on the line. Something dramatic had to happen. Something so compelling that it drew immediate attention to the band. Something that sucked the oxygen out of the room. He swallowed long, painful chestfuls of stale air. No matter what the current entertainment news was, he had to invent a story that screamed headlines. Something that sold millions of records. It was that simple.

His pain subsided. Oh, there was throbbing, but way below the top of the threshold.

And he was still gasping for air.

The drugs and the alcohol clouded his mind. But there was a mission to accomplish.

Johnny Run had a new manager, a new attitude, a new producer, and a new sound. Maybe they could make it on their own. Maybe they could once again own the music world. Probably not. They probably needed a shove. And he'd been designated to give them that shove. He had no idea what to do, but it was more than obvious that he'd better figure it out, and figure it out fast!

CHAPTER ELEVEN

Teddy Bartholomew watched the session, but Britt controlled it. *Resurrecting the Dead* was the title of the album. Resurrecting the dead was Bartholomew's job. Turn this band around and sell the hell out of this new record. The scrawny gray cat brushed against his leg and he pushed it away. He hated cats.

"Jonah, is this song strong enough for the closer? Man, I just don't think this is the song to end on."

Britt squinted, as if questioning the audacity of this little man.

"Teddy, you show up at about half the recording sessions, yet you want to jump right in and tell me what to do?"

"Well, it's just that—"

Britt turned from the board, his eyes bright and a frown on his face. "I've told you before. Shut the fuck up and let me do my job." He'd told Bartholomew that he heard a song in his head. He always heard it in his head, playing as if it had already been recorded. Playing as if it had been produced, filtered, and mixed. This song was a long way from being finished, but it was already a done deal in Jonah Britt's head and he had told Bartholomew that it would be the strong finisher it was intended to be.

He spun around, continuing to concentrate on the vocal overdub.

Bartholomew bristled. "Jonah?"

"Teddy," he took a deep breath, "you may be the manager, but let's keep it there. Handle their affairs, their money, make sure I get my check, but don't question what I'm doing."

Bartholomew's eyes burned. He felt the heat of a fever in his face. "Look, you arrogant prick, I'm in charge of this project."

Britt turned once again, shoving his index finger into Bartholomew's chest. "As I pointed out, you don't even show up half the time. You probably are out getting stoned or you've got your dick up some tourist girl's ass, and that's fine. That's probably where you should be. Go enjoy yourself, because you're not making any decisions on this project. You like it or not, Teddy, I'm the one that's going to determine how this album sounds. Got it?"

"I've got every right to question what you're doing." Bartholomew's ire raised its head. "This studio fucked up the last production and —"

Britt raised his voice, about two times the current decibel. His eyes blazed and he pounded the mixing console for emphasis. "This studio did not 'fuck up' the last production. You know that, and I know that. You did get some excellent reviews. Would you like to see them? Huh? I've got a file, Bartholomew. You know who fucked it up? The former management may have fucked up the promotion of the last project. The band may have fucked up the tour. And you, you tend to be a fuckup when it comes to bothering me."

Bartholomew had taken two steps back and now wished he'd just left the room.

"And, one more thing, Teddy. You above anyone else in the business, should know that shit happens. How many shit positions have you had in your putrid career?"

Bartholomew had been with the engineer before the session and Britt didn't hide the fact at all that he had had a line of coke and a couple of beers. He'd smoked a joint on the outside porch and told Teddy that it usually gave him the edge to mix a great track. Now, it was fueling him to vent. Really vent. Vent about the last production for Johnny Run.

"Now, leave me alone. I'll turn this thing around, you'll look like a hero even though you had nothing—absolutely nothing—to do with it, and all you have to do is just babysit this bunch of immature rock stars. I ask you again. You got it? Do you understand? Are we clear?"

"Yeah." He pouted. "I got it. But this thing had better kick ass, Britt. My ass is on the line and your ass is on the line."

Britt gave him a grim smile. "My ass is on the line with every project I create. You, on the other hand, don't really do anything. You're a conduit. That's it. You have no creativity, no imagination, and no talent, so don't tell me about my business. If this album falls on its face, I'm the one on the bubble. You? You'll just go back to your puddle of slime and beg for another job."

It was true. Bottom feeding was the way of life for a lot of people in the music business.

"I'm the one who makes this happen. Without me, the only thing you've got is a bunch of self-absorbed, rich, asshole musicians. It's the only thing you've got. And there's not a lot anyone else can do with them."

Bartholomew backed down, biting on his own index finger like a disciplined child, standing in the corner pouting as the producer turned around and worked his board. He stared at the bad-tempered engineer, wishing he could cast an evil spell on him. Instead, he sulked in his corner.

The lyrics were strong, bouncing with a slight echo, and Stretch was doubling the lead.

> *I'd rather die young and leave 'em wantin' more,*
> *'Cause when you're past your time you can be such a bore,*
> *The people they ignore you and the women walk away,*
> *And then you're all alone do you hear what I say?*

And the chorus came in like a Queen song from years gone by.

> *Dust to dust, it's all the same to me*

Dust to dust it's how it's meant to be
Six feet under, no one knows your name
Deep in the ground, now there's no one to blame.

Bartholomew watched Sever, sitting in the semidark control room, leaning back in an uncomfortable chair, and watching the fireworks between the engineer and the manager. Even with the lights low, the bemused look on Sever's face pissed him off. The reporter was getting a kick out of this. And the fight would probably end up in some story he was writing about Jonah Britt or Johnny Run. Fuck 'em. Fuck 'em all. Somehow he'd make this record go, and everyone would know that he was responsible. Everyone would know that his promotional savvy, his marketing expertise and knowledge of the industry helped push *Resurrecting the Dead* to the top of the charts. Maybe someday the syndicate could look back and say *Resurrecting the Dead* made $45,000,000, and maybe they would thank Teddy Bartholomew for his shrewd business practices and recognize that he really did know a thing or two about the music business. And, maybe Jonah Britt would still be the prick that he'd always been.

Sever's gaze seemed to be on him, as if he were trying to make out the new manager in the dim light of the control room. Teddy Bartholomew, a guy who'd been lurking in the shadows of the music industry for ten or fifteen years. A guy who'd been trying to break new groups, new artists, who'd been signed with a couple of upstart companies but had never amounted to much. A guy who'd been rumored to be a drunk, a loser, and here he was, the man whose mission it was to put the life back in Johnny Run.

And by God he was going to get it done. He finally had the band and the chance. And Jonah Britt could fuck himself, as long as he produced a hit. That's all that mattered. Just put magic into the product. Give them a hit and all would be well.

Britt glanced at the wall clock, signaled to Stretch with a finger across his throat, and pointed at his wristwatch. He turned to Bartholomew. "As if it matters to you, we're calling it a night."

"Any chance we can get another hour in?" Bartholomew pretended to be contrite, speaking barely in a whisper. He wasn't happy about being chastised, but was still trying to squeeze as much as he could out of the recording session.

"I'm tired, Teddy. Do you have any idea what time it is? Two thirty a.m. Stretch has been going at the vocals for almost two hours. It's enough."

Bartholomew had heard the raspiness in the singer's voice. And they had a session scheduled for tomorrow, too, if the band was up to it. Teddy wasn't going to be there. He had an afternoon planned with a native honey who had promised him a home-cooked meal and whatever else followed.

He couldn't be too upset about shutting down the session. He needed his rest. The manager nodded, bowed his head, and walked out into the hall. He reached for a joint in his shirt pocket. House rules, don't smoke in the house. It was bullshit. Jonah and Rita smoked in their apartment. He'd seen Jonah Britt smoke on the porch outside. Even do a line of coke. He was sure that Sever knew it, too. The engineer and his wife were recreational drug users. Not much of a secret.

He could smell that sweet odor every morning when he came over for the first cup of coffee. But, there was no reason to start another fight. He walked down the hall and outside, glancing back at the studio and wondering if this project from hell would ever be finished. An engineer that did coke and grass, a band that lacked discipline.

He flicked the cheap plastic lighter, and as the weed caught fire, he inhaled deeply, reveling in the immediate floating sensation.

"Got anymore of that?"

Bartholomew jerked his head, seeing the figure in the dim light. Bernard, the crazy kid from next door. Twenty-two, twenty-three and he acted like he was in grade school.

"More what?"

"Grass?"

Bartholomew shook his head. "No. This is it."

"Let me have a drag, man." The young black moved closer, and

Bartholomew sensed tension in the air. He handed the boy the joint and watched in the dark as the neighbor took a deep hit.

"Good shit."

Bartholomew nodded and took back the cigarette.

"We can smoke in the Caddy."

"Caddy?"

"Elvis's car." The boy pointed to the rusted car sitting on blocks.

For some reason Bartholomew followed him, taking another drag. He held it for five seconds, then slowly let the smoke escape. It had been a rough night, and now, now he had to share his last joint with this freak kid?

Bernard opened the creaking car door and got into the driver's seat. Bartholomew walked around the car and slid into the passenger side. "So, this is your car?"

"Elvis's car."

"Some guy named Elvis owns it?"

The kid sighed. "Elvis Presley owned it, asshole. Let me have another hit." He reached and grabbed the joint from Bartholomew. One more deep puff and he handed it back.

"Honest to God?"

"He owned it. My momma told me."

"Wow."

"Lots of musicians smoked in here." The boy offered nothing else. They were both silent for a minute. "Me and my brother, we own this car. Momma says it's worth a lot of money."

"Who? Who smoked in this car? Besides Elvis?" Bartholomew passed the joint to Bernard.

"I don't know if Elvis smoked in here, but the musicians? Hell, if they recorded there," he pointed to the recording studio, "they probably smoked in Elvis's Cadillac. My mom gets really pissed."

Bartholomew laughed. He tried to picture some of the big names sitting where he sat, toking with a kid who believed Elvis had owned this rusted, rattletrap of a car. He laughed out loud, finding the idea funnier and funnier.

"Shush. My momma will hear you!" The boy had a serious tone. No humor there.

"We'll let her have a hit." He laughed again, coughing as the smoke tickled his throat.

"Give it to me." The young man grabbed the joint from him and took another pull deep into his lungs. He held it for what seemed an eternity, then blew it out quickly, catching his breath. "I gotta go in. Momma's gonna worry."

"You mind if I sit here for a while?" Bartholomew was comfortable. There was no reason to smoke and run.

"You can stay as long as you like. Just be careful of the car. It's worth a lot of money."

Bartholomew's eyes drifted to Bernard. The kid didn't know the meaning of a lot of money. He saw the boy leave the car, carefully closing the door behind him. Didn't want to disturb the tribute to Elvis. Teddy Bartholomew closed his eyes, leaving the cigarette dangling from his fingers. Elvis owned the car? How many memories could one car hold?

The heat burned his knuckle and he dropped the short stub of the joint, stomping at it with his foot where he saw the red-hot ash on the car's floor. He stomped it again for good measure. He'd fallen asleep for maybe a minute, and as he looked up through the windshield, he could see the stars in the sky, hanging over the water just past the pastel-colored cottages of the Compass Point Hotel. Serene, peaceful.

He closed his eyes again. The passenger car door opened, and he breathed deeply. "Bernard, there isn't any more, man. It's all gone."

A hand gripped him, grabbing him by the throat and yanking him out of the car. He hit the ground, his face in the dirt. It all happened in a second and he tried to catch his breath. As he attempted to roll over, he felt the foot come down on his larynx, crushing his throat. Bartholomew cried out but there was no sound. Mercifully the weight was lifted and he tried to stretch. If he could only roll. Get out of the path of this foot and roll to safety.

This time the foot came down hard, cutting off his air. He lay there, his mouth open wide, panic building inside his oxygen-starved brain. Pressure in his head caused his eyes to bulge. His chest, his lungs, his heart, his head, he could feel the pain building panic. This wasn't going to end. He was aware of it all, and very much aware that he was going to die.

He knew that man could live for a short time without water, a long time without food, but he couldn't exist at all without oxygen. He tried to see, his wide eyes staring up, but all that was visible were stars, flashing, brilliant explosions of light that were far more bright than the ones he'd seen in the sky. His lungs ached, his throat was on fire, his brain exploded, and Teddy Bartholomew died, wishing he'd never had that last joint.

CHAPTER TWELVE

Sever swallowed the Scotch, feeling it burn his throat, then his stomach. He was on his first glass, and Britt was on his second glass of rum as they sat around the small kitchen table.

"You've heard some of the stuff we're doing, Mick. Honest opinion."

"It's great stuff, Jonah. You haven't lost your touch."

The man held up his glass, staring through the dark amber liquid. "Maybe I'm getting too old for this shit. I think I'm doing a good job, think my finger is on the pulse of these young people, then I hear something that is so far-out, so much different——"

"You'd be foolish if you didn't listen and compare. Maybe you can learn something from these new guys."

"Maybe I'm too old to change."

"And maybe these other guys are listening to you. Maybe they want to learn from the master."

Britt laughed loudly.

"Everything all right in there?" Rita called from farther back in the small apartment.

"We're just loosening up a little."

Sever detected the faint, sweet aroma of smoke. Rita was probably having a joint. "Jonah, this thing with Johnny Run—"

"There's a lot of pressure on that one. The label, the management team, the investor group."

"But Teddy Bartholomew? This guy is a washed up hack, and—"

"He's a fill-in."

"A fill-in?" Sever frowned. He of all people should know the music terms. "What the hell is a fill-in?"

"It's what I call him. They needed somebody to keep the guys straight and shepherd the project to completion. He's done it before. It's pretty much a babysitting job. It takes no talent, no brains, just the ability to make sure they show up for the session. That's really about all he's good for."

"So he's not been with them long?"

"No. And I don't imagine he'll be with them much longer. You saw the guy tonight? He's a burnout. I couldn't do another album with him. Has no idea why he's even here."

"He's here because the last album didn't do so well?"

"Didn't do so well?" Britt took another swallow. "That's kind. It went into the toilet, okay?"

"Well, I got that impression. But I heard you tell Bartholomew that it wasn't the fault of the studio or the album. Right?"

"That's exactly what I told him."

"So was it the management's fault? Who?"

"After the last album, the management team was screwed. I don't like to think about it, Mick. It tanked. I mean, it didn't make enough to pay the bills. Grant Davis was the manager for the last album. He had a financial stake in it too, but—"

"What exactly happened?"

"Off the record?"

"I'm not going there, Jonah. Just curious."

Britt took a deep swallow of his rum and refilled his glass. "You know, I probably made a mistake on their last album. I'm not saying the band, the record company, and the management company didn't buy into it, but I probably should take some blame for the fact the project never took off."

"If I recall, you said you didn't even mix it."

"I didn't." Jonah thumped the tumbler on the table. His speech was a little slower than usual, the alcohol starting to have its effect. "That's the problem." He stretched the word *that's*.

"You want to explain that?"

"I wanted the money, I needed the money, so I booked the session. I knew I couldn't do it, so I gave them Be-Bop."

Sever nodded. "Be-Bop."

"Bobby is okay. I mean, I told you he's a little dated. But he still can function. He still has ideas. There were a couple of groups who actually demanded him in the last year or so. So, I figured what the hell."

"You knew Be-Bop couldn't do the job, right?"

Britt was quiet for a minute. No sound except the clicking of a clock on the kitchen wall. "I told you. I needed the money, Mick. I got greedy, okay?" Britt looked at him with red, watery eyes. He shrugged his shoulders and threw back another swallow of rum. "All right. I knew Be-Bop couldn't do the job. But they accepted him, so I can't beat myself up over this."

"So what happened to their manager, Grant Davis?"

"You don't stop, do you? You just push and push, question after question. Don't you ever get tired of it?"

"It's what I do." Sever gave him a smile and took a sip of the Scotch. "I ask questions. What happened to Grant Davis?"

"Well, Davis was fired."

"Because?"

"Because Johnny Run's last album didn't sell. Didn't chart. Haven't you been listening? And they blamed the management."

"And you think it was something to do with Be-Bop's mix?"

"Should have done it myself, Mick. Should have done it myself." Britt drained the last of the rum, stared at the bottle for a moment, then stood up, walked to the sink and placed his glass on the counter.

Rita walked out from the back room, an oversized T-shirt apparently the only item of clothing she had on. She smiled at Mick. "Boys, it's almost three thirty in the morning. Time for bed, Jonah."

"Yeah," Sever tried not to stare. "I've got to get some sleep."

"I suppose you could join us." She laughed out loud. Sever wasn't sure whether she was kidding or not. In her younger days, Rita had gotten around. There were rumors about her, and he knew her just well enough to believe that she'd had threesomes in her life. Maybe more than three.

"It's late, man. We'll start around noon tomorrow if you're up." Britt looked a little tipsy. Sever detected a slight slur. Three rums to his one Scotch. He nodded.

"I think I'll walk outside and finish this if that's okay."

"Sure. You can leave the glass on the porch when you walk back to the hotel."

Britt walked him to the door, and Sever heard the latch click when he closed it. Locked up tight. Sever wondered if Britt had on occasion gotten a little drunk, or a little stoned, and had forgotten to lock up. Forgotten to set the alarm. He'd already admitted to being a little lax in that department.

No cop car this late. Apparently Eric the cop didn't spend every night with the lovely Etta May. Or maybe he was on patrol this evening. Etta May and a cop. There was somebody for everyone. Apparently.

Elvis's Cadillac was silhouetted against the horizon, the half moon lighting the sky with a pale yellow aura. Sever started down the driveway to cross the road to the pastel-colored Compass Point Hotel. He looked back and realized how the moonlight and the scrub bushes and trees that grew next to Etta May's little block house played tricks on the eyes. The shadows made it almost look like Elvis was sitting in the driver's seat.

CHAPTER THIRTEEN

It sounded like someone was trying to kick the door down. His eyes flew open and for just a second he wasn't sure where he was. The domed, cathedral ceiling of the cottage loomed above him, the ceiling fan turning lazily, barely moving the humid air.

Bang! There it was again. Someone was pounding somewhere. Somewhere close. Didn't they realize he was up on stilts? The Carribbean pastel cottage sat high up from the ground. The colors ran together, swimming in a pool of water and alcohol. Who the hell had ever chosen those outlandish colors? And what was the pounding? Maybe it was an earthquake. But if someone was pounding on *his* cottage, they might just knock the damn thing right off its foundations.

"Mr. Sever. Please, open this door."

His eyes snapped open again. This wasn't a dream. Someone was trying to break into his room.

Sever stood up, stretching and reaching for his jeans.

"Mr. Sever?" Bang! An African vase on the dresser shook and Sever hoped it wouldn't crash to the floor. They'd probably charge him for it.

"I'm coming."

"Mr. Sever, we're going to break down the door."

Break down the door? He'd been right. They were coming in with force. He struggled into a T-shirt and sandals and hobbled to the door, his stiff knee not limbered up yet. He didn't even want to think of how many years ago he'd torn that up in a drugged-out evening with The Who.

Sever pulled the door open, and two uniformed officers stood there, stern looks on their faces. Mutt and Jeff, from the old, old comic strip. One short, squat, one tall and painfully thin.

"Mr. Sever, I'm sorry, sir." A small black man behind them waved his arms. "I wanted to call you on the house phone, sir, but these gentlemen demanded that I take them directly to your room." Sever recognized the desk clerk. The man smiled sheepishly.

"What? Was I snoring too loud?"

"Oh, no sir. We —"

The tall, thin officer put his hand up, effectively silencing the hotel clerk.

The two men pushed their way into the room, Sever backing up. They glanced around the small area, looking for something, but for the life of him, Sever couldn't figure out what it was.

"Where were you last night between the hours of eight p.m. and three a.m.?" The shorter officer, slightly overweight, had taken off his hat and stood at attention, looking up into Sever's eyes. Tough guy. Napoleon complex.

"I was at the studio across the street."

"The entire time?"

He was still groggy. There was no place else he'd been. Still, he had to think. Maybe it was the years of alcohol or the drugs, but his memory, short- and long-term, wasn't quite what it used to be.

"I was. We even had food brought in, and I was drinking with the owner in his kitchen till early morning."

"Mr. Sever," the short man continued, "did you at any time last evening go outside and have a cigarette?"

"I don't smoke. Quit several years ago. Why?"

"Marijuana, Mr. Sever?"

Sever looked back at the taller officer standing just inside the doorway. He was ramrod straight, almost at strict attention. "Guys, is this a drug bust, because if it is, you've come to the wrong place. I've been clean for years."

"Would you come with us, sir?"

"Why?"

"It's a matter of some questions."

"Am I under arrest?"

The short officer shook his head. "Not at this moment."

The two uniformed men watched Sever finish dressing, then walked on either side of him out to the front of the hotel where their car was parked. Sever smiled. "One of you named Eric?" He'd bet on it. The short guy with the gut.

"My name is Eric." The cop gave him a surprised look, a crease across his brow. He hesitated, then opened the rear car door and motioned to Sever. "How did you know that?"

"Before I go with you guys, can you tell me where we're going and why?" He wasn't quite sure about the laws on this island. Any time a cop, in any country, asked you to come down to the station, it was trouble.

Eric the cop squinted in the morning sun, pulling a pair of cheap sunglasses from his shirt pocket and putting them on, completing the image. This was a guy who could couple with Etta May. He could see the fit. It wasn't attractive, but he could see the fit.

"You know my name?"

"I do. You have a reputation."

Eric nodded, as if that was common knowledge. "Mr. Sever, do you know the penalty for murder in the Bahamas?"

"What?"

"Do you know the penalty for murder?"

"Who the hell was killed? That's what this is about? A murder?" It exploded out of him. He only knew a handful — not even a handful of people on the island. If they were taking him in for questioning, it had to be someone he knew. That scared the hell out of him. "Wait a minute, is Jonah okay? You've got to tell me."

"It's hanging. Death by hanging."

"Why are you telling me this?" Now he was very concerned. Somebody was dead, and they wouldn't tell him who it was. The taller officer was pushing him into the backseat. "I ask you what this is about. And you ask me my knowledge of Bahamian law? Tell me what's happened, Eric. *Officer* Eric."

"There was a murder across the street last night. We're simply going to take you to the station and ask you some questions."

"Who was killed? For God's sake, tell me that much. It wasn't Jonah? Rita?" Who the hell else could it have been? Maybe the neighbors? Etta May or the kid, Bernard? Or another kid back in the alley? Somebody dead in the fire, now another one murdered? He was still trying to wake up and they'd already got him in the car and were taking him to some undisclosed station? And if he was never heard from again—

"Are you going to tell me?"

Eric started the engine, glancing back at Sever through the metal-mesh screen that separated the front and back seats. "Are you sure you don't know already?"

What the hell did that mean?

"I get this impression you think I know more than I do. I am not aware of any killings last night or this morning."

"And we're not accusing you of knowing anything, Mr. Sever. I'm just asking."

"Can you please tell me who was killed?"

Eric glanced at his partner. The thin man shrugged his shoulders.

"All right. A Theodore Bartholomew."

Theodore Bartholomew? Teddy Bartholomew. *No.* He'd just seen him this morning. And Jonah, he'd been talking about him. Jonah. Just a little bit drunk, a little bit testy about Teddy. God, no. Sever felt like he was losing it. Certainly not Jonah. The legendary engineer/producer just didn't like the guy. He'd never get carried away. Jonah Britt wouldn't kill a fly, no matter how messed up he was. Sever was sure of it. "Teddy? Bartholomew? You're sure?"

"Mr. Sever," Eric looked over his shoulder, "we don't make

mistakes on matters of dead bodies. It was Theodore Bartholomew. I'd be happy to take you by the morgue as well so you can discover this for yourself."

"Uh, no. No, thank you."

"We can discuss this when we get to the station."

Sever knew better than to say anything. If he was under any suspicion, he should call his attorney stateside and just shut up. But he couldn't do it. It wasn't in his nature. He needed to clear himself, and he needed some answers. And now seemed like as good a time as any to get them.

"I was with him last night. This morning, actually. He left maybe an hour or so before I did. Did someone shoot him? Guys, I had nothing to do with this."

Eric and the tall, silent man said nothing.

"Where did they find him? The body?"

Eric looked back for a second. "Mr. Sever, I told you, we'll cover this when we get to the station."

A reporter asked questions. It's what he did. "Just tell me where they found the body."

The tall silent one spoke up. "They found Mr. Bartholomew in the Cadillac."

"The Cadillac? What Cadillac?"

Eric cleared his throat. "Elvis's Cadillac, Mr. Sever. He'd been smoking ganja and somebody killed him."

CHAPTER FOURTEEN

He opened his eyes, feeling the starched sheet beneath him. The faint odor of bleach was in the air and everything around him was white. Maybe he'd died and this was heaven—white and sterile. Then he remembered. The sisters. He'd wandered through the halls with them, listening to them chat, catching him up on the ladies no longer living there and on several who had passed away. One had retired to Washington state. They told him that they no longer made the journey to do mission work in Bimini. The numbers were thinning, the money was tight. Things weren't as they had been when Bobby had lived there.

They'd walked him to the library, where he used to read as a child, to the cluttered souvenir shop, and upstairs to his old dorm room. The beds with the sagging springs were still there, the mattresses on each bunk. Woolen blankets were folded neatly at the foot of the bunks as if waiting for the next generation of orphaned boys to march in, one by one and take possession. For a moment he felt a sense of longing. He shook it off in a second. There was work to be done. No time for emotion.

No one asked about the grotesque surgery. No one mentioned the hideous scars on his face and hands. He was Bobby, back for a visit, and for that he was thankful. And the sisters seemed thankful as well. Glad to see him.

They showed him the quiet courtyard, with the graceful palms, the spotty grass growing in the sandy dirt, and Sister Mary proudly showed him the fifteen stalks of corn, about knee-high.

"About as tall as you were when you were here," she said.

And then they'd gone to the kitchen, and Sister Annie brought out a plate of warm cookies and a glass of milk. As if they knew he was coming. Again he marveled at how things hadn't changed. As if they were on pause, ready for another group of boys to take over the upstairs of the old building. He felt somewhat nostalgic and chilled at the same time. The entire experience had been seductive.

Now was the second time he'd seen the morning. He'd left late at night and rolled in during the wee hours of the morning. He'd watched the sun come up, finally drifting off to sleep, and was now awake for the second time. He looked around for a clock. Nothing. Walking to the window he gazed at the sky, guessing the time to be around nine o'clock. He needed a cigarette, and he could use a joint. To calm him, to help with the pain. Baron walked out into the reception area. Sister Annie was gazing out the window. She turned when she heard him approach, his shoes clicking on the bleach-white tile floor.

"The dogs, Bobby. There are more of them everyday. They're in a pack, and some of the sisters won't even go out when they hear them. They can get pretty vicious."

He walked to the window and looked out. They were mean looking, standing around in a group, like a street gang waiting to rumble. He could hear their low growls. "Sister, how many of us were there?"

"Oh, fifteen, twenty." She continued to look at the pack of fifteen to twenty dogs.

"And all of them, all of our parents —"

"Most of the parents had been incarcerated. It was our mission to make a home for you and the other boys while your parents were in prison."

"My parents?" He knew. He knew what they were, but he needed to hear it.

"Goodness, Bobby, I can't remember every set of parents for

every boy who stayed here. I'm sure they loved you. It's just that, adults sometimes tend to —" she hesitated. "Well, you're an adult. I guess you know."

It was all so vague. Explaining adult behavior. She was uncomfortable, ill at ease, and he didn't want to push it any further.

"And what happens now?"

"What happens?"

"To children? Kids whose parents are in prison?"

"Oh, heavens, other charities took over, the government got involved, and we ran out of funds. It's not easy, Bobby." She looked at him, and he knew it must be difficult. To see him in this condition. "Are you Catholic, Bobby?"

"I'm not certain what I am."

"Here, in the Bahamas, eighty percent of all our population is Protestant. Less than twenty percent are Catholic. While I think we're well respected and people appreciate what we do, we don't have the resources to do a lot of things."

He nodded. The sisters had had the resources when he needed them the most. When his father and mother were in and out of the hellhole prisons of the Bahamas. His father was a thief, his mother had been a part-time prostitute. They'd done a lot of time in the system. And the stories from there were horrific. Beatings, raw sewage, rotten food, the list was endless.

"So I can stay here for a couple of days? I won't be in the way?"

Sister Annie smiled. "Of course, Bobby. Of course. But you haven't told us why you came. What brings you here?"

He nodded. "It's a long story, Sister, but you'll appreciate what I intend to do."

Her face lit up as she smiled. "What is it, child?"

"I intend to right a wrong."

"The Lord gives strength to those who work in his name. I speak from firsthand experience."

"I'm not sure this is the Lord's work, Sister, but it must be done."

"Always try to do the Lord's work."

He put his hand out and covered hers. Getting revenge. It wasn't necessarily the Lord's work, but when he decided it was righting a wrong, it seemed to make it right.

"Our house is your house, Bobby Baron. Stay as long as you wish."

They watched the dogs nipping at each other and snarling at an elderly man who walked a little too close. The old gentleman wisely scurried to the other side of the street.

"Bobby," Sister Annie kept watching out the window. Whether the view was still interesting, or her eyes wanted to avoid his looks, he couldn't tell.

"Yes, Sister Annie?"

"If you want to talk—"

It was their job. To counsel, to minister, to listen.

"Thank you."

"No, please, don't thank me. I just want you to know that I'm here if you—we're here if you need us. And you can tell us anything."

No, he couldn't. He couldn't tell them anything at all. Quietly he repeated the prayer he'd learned those many years ago, in the chapel in this very building.

> Many sins I've done today
> Please, Lord take them all away.
> Look upon me in Thy grace
> Make me pure before Thy face.

Baron hadn't prayed since he was a small child. Except that one night. The night the fireball came blasting down the hallway. For a brief second he'd prayed for his life, and now he wasn't sure that it was worth it. He might be better off dead. Like the motorist had said. "You should have been dead, asshole."

"Thank you, Sister Annie." Bobby nodded. He'd be gone in two or three days tops. All he needed to do was right a wrong.

CHAPTER FIFTEEN

The reporter from the *Nassau Guardian* was waiting for him when he left the station. A young lady named Audrey. She had long auburn hair that caught the sun and turned a coppery red. And, Sever noticed, she was white. You got used to the black skin in Nassau.

"Mr. Sever?" A British accent. "I'm from the island newspaper and I wondered if I could have a word with you?"

Hated it. Purely hated it. Interviewers. They asked the most intimate, embarrassing questions. And he should know. Oh, he could do it to others, but don't let them do it to him. But what was he supposed to do? If he refused to talk to her, the headlines would read "Famous Person of Interest Refuses Comments to Guardian." Hell you couldn't win.

"Mr. Sever?"

He felt like asking for her credentials. How long have you been a reporter? What's your background. Turn it around on her. But, of course, that was out of the question. He stopped. "Yes, of course."

"We heard you were brought in for questioning in the death of Theodore Bartholomew. Can you tell us what you know about last night's murder?"

"I sincerely hate to disappoint you, but I know very little. I saw the man briefly yesterday during a recording session, and found out this morning someone had strangled him."

Eric-the-short came up behind him. "Come on, Sever. If I'm

driving you back, let's move it." He grabbed Sever's arm, and Sever wanted to coldcock the arrogant cop with his other fist. But he didn't. Taking him in for questioning, it had been Mr. Sever. Now it was just Sever. They didn't need him anymore.

"One more question, Mr. Sever." At least the reporter showed some respect.

"You can talk to him all you want to, Audrey, after he gets back to Compass Point. Right now I've got to get him back there." He opened the back door and gave Sever a gentle nudge. The journalist wanted so badly to swing around and —

"Get in."

Eric drove without his partner, carefully hitting every pothole in every road they took. The car took a particularly nasty jolt, and Eric turned around for a brief second, speaking directly to Sever.

"Drugs. American music and drugs."

Sever wasn't sure if it was a statement or a question. The cop looked straight ahead and was silent for several minutes. Sever stared out the window, watching the colorful shops up and down Bay Street. Expensive to trashy, with merchants selling everything from cheap souvenirs to Coach purses and expensive evening wear. From diamonds to Tommy Bahama jeans, and T-shirts with witty sayings to Rolex watches.

They passed by buildings of mint green, avocado, faded yellow, and rose red, and he realized how hungry he was when they passed the rum cake factory.

"Do you know Bernard, the boy who lives next door to the studio?" Eric was engaging him in conversation. The short little man had been belligerent, rude, and obnoxious during the entire interview, and now he wanted to have a pleasant conversation?

"I've met him. Wanted to sell me the Cadillac."

"Let me tell you something about Bernard."

Sever smiled. The little guy was banging Etta May so he probably did know the kid.

"He's very fragile."

"Fragile?"

"He was born with some problems, and his maturity has been stunted. Not entirely by the birth problems."

"Oh? What other problems does he have?"

Eric kept his eyes on the road, making sure to jerk and bounce the car as much as possible. "American music and drugs."

"What does that mean?"

"It means that he has been offered drugs from many of your musician friends at the studio. And it has greatly affected his ability to learn, socialize, and comprehend. He's had several overdoses." Almost a sneering tone to his voice. So much for the pleasant conversation.

"If this is true, why haven't you arrested the musicians? The ones who provided him with drugs?"

There was a long silence from the driver's seat. Eric pulled up to a stop sign, sharply stepped on the brake, and turned around. "Because we can't prove it."

"If you could—"

"If we could, I'm afraid that we still would be hard-pressed to arrest these drug-pushing musicians."

"Why?"

"For two reasons, Mr. Sever." He turned around and touched the gas pedal, bouncing the car through a pothole the size of Rhode Island. "One is that, as much as I don't like to admit this, drugs are almost part of the culture here in the Bahamas."

Sever nodded. "And?"

"And, we are supposed to encourage American entertainers to come to Nassau. To drink, take drugs, gamble at Atlantis, make love to our women."

"And record at Highland Studios. It's good for business, right?" Sever knew the story.

"Tourism is the primary industry here. But the boy, Bernard, I have a special feeling for him. I will do whatever is necessary to protect him from your friends. Do you understand me, Mr. Sever?"

Sever took a deep breath. The guy was defending his girlfriend's honor. "Sure. Except I'm not involved in the studio or with these musicians. I'm simply here to do a story. You should know that. Why tell your story to me when I can't do anything about it? Why not talk to Jonah?"

"We have. And we will continue to do so."

"Look, I'm simply here doing a report on the new studio. The drug thing is an entirely different —"

"Do you know what the United States culture has done to this country?"

Sever watched the back of the cop's head. Now the guy was talking culture?

"You've tried to turn us into one of your states."

"Believe me, *I* haven't tried to —"

"You've tried to turn us into a materialistic society, Mr. Sever."

They swerved around a corner on the wrong side of the road. Sever closed his eyes. Driving on the left side in Nassau. He couldn't get used to it.

"Our women, they want a man with more money. All because of your culture. Our young people," he paused, choosing his words and thoughts, "they don't understand why they can't have everything as soon as they become adults. Give me this, give me that. All because of your culture."

Sever let him run on. Obviously he needed to vent.

"Do you know that we took BET off of our cable systems? Black Entertainment Television was preaching a culture that's not our culture. Do you understand me, Mr. Sever?"

They were in the homestretch, and Sever recognized the road leading to his hotel. Anything to get away from this guy.

The officer was quiet as he pulled into the parking lot. He stepped from the car and opened the rear door. Sever climbed out, feeling the stiffness in his knee.

"You're doing a story for a magazine in the States." It was a statement, not a question. "I hope you will treat this incident carefully."

"What incident? Dragging me down to the station?"

"I hope you will treat it carefully."

"Carefully?" Hell, if he wrote about it at all, he'd humiliate the law enforcement agency.

"The United States is responsible for a lot of our troubles, Mr. Sever. I would lay this murder solely at your feet."

"You're crazy." He didn't want to go back to that station, but the cop wouldn't let it rest.

"Be careful how you write this story."

"Why? Because you don't need the bad publicity?"

He glared at Sever.

"Come on, Eric. You're afraid this is going to reflect on your ability to enforce the law. It's going to make some people a little wary about coming to Nassau and dropping a lot of money on your island. An American businessman is strangled in Nassau, and that's not going to reflect positively on the Bahamas, is it?"

Jamaica, Aruba—tourism took a hit when an American was killed or came up missing.

Eric tugged on the brim of his hat. "You have all the answers, Mr. Sever. But there's something you haven't yet mentioned."

"What's that?"

"This killing is going to bring a lot of attention to the recording act Johnny Run. And that attention, that curiosity, will probably sell a lot of records. Tell me I'm wrong about that."

Sever watched him climb back into the squad car and drive across the street. Eric parked next to the rusty Cadillac and walked up to Etta May's small block house. The cop had a point. The recording industry would be buzzing about the murder, and the bad news could help sell a lot of records. What a crazy—What a fucked-up—business. And it was his job to report on it. Maybe it was time to retire and just walk away from the whole thing.

Sever walked into the hotel and opened the door to his room. The message light was blinking and he pushed the playback button.

"Mick. Lee Jenson, *Newsweek*. Hey, we're paying for the studio story, so I would hope you'd give us your exclusive on Teddy Bartholomew's murder. Call me."

"Mick, it's Jeff Bloomfield." *Chicago Tribune.* "Call me the minute you get this. I need to know about this murder, man."

"Mick."

"Hey, Mick!"

"Mick?"

There were seven altogether. They'd probably called his agent, got the message he was in the Bahamas, and tracked him down. Unbelievable. Bad news traveled fast. When anyone in the music business wanted a story on a band, a musician, or the underbelly of the industry, they called Sever. A crazy business. And he kept getting sucked in. He wanted to get to the bottom of it just as much as everyone else.

Sever dialed *Newsweek*'s number. He'd tell them what he knew and promise to dig deeper. They'd offer him a bonus and he'd accept. It might not be as big as the Anna Nicole Smith story, but Sever bet himself that it would still be big. Very big.

CHAPTER SIXTEEN

He'd had one too many rum and colas. One, hell. He'd slammed them down one after another, finally losing count and losing any sign of sobriety. And there'd been the girl next to him who was hanging on his arm, resting her hand on his leg, nuzzling her face against his neck. And he had no idea what had happened to her.

He held his head between his hands as he sat on the edge of the bed. It was coming back to him. She'd convinced him to go to another club—Fluid. That was it. A dingy basement operation with some couches, a disc jockey, and a bar. The hottest bar in Nassau, she'd said. And the bartender offered to sell him a gun. Even showed him a pistol he'd hidden under the bar. Said he'd need it in the rougher parts of Nassau. And Davis had never owned or fired a gun in his life. He remembered declining the offer.

And later, when he could barely walk, he'd found a cab. And he'd given the guy the address. Highland Studios. Because that's where Johnny Run was recording. Because that's where the trouble had all started. That's where the last album had been produced, and that was the reason he'd been fired. It all made sense at the time.

And now he was back in his little rental with no recollection of how he'd gotten there or what had happened in the meantime. No recollection at all.

There was no girl, so he must not have scored. He picked up last night's wardrobe and whiffed the stale odor of marijuana on his T-shirt and jeans. He'd either been around it or maybe he'd had a joint. Or two or three. Actually, he kind of remembered smoking with some guys from Fluid. Outside. On the street. It was hard to tell. He threw the clothes back on the floor.

They'd threatened him. They'd told him that he had to find a way to draw attention to the record. Johnny Run was on the island. Davis was on the island. The people who were threatening him were on the island. Now would be a good time to make something happen.

His head throbbed. Grant Davis pushed himself up and staggered to the bathroom. He poured four aspirin from a bottle and put them all on his tongue. He reached for the fifth of Jack Daniel's on the counter and poured liberally from the bottle, swallowing the amber liquid and the small white tablets. Never failed. He'd be rid of the headache in fifteen minutes and would start to feel somewhat normal in an hour. He took another pull of the whiskey just to make sure. Hair of the dog.

His cell phone rang, and he looked around the tiny room, trying to track down the sound. In the jeans pocket, on the floor. He pulled the phone out and glanced at the number. Blocked.

"Hello." His voice cracked and he coughed up phlegm.

"So, you took us at our word."

He thought for a second. Could be a wrong number. Not too many wrong numbers on the cell phone, but still—

"Grant?"

"Yeah." He cleared his throat, trying to place the voice.

"There should be a lot of buzz once the story breaks in the States. I understand there's already a lot of people who are very interested in the story."

"Who is this?"

"Davis, you know who it is. And we know what you did. We want focus, Grant, focus. On the new project. Do you understand?"

Focus?

"You've brought a lot of attention to the project. Not necessarily positive attention, but everyone is talking about it. Honestly we were a little surprised, but I'm glad you took us seriously. Whatever it takes, Grant. Just remember, this one had better be at the top of the charts."

"Listen, I'm not sure you —"

"We've said enough."

"But —"

"Grant, we shouldn't have to talk again."

Maybe that was a good thing.

There was a soft click and Davis held the phone to his ear for another twenty seconds. He had no idea who it was. He had no idea what they were talking about. Maybe about Johnny Run? He couldn't be sure. But he did know he needed some food. Some eggs, bacon, toast, strong coffee — they had strong coffee in Nassau — and another shot of whiskey. Just to take the edge off. Davis picked up the bottle and sat down on the edge of the bed, feeling just a little better. He'd told friends that he wanted an IV with nothing but Jack so he could just mainline it. It sounded like a good idea. He took one more long swallow. Time to go face the day.

CHAPTER SEVENTEEN

They ordered conch salad and a pitcher of Bloody Marys. Tommie brought them a plate of lemon slices, tartar sauce, and some extra hot sauce for the drinks.

"How hot do you like yours, Mick? I'll bet plenty hot." She gave him a mischievous smile, and he watched her walk away, her shorts showing off her long brown legs.

"Come back to earth, Mick." Rita shook her head. She squeezed a lemon slice on her salad and took a sip of the Bloody Mary. "Do you realize I'm the only one who hasn't been summoned to headquarters so far?"

"They never think a woman is responsible for anything." Britt took a bite of the salad and washed it down with his drink.

"I haven't heard much. One of your island reporters tried to fill me in, but Eric didn't let her say much. What have you heard?" Sever watched Britt, wondering if the soundman had something to do with the killing. He'd really ripped Bartholomew yesterday, but he just didn't seem to be the type to kill someone.

"Same as you, Mick They woke me up early this morning, dragged me downtown, and asked me what happened last night."

"And?"

"I'm sorry, Mick. You never should have been taken down there. All I did was say that we'd been recording late and that you and I sat up and had a couple of drinks." He took a long drink of his spicy beverage. "Right away they jumped on that. I never meant to involve you. It's just what happened."

"Jonah, I'm not upset. I'd just like to know what *did* happen."

"Because it's going to juice your story."

"Hey," his defenses took over. "I told you I wasn't going to write about the strange things that are happening at your studio. But this, this killing of Teddy Bartholomew, it's not going to stay quiet. I got seven calls this morning already from the States." Damn it, he was not going to give in to Jonah on this one. "Do you understand that it's probably front page news on *Billboard* and most of the tabloids this week. *Entertainment Tonight* will have a field day with it, and I'll lay odds it will be the cover story of *People*, *Us*, and possibly the *National Enquirer*. The *Star* will have it, and *Newsweek* would like a piece by three this afternoon. So listen, partner, there is absolutely no way I'm laying back on this one."

"Mick, I didn't mean to imply —"

"Then don't. This is a big story, and I've got a job to do. Does it involve your studio? I don't know. Maybe it was a robbery, maybe it was a local drug thing, or maybe it had something to do with Johnny Run. Whatever it is, whatever comes out, I've got to write the story."

"Mick, all I meant was —"

"And I've got a good sense that you'll like my version of the story a whole lot more than someone from the outside." Sever took a deep breath. Time to calm down and give it a rest. He'd said his piece, and almost had a heart attack while doing so. He wanted to make it perfectly clear that no one, not Jonah Britt, not Rita, or anyone else, was going to take this story away from him. It's what he lived for. It's what made him tick.

Rita reached out and put her hand on Jonah's. He looked at her, and she turned to Sever. "It's tough, Mick. We've got a lot invested in the new place, and we just don't need this kind of reputation. Not now. Not ever. Surely you can understand that. For one quick story, we could suffer a lifetime of crap."

Sever nodded. "But," he held up his index finger, "this story is going to draw a lot of attention to Johnny Run's new CD. And it may very well help sell the hell out of it."

Britt let out a deep breath. "Is that what it takes to sell records today? A lurid story about drugs and murder? Jesus, I thought a solid production might be just the answer. Apparently not."

"Your production is going to sell the record, Jonah. You know it, I know it." Sever shrugged his shoulders. "If the album sells well, you'll get back some of that good reputation that you want." He saw the tiredness in Britt's eyes. "Jonah, the story about the murder is already out there. There's nothing you, Rita, or I can do about it. Think about the album. Think about turning the bad news around. Who cares if the killing helps sell records. If *it's* a hit, *you're* a hit."

Britt's face was pale and drawn. "Groups are strange, Mick. I don't have to tell you. They can be very superstitious. An artist wants to record in a studio where the magic has happened. I remember visiting the Abbey Road Studios in London years ago. They'd kept the Beatles' studio the same — yellowed walls from the cigarette smoke, baffling that was old and matted, worn carpeting, but it was the Beatles' studio. The Beatles. And the room was booked for months, for years, in advance."

"As you said, it's where the magic happened."

"And it's one of the reasons so many of the big acts recorded here in our old studio."

Sever nodded. Legendary artists, legendary productions.

"This isn't that studio. The old studio had history. Major acts, number-one hits. It meant something. The new studio doesn't have the track record. It doesn't have that reputation. And we need to build it. As fast as possible."

"You'll build it, Jonah. And I firmly believe it will be bigger than before."

"But it also might have a reputation of murder. Spirits, strange things going on? You heard Stretch last night. He's worried about it. It'll end up killing us, Mick. That's my greatest fear."

Sever couldn't argue the point. The public would come to their own opinion. But the story of the murder was already told. There was nothing anyone could do about that.

Rita gave a slight shudder. "Maybe now isn't a good time to bring this up, but I think you two should know." She took a deep breath. "I talked to Etta May this morning. Bernard found the body." Rita gripped Britt's hand a little tighter.

"What?" Britt pulled his hand away and frowned. "You didn't tell me this."

"Jonah, you spent most of your morning downtown. This is the first chance I had to tell either of you." She topped off her glass and poured some of the drink into Britt's glass as well.

"Was she shook up?" Sever wished he could take notes, but the tension at the table was a little too much for that.

"She was upset because of the effect on Bernard. Apparently he came screaming into the house. The kid can be an emotional basket case."

"The kid?" Jonah rolled his eyes. "Etta May qualifies for the emotional basket case as well. Bernard's twin, Samuel, was the only one in that family that was normal."

"Whatever. Finding the body, that couldn't have been pleasant. Anyway, Etta May says that it's just one more event in the traumatized boy's life. I agree with you. Mother *and* son have some loose screws."

"So, what did she say happened?" Sever could sense she was agitated.

Rita's eyes left his and she stared out at the water. Kids in bathing suits were laughing and playing in the sand, a volleyball game was going on not thirty feet from them, and just offshore a catamaran skimmed across the clear blue water heading out to sea. Sever wondered what was going through her mind.

Finally she looked at him. "I know it sounds silly, but I can't rule out the spirit thing. There was a dead body in the fire, and how can we say that the ghost of that person isn't out there, looking for redemption?"

"Rita, that's crazy. You know —"

She cut Britt off. "No! It's something that the Obeah man said."

"We're back to the Obeah man?"

"Just hear me out. He said that we are housing a spirit that was disturbed by the fire and isn't happy. The spirit is trying to destroy sights and sounds."

"Jesus! Rita, speak like a sane person, okay." Britt reached for his glass and swallowed half of his drink.

She didn't seem upset. Almost calm. "Etta May said something had crushed Bartholomew's windpipe. And when Bernard found him, he was sitting upright, in the Cadillac, with a joint in his mouth. Apparently like he had been smoking it when someone crushed his throat. Very staged."

The three of them sat there, each picturing the gruesome discovery. Bernard had a reason to go screaming back to the house.

"So why the mention of a spirit? Why bring up the Obeah man? Spirits may knock a guitar off the wall. I suppose, if spirits exist, they could interfere with digital recording and erase music tracks," Sever felt foolish even discussing the topic, "but it would take someone of some serious strength to strangle Teddy Bartholomew. I'm convinced of that."

"I didn't see the body, Mick. Apparently Etta May ran out as soon as Bernard reported to her. She said the throat was swollen and the skin was red and raw. She listened for breathing, put her hand to his chest to detect a heartbeat, and then looked into his face."

Sever took a long swallow of the drink, letting the alcohol work its way through his bloodstream, calming him down. "His face. And then?"

"And what?" Britt was staring into her eyes. "You're leaving something out."

"I don't know if the police will release this information or not. Maybe they don't want anyone to know." Her face was pale and drawn. "Etta May tells me that she finally looks up into his face and —"

"What? Rita, don't be cryptic."

"You think I'm crazy because I suggested that the 'ghost,' the dead body they found in the old studio, may be haunting us. Or some spirit from the past may be trying to get some satisfaction. You think I'm crazy because I talked to an Obeah man. Don't you? You think I'm a little crazy."

"Rita, what does this have to do with the cops?" Sever folded his hands on the table.

"The Obeah man said that this spirit wanted to destroy sights and sounds."

Britt let out a long sigh, shaking his head ever so slightly. Sever could tell they'd had the conversation about this a few times at least.

She looked at Sever, not her husband.

"The cops didn't share anything with you?"

"The basics. Teddy was strangled and they found him in the Cadillac. Apparently they think he'd been smoking grass."

"Etta May says there's more."

"How much more?"

"You're not going to believe it."

"Try me, Rita."

The noise from the restaurant, the dishes banging on trays, the silverware clanking, and the melding of conversations from the tables and booths seemed to fade away.

"Mick, I'm not saying I'm convinced that a spirit was responsible for all this stuff. But I try to keep an open mind. And keep in mind, I didn't see the body."

"What did Etta May see?" She was dragging it out, almost as if she didn't want to get to the end of the story.

"The throat had been crushed. Sound had been cut off."

"Okay."

"And there were holes where the eyes had been."

Jonah stared at her as if he hadn't heard. "Holes?"

"Somebody had removed the eyes, Jonah. Teddy Bartholomew had no eyes."

CHAPTER EIGHTEEN

His head throbbed, his dreams ready to spill from the cavities. His mouth, his eyes, his nostrils, his ears. To once again make the killer record. To be raised up, honored, awarded as a world-class producer. To have the material wealth that comes with it all. The fame, notoriety, the halcyon days of wine, women, and song. It was in his far distant past, yet he could taste it like yesterday. And the final dream, the dream that would stay just a dream, to have his body back. To have his face, his hands, his legs and arms as they were just a year ago. That dream brought tears to his eyes. Somebody was going to pay dearly for that.

Bobby Baron's empty coffee cup sat in front of him, the remaining drops now cold. He'd checked the finances and realized he was running dangerously low, but a cup of coffee was almost a necessity. When you were conserving your stash, and you didn't have alcohol, or any other illegal substance to give you an edge, a little caffeine helped to sharpen the senses.

Starbucks. They were alive and well in Nassau. Six locations and he'd visited every one of them. There was something about the buzz. Could alcohol be any more potent?

"Excuse me."

Baron peered up from under the brim of his cap. He wore his sunglasses, but even through them he could see the man was dark.

Darker than most blacks on the island. And he wore a stern look on his face.

"Yes?"

"Your coffee?"

"Yes?" What about his coffee?

"You finished it fifteen minutes ago."

Baron blanked out. He slowly closed his eyes. Confrontation was a bitch.

"Sir?"

The man was insistent. "Are you going to sit there forever? I have three friends who would like a table."

Pushy. Rude. And he'd think of an entire list of other terms he could use. He watched the heavyset man through watery eyes.

"Well, are you going to give me your table or not? What is it?"

Baron glanced around the room. Every table, every seat was taken. Ladies with fancy whipped cream drinks, groups of young people, and a handful of men with laptops, working the keyboards into a frenzy. Baron came back to focus on the big man. "The what it is is that I come here often. Not like some of the slimy tourists who frequent our island."

"Look, friend," he was growling, "I'm trying to find a seat. You seem to be just taking up space. Either you have business here or you don't. Now, please, give me an answer before I kick the shit out of you."

Baron looked into the man's face. In a brief instant he realized the speaker spoke the truth. He would kick the shit out of Bobby Baron. And with all the pain that Baron had been through, he didn't need to be kicked again.

"I'm sorry. So sorry." Baron stood up, slowly, awkwardly, then turned to the accuser. He pulled off his cap exposing his hairless scalp, and slowly removed the sunglasses. Staring at the big man from under the stretched skin of his reconstructed eyelids he watched as the man's face crumbled.

"Oh. My God. My God."

"I'm sure you and your friends will enjoy your coffee. I'd be more than happy to give you my seat."

He could tell. The man wanted to look away, look anywhere but at Bobby Baron's deformed face. The scars on his head where the flames had burned away his hair and follicles. The man wanted to close his eyes, but he couldn't. Like watching a bad train wreck. He couldn't take his eyes off Baron.

"Is there something else? I certainly don't want to get my ass kicked."

"No. No." The big guy bowed his head, turned, and walked out of the building, followed by two other men. Sometimes you had to use what you had. Baron pulled the cap back on, put the sunglasses on, and sat back down. Others in the coffee shop quickly looked away, in shock, in awe. Baron didn't care. He'd become a freak, a sideshow character. Maybe he'd have one more cup of coffee.

He pulled a folded sheet of paper from his shirt pocket. An aerial photograph of the new Highland Studios was on one side. He ran his finger around the outside of the building, then opened his hand and placed it palm down on the structure. If he was a giant, he'd have squashed it. He noticed how far each of his fingers reached out and he studied the distance each finger represented. The neighborhoods that surrounded the building, the hotel across the street, the house next door with the small dark spot that represented the ever-present Cadillac. He looked at each one of them. He'd go back again tonight. Needed to go back. There was business to take care of, and he was the only one to do it.

CHAPTER NINETEEN

She stroked his chin, running her finger over his jawbone.

"You have a strong face."

"Is that a good thing?"

"You have other parts that are strong as well." She stretched out and he marveled at her lithe limbs. There seemed to be no shyness about her at all. She was proud of her naked body and he was glad because he admired every inch of it.

"Mick, I have to go. I start the second shift in half an hour."

"Bartending, right?"

"I am a very good bartender. Almost better than a waitress. I can make drinks like love potions or drinks that can cast a spell on you. I'm very good. Voodoo queens seek me out when they want a special magic." She laughed. "Do you believe me? Do you think I could cast a spell on you with one of my magical drinks?"

"I'm not exactly in the market for the woo-woo factor, Tommie. Not right now. But, you have some other talents that I didn't know about."

She smiled seductively. "I'm very good at those talents, too, am I not?"

"Oh, you are."

She put her bare feet on the floor, blew him a kiss over her shoulder, and walked to the bathroom. "You know, Mr. Sever, this could mean my job."

"They'd fire you for looking after the needs of your customers?"

"Well —"

"Then I'd hire you."

She turned on the shower and he watched her bend over, adjusting the water. The best view on the island so far.

"To do what?"

"I'd find something."

She looked up at him. "Do you like what you see?"

"Very much."

"Then maybe you would hire me to see things for you."

"What?"

"You need eyes on the island."

"That makes no sense."

Leaving the curtain open, she stepped into the shower, the water caressing her body. When he showered, it just bounced off. The water seemed to cling to her brown skin, and slide down like oil. He wasn't ready for her to go back to work just yet.

"Mick, I see things. I hear things. If you are doing more than just a story about the studio, if you are trying to find out who killed this man, who is stealing bass guitars, I may be able to help."

Her coal black hair hung in ringlets, and finally she pulled the shower curtain closed. "I'm very good at a number of things." She spoke loudly over the cascading water.

"Tommie, I'm no longer surprised by your endless talents."

She laughed. When she stepped out she wrapped herself in a large, terry cloth towel. "No more this afternoon, Mick. Maybe around three when I get off work?"

"You get off at three? Long past my bedtime."

"Oh, you can stay in bed. I may even join you. Would you like that?"

Sever watched her dry her hair, using another large absorbent towel. "You get off at three?"

"Yes. Why do you keep asking?"

"And what do you do?"

"Usually find a rich guest to sleep with." She flipped her hair and stepped into the bedroom. "What do you think I do? I go home. Seven miles from here."

"That's it?"

"No. I sometimes take a glass of wine and go outside to see the moon and the stars. And I think about my life, my dreams —"

"Last night, did you have the glass of wine?"

"I did."

"And did you happen to look across the road? To the studio?"

She studied him, still toweling the hair. "And if I did?"

"Did you see anyone? Did you notice anyone smoking. Possibly in the old Cadillac car that sits on cement blocks?"

"Mmmm. I wasn't looking for anyone."

"Think."

"I may have seen someone in the car."

"You really did? Are you just saying that because I asked?"

"No. I hadn't thought about it." She turned on the hair dryer, spreading her shiny mane as the dryer evaporated the water from it. Ten minutes later she was done.

"The car? Smoking?"

She pulled on her underwear, then her shorts and blouse. He missed her already.

"No. What I saw were reflections of the stars." She ran a brush through the hair, and it was as if they'd never made love. She was cleaned up, as if it had never happened.

"What kind of reflections?"

"Stars."

"Where?"

"The windshield of the old car, Mick. A twinkling light, moving across the windshield. I only paid attention for a brief time. I watched the orange glow move back and forth across the windshield before I finally realized that it must be a star in the sky."

Or the burning tip of a cigarette. "You could see all that from over here?"

"Mick, is it so important? I probably imagined it all." She slipped on her sandals and walked to the door. "Please, visit me for dinner if you'd like. Or for drinks later. And if I don't hear from you, you might find me at three a.m. under the stars, sipping wine."

"I'll find you."

She walked out the door, never looking back. Sever rested his head on the headboard. An orange glow that moved back and forth in the windshield of the Cadillac.

A reflection? Or someone smoking? But she said it moved. It was a long shot, but two people sharing a joint might appear that way.

He tossed back the sheet, and stood up to take a shower. He could still smell her musky perfume. It was on the sheets, in the towels, and he knew he'd count the hours until three a.m.

CHAPTER TWENTY

He walked across the street, wanting a closer look at the car. She stepped out of her doorway, arms folded, almost daring him to come closer.

"Etta May."

"What you want?"

"We met. Remember?"

"So?"

"I . . . I wanted to see the car again."

"You gonna buy it?"

"No."

She was quiet. Arms folded. Frown on her pudgy face.

"Can I look inside?"

"What? You want to see where the rock-and-roll man died?"

Why not be honest? "Yeah."

"You're not gonna buy it? Not interested? Maybe a little?"

"I'm not. Interested in buying it, I mean. I'm interested in seeing where Teddy Bartholomew was last night."

She nodded, her arms still folded. "Elvis owned this car. It would be a nice car to own. Especially for a writer, like yourself. Your writer friends would be envious."

"I appreciate your effort, but I'd just like to see the inside of it. Can I do that?"

"Eric was here. They took pictures, looked for fingerprints, and dusted. They were looking for somethin' from the killer. But," she unfolded her arms and shrugged her shoulders, "I think they found nothin'. Now, he's done with the car so I suppose it's okay."

Sever pulled on the passenger door, the squeaky hinges grating on his nerves. If he ever found a can of WD40—

"What are you lookin' for?" She eyed him warily.

He glanced up. She wore what his mother would have called a "house dress." A single garment that was buttoned high at her neck and hung low on her hefty calves, thin but patterned with some overdone tiny flower. Very matronly. Sever forced the image of Eric, the short cop, and Etta May out of his mind. It wasn't a pretty picture.

"I asked you, what you want?"

He put his hands up. "Easy, Etta May. I'm a reporter and I'm just naturally curious. I told you, I just wanted to see where Teddy Bartholomew died."

"You want to see *how* he died. You lookin' for the killer like Eric is?"

"I'm not trying to take on Eric's job. I just wanted to see where it happened. I'm probably going to do a story on the murder for a magazine back in the States."

"So you'll write about the Cadillac?"

How could he not? And the strange woman and the twin sons who owned it. It would actually make a great background for the story.

"This Cadillac, here — rock-and-roll history, Mr. Reporter. Elvis lived in that car, drove it to concerts, to the homes of beautiful women, and this slimebag Teddy somebody died in Elvis's car."

Sever stuck his head in the door. The smell of stale ganja was strong. He glanced at the windshield, remembering Tommie's recollection of the floating orange glow. Passing a joint? Or stars and lights playing tricks in the reflection?

"Somebody smoked in that car last night. Wasn't just no cigarette." She stood there, a frown on her face.

Elvis had died from polypharmacy, a lethal interaction of drugs.

There were something like fourteen different drugs found in his body at the time of death. Maybe Elvis had smoked grass. Maybe the odor had permeated the car. He breathed deeply. Strong odor. And he reminded himself—Elvis had never owned this car. Never even laid eyes on this car. Probably had never been within two thousand miles of this car.

"This man who was killed here, he was one of them."

"One of who?"

"One who smoked the weed, did the drugs, did the deed. There's a string of them that come through that building." She pointed at the studio.

Inside the car, there wasn't much to see. The leather upholstery was worn, torn, and missing in places. The gearshift handle was missing as were the knobs on the radio. Vandals who were using them as replacement parts, or possibly someone who thought the car really belonged to the King. They were probably listed on eBay.

"You seen enough?"

The ashtray was gone, and the turn signal lever had been broken off. There wasn't much left of the car. Sever was surprised that the frame of the steering wheel was still intact. Chunks of plastic from the wheel were missing, and again Sever figured that someone, somewhere, had sold the pieces for a tidy profit.

"Your son found the body?"

She nodded, still eyeing him suspiciously. "Bernard. He found the man. It wasn't a pretty sight."

"Rita says you told her that the face had been disfigured."

"She told you right."

"They eyes were —"

"Gone. Just holes in the head."

She said it in a matter-of-fact tone. Sever shuddered. "Etta May, there's no blood in the car."

"He was strangled. That's the way we found him. There's no blood when a body is strangled."

"If the eyes are cut out, there would be blood."

She studied him, sullenly, quietly, and he felt like she was casting a spell. That's all he needed. A spell.

"No blood, Etta May." He looked back into the car. No blood.

"Maybe it was the spirit. The ghost. Maybe the ghost took his eyes. There's things that we can't explain, Mr. Reporter."

"This ghost, these spirits, they can mutilate a body with no blood?" Sever tried to keep a smile from his face. He didn't know much about the lady, but he didn't want to offend her. She seemed to be the type of person who would take offense, and he didn't want to face her wrath.

"There are spirits in this world, Mr. Reporter, who can do all kinds of things. Things that a mortal can't understand."

Trying to reason with Etta May wasn't getting him anywhere. "Is your boy okay?"

She squinted, staring intently at Sever, still working her magic. "Samuel?"

That didn't sound right. Samuel?

"Bernard? Are you talkin' about Bernard?"

He'd forgotten. There were twins. Of course he meant the one living with her. "Bernard. Is he okay? I mean, after he saw the body?"

"He's never okay. Not for a long time. This," she waved her hand at the car, "this didn't help."

A burned black smudge on the floor mat told him that someone had lost a hot ash. It appeared to have done little damage, not that damage to this rusty bucket of bolts mattered. Who knew how many people had sat in this seat? Who knew how many people had put their hands on this steering wheel? Maybe the King. Maybe Elvis actually sat in the Cadillac. Dust covered everything and the musty smell watered his eyes.

"Elvis drove this car, sir. Include that in your story if you will. We would appreciate it. And nothin' says you can't mention that the car is for sale."

"Etta May, just for my own education, how do you know that Elvis owned this car?"

She squinted in the fading sunlight, folding her arms again and staring him down. He thought about the Obeah man, a person of hexes and voodoo magic. Etta May seemed to possess some of the same characteristics.

"Are you sure this was his car?"

She frowned, and finally turned her back to him, walking into her opened doorway. Sever felt a slight chill in the air. Hell, if she believed it, why argue with her.

She spun around and pointed her fat index finger at him. "Mr. Reporter, you want to write a story?"

He nodded.

"Write about my son. The one who lives with me now. Both of my boys are good sons. Samuel was a wonder. But Bernard was born a special child. And he would be amounting to something by now. The boy would be working, making a good living, and maybe have a wife and a child. You and your musician friends, you've introduced Bernard to drugs, to wicked ideas. I lay it in your lap, Mr. Reporter. But we had money, we had everything you could want. I had whatever it would take to make my son healthy."

He watched her expressions. She was suddenly animated, not the sour, dour overweight homemaker he'd seen just moments ago.

"What about your other son?"

"Samuel?" She frowned. "He lives with his father on Grand Bahama. I don't care to discuss Samuel." Again with the look. "Or his father."

"I respect that." Don't push an interview where it doesn't want to go.

Etta May spread her arms. "I could have had the world. Do you understand?"

He nodded again, afraid to say anything and break her train of thought.

"Hell's fire, I *had* the world. This fine man I knew was giving me money, and would have done anything for me. Anything. And in a flash it was gone."

All of a sudden, Sever had questions. But she plowed ahead.

"It was the drugs. The pot, the prescriptions, anything he could get his hands on. And I was left by the side of the road. It was over. The drugs were more important. And now, my boy — my pride and joy — *he's* doing the drugs too."

"Etta May . . ."

"Oh, Bernard don't buy them. Hell no. The boy's got no money. These crackhead musicians keep him supplied. Your friends. Do you hear me Mr. Reporter? Your friends. And try as I might, I can't seem to control it. The boy is bad enough as he is. He don't need drugs to make him any worse, but these men, these women, they share with him. All for a chance to visit Elvis's Cadillac."

"This guy, whoever he was, the guy with all the money. He was willing to take care of Bernard?"

"It was before Bernard. It was a long time ago. Long time." He thought there were tears in her eyes. She wiped at her face and he was sure of it.

"And now this man, this man who happened a long time before Bernard, he's no longer in the picture?"

"He's gone. That is that."

"Aren't there treatment centers for Bernard? Somewhere, someone on the island who could help him?"

"I'll help him just fine." She'd erased the tears and pointed that finger at him. "You. You help keep these musicians away from my boy."

The second time someone had starting accusing him. Giving him orders. Hell, didn't they realize he was simply on assignment? He didn't even do drugs. Anymore.

"You make sure the car is closed and the windows rolled up, you understand?"

"Sure. I'm done here."

"You ask permission if you want to come back. You do what I say."

Sever smiled. What a bossy lady. He wondered where the kid was now. And, he wondered just how addled Bernard really was. He was smart enough to score off the recording acts that passed through.

Smart enough to do the drugs and get away with it. It seemed that Etta May only got involved after the fact.

"I'll expect you to take care of the car."

"I will."

"One more thing." She was sounding like Eric, the boyfriend cop. Always another question.

"What?"

"Don't take the idea of a spirit too lightly. I believe the dead roam the earth, and I've seen the proof. Those who doubt it will roam it forever. That's your punishment."

"Roaming the earth?"

"Spirits haunt us for a reason, Mr. Reporter. Listen to their message. I believe that the dead are still in our lives, sir. You would do well to believe the same thing."

Sever nodded. "I'll remember that."

"Oh, Mr. Reporter." Sever smiled. One more thing. She stopped just before entering the small block house. "You asked how I knew the Cadillac was Elvis's?"

"I did."

"You won't believe me if I tell you."

"Try me."

She pursed her lips, studying him. He could tell she wasn't sure he could be trusted with the information. Finally, Etta May licked her lips and in steady tones said, "He gave it to me."

She turned and walked into the house, slamming the door behind her.

CHAPTER TWENTY-ONE

He took a puff on the cigar, savoring the tangy smoke. It drifted from his mouth in a final haze and he snuffed it out in the large glass ashtray. Sever shifted in the outdoor lounge chair, sipping his strong, rich Bahamian coffee as he watched the cop car pull into the crushed-shell driveway that led up to the little house, and Eric step out.

"No eyes, Mick. What do you think about that?"

Sever looked up as Britt walked out of the studio.

"Almost like a ghostly kind of ritual."

"Jonah, are you starting to buy into the spiritual thing?"

Britt sat down with him and they watched Eric walk up the two steps onto the porch and knock on the door. Etta May let the police officer in, giving Sever and Britt a hard, cold look before she closed the door.

Britt ignored the question. "Rita's got a strange sense of what's real and what's not. However —" he paused.

"However what?"

"Are you a religious man, Mick?"

"Religious?"

"Did you grow up with the Church?"

Sever laughed. "My parents never saw the inside of a church. And they certainly never steered me anywhere near one."

"I grew up Catholic. Pretty intense. Filled with symbolism, rules, no-meat Fridays, statues of saints on the dashboard, crossing myself before I ate, and believing a wafer on the tongue will help absolve my sins. You may not understand all that, but I —"

"Jonah, I wasn't raised in a religious environment. That doesn't mean I don't know what goes on."

"No, no. I'm telling you this for a reason. Rosaries, patron saint medals, statues of Jesus in the garden, crucifixes." Britt sat down across from Sever and unbuttoned the first two buttons on his shirt. "A gold cross, Mick." It hung low on a thin gold chain and he rubbed it between his fingers. "Not just jewelry, but it's more of that symbolism. I suppose, down deep, I believe that this cross will save me someday. From what, I'm not even sure."

"What's your point?"

"What's the difference?"

Sever watched him button the shirt back up, hiding the necklace. "Difference in what?"

"In what Rita is suggesting."

"The Obeah man?"

"Sure. Hexes, black magic, voodoo, religion. Look at *me*, Mick. Genuflecting, going to confession, praying to a higher power that my studio will be a success. What's the difference. The Obeah man comes out, waves some burning leaves, says some mumbo jumbo, and the spirit goes away. Hell, Mick, we have priests, the Catholic religion has priests who perform exorcisms. Think about that."

He'd raised his voice, emphasizing his words with a clenched fist. Sever wondered if the man was defending his religion or mocking it.

"Mumbo jumbo, my friend." Britt pounded his fist. "Spirits are at the heart of every religion. I'm not sure there's a difference. It's not so hard to believe that she'd buy into this."

"You do? You buy into it?"

"Maybe. A little. But somebody, something, killed Teddy. And I feel certain that it was a real person."

"You're right." Sever shook his head up and down. "Somebody killed Bartholomew. A *real* person. But I talked to your neighbor, Etta May. Jonah, I brought up the fact that there was no blood in the car."

"Blood?"

"Come on, man. Somebody took his eyes out. Bartholomew's eyes were removed. I'm not a doctor, but I've got to believe that blood would be all over the corpse, the car, wherever Teddy was killed. Jonah, she said that spirits could accomplish any disfiguration without the spill of blood."

"The lady is certifiable. Crazy. A *real* person killed Bartholomew. A real person took his eyes out. There is no question about that."

"Glad to hear *you* haven't entirely lost your mind."

"You still don't get it. I think," he paused, trying to gather his thoughts, "I think that maybe spirits work through people."

Sever shook his head. "Fillet of a fenny snake, in the cauldron boil and bake; eye of newt, and toe of frog, wool of bat and toe of dog."

"What the hell is that?"

"Ahh, Jonah. It's from the Bard. Haven't you ever read *Macbeth*? I had to memorize something from Shakespeare when I was in tenth grade and that seemed like the cool phrase. You remember, Double double, toil and trouble, fire burn and cauldron bubble."

"Look, Sever, you can make fun of it, but there are a lot of things we don't understand."

"I'm not making fun, my friend. We've all got a dark side, Jonah. But I don't know that spirits play a part in it."

"Catholics believe the devil gets inside some people, Mick. That's all I'm saying. The priests exorcise demons from real people. The demons live inside these human beings. The Obeah man believes there are spirits, some good, some evil, and he's suggesting that they live on after the person is dead." Britt took a deep breath. There was a long moment of silence and he leaned back in the chair, lacing his fingers behind his head. "What scares me is that maybe he's praying to the same God I'm praying to."

Sever took another sip of his coffee. "And I can't believe we're having this conversation." An Obeah man? What the hell was this all about? Sever dealt with facts. Not some witch doctor who scared away spirits.

"Well, whatever the case may be, somebody propped Teddy up in that car after they carved out his eyes. That's scary. That's just bloody scary."

Sever nodded. It was time to do away with spirits, do away with the Obeah man. "Somebody is very sick."

"Yeah. And you know what scares me more than the fact that someone did that?"

"What?"

"Why. Why they did it."

"You just told me." Ghosts. It wouldn't go away. "You think spirits made them do it."

Britt pursed his lips and nodded. "Even spirits have their reasons, Mick. And there must be a reason."

They both sat back, watching the fading blue in the Bahamian sky. Sever found his eyes drifting to the Cadillac. He'd seen the body the night before, he was convinced of it, but thought it was just the shadows playing tricks on him.

"Rita's shopping. You got any plans?"

"There's a mixologist over at the hotel who makes a great rum drink — among other things. I was thinking about going over there."

"Something going on between you and this mixologist?"

Sever smiled. "As I said, she knows how to mix things up."

"You want some company?"

"For the drink?"

"I think I'll leave the rest up to you and the young lady."

"Sure. Let's go."

Britt stood up and walked to the door. Sever watched as he pulled out a key and locked the front door of the studio. He dropped the key back into his pocket.

The two men walked down the drive to the road, the last light in the sky fading fast as they crossed to the hotel.

"Have you known Tommie long?"

"She's been at the restaurant for the last three years."

"A very sweet girl."

"Yeah." Jonah agreed. "Sounds like you'd like to find out a little bit more about that sweet girl."

"Maybe." Sever kept his eyes straight ahead, focusing on the pastel-colored buildings in front of him. As they crossed the street he glanced at Britt. "I'll let you know."

He left Britt in the bar as he walked to his cottage, down the tree-lined path, up the multicolored wooden staircase to the porch that looked out over the ocean. He put his key in the lock and before he could turn it, the door swung open. Sever almost fell into the room.

He stood in the doorway for thirty seconds, trying to remember if he'd locked the room. Maybe housekeeping had left it open. That had to be what happened. He didn't have much that someone could steal. One suitcase, toiletries, and several changes of clothes. Three pairs of jeans, some T-shirts, and underwear. He checked the closet, the bathroom, and the sitting area. Nothing. The African art that adorned the room all seemed to be in place. Vases, baskets, a couple of small statues. They were all where they had been. It must have been housekeeping.

Picking up the phone he checked for any hotel messages. He didn't want to call the Stateside answering service again. He knew that would be on overload and he didn't need any of it. No more requests to cover the murder story for anyone. He just wanted to see if anyone had called the hotel. Only three people even knew he was here, and one of them was Ginny. He'd left a message on Ginny's machine. He always left a message, to tell her where he was. It was habit, but maybe, just maybe, she'd called. Hell, she hadn't called in six months. There were no messages.

With the phone still in his hand, he saw it on the bedspread. The tightly stretched bedspread with the crisp linen sheets folded at the top. With the duvet folded at the bottom and the seven pillows arranged in a pattern. He placed the receiver back in the cradle and stepped closer for a better look. It was a black cloth doll, slightly bigger than his hand. He didn't touch it, but studied it carefully. The rag doll appeared to be homemade, a crude sewing job of cloth and stuffing, but the doll's skirt was a course fabric of festive colors. He admired the tiny kerchief that wrapped around the doll's head, and the face that was roughly drawn on the head. Sever glanced around the room again. Just to be sure there was no one. No human presence. But someone had been in this room, leaving him the strange present. Walking to the door, he opened it and gazed out at the array of shadowy cottages and at the dark water.

It wasn't the doll itself that concerned him. Not even the fact that someone either had a key or knew how to pick the lock. What bothered him were the two large sewing needles that were shoved through the eyes of the doll, pinning it to the bedding. That bothered him just a little bit.

Strings of lights twinkled above the crowd of diners and drinkers, and a local three-piece band played on a small stage under the stars. Steel drums, guitar, and keyboard. Sever shuddered. They were playing one of the tourist favorites, "Yellow Bird." Someone should put the damned bird out of its misery.

Britt was standing just inside the bar, nursing a drink. "Everything all right, Mick?"

Sever smiled. He hadn't decided to tell anyone yet. See if someone tipped his hand. See if someone, even Britt, expected him to say something. It could all be a big mistake. His guess was that it wasn't.

"Yeah. No calls. I guess that means no problems."

Britt and Sever walked around to the crowded bar, where tourists and locals mingled in a bright array of colored shirts and skirts.

A small black man waved at Sever from a nearby table, and Sever waved back.

"You know everyone everywhere," Britt said.

"That's the problem. I don't. I think the guy is a regular on some cable series, but I'm not sure."

"And he's hoping you remember and mention him in a story?"

Sever nodded. "Something like that."

"Mick Sever."

Sever glanced at the end of the bar. A bald man in a bright orange shirt waved him over.

"Mick, did you hear about Teddy Bartholomew?"

Mark Holly, an entertainment journalist from — Sever couldn't remember who the guy worked for. The point was, the guy worked for someone and had probably jumped a plane as soon as he'd heard the news.

"Yeah. I heard."

"That's why you're here?" Holly's eyes were big and wide, and he took a big gulp of some lemon-colored drink.

"No." There was no reason to share.

"Well, we heard about it, and they wanted me to come over right away and do a —"

"Yeah, I understand, Mark. I don't mean to be rude, but I've got an appointment at the other end of the bar."

"Sure. Sure." The man was slurring his words. More interested in the drinking and the possibilities than in the story. *Miami Sun*. That was it. Holly worked for the *Miami Sun*.

Now the band was playing some Harry Belafonte song from the fifties. "The Banana Boat Song" or something equally lame. Sever and Britt walked down the bar, weaving between customers with drinks in their hands. Across the room Sever saw an attractive woman. Another celeb he couldn't quite place.

"Mick, isn't that the girl who played one of Cosby's kids on *The Cosby Show*?" Britt nudged him.

That was it. Tempestt somebody.

At the other end of the bar Tommie was pouring a neon blue drink from a mixing tumbler into a martini glass. She pushed it to a portly gentleman in shorts and a flowered shirt who was leering at her. Sever felt a moment of jealousy. Then she picked up a mixing glass and seamlessly filled four short glasses with a raspberry-looking concoction. She looked up and grinned, leaning across the bar to be heard above the din of conversation and music. Sever admired the lean figure, the sexy, trim body of the very attractive bartender.

"Ah, two of my favorite gentlemen. Have you come to let me mix some special spirits for you?"

"Spirits?" Sever smiled and glanced at Britt.

"Can't get away from them, Mick."

She gave them a questioning glance.

"It's nothing, Tommie. An inside joke."

"Well, then tell me what kind of spirits you would like to drink tonight."

Sever and Britt looked at each other, both breaking out in laughter.

"Jonah, you were right. I never should have doubted you. I'm sorry." Sever patted him on the shoulder. "I guess all of us can have spirits in us at one time or another."

CHAPTER TWENTY-TWO

It was still early. Dark outside, but early. He'd watched them walk across the road to the hotel, and earlier he'd seen the Mrs. drive toward town. No bands tonight. No music being made. So there was no one home. No human in the house. He said it to himself several times, vocalizing it as he stood in the shadows, smoking his cigarette. No human in the house. No human in the house.

He briefly glanced around the area, not really expecting to see anyone. It was still early, and there were no humans in the house. He walked to the rear of the building, staying close to the walls so he wouldn't be noticed. They lived back here. Back here when the bands were in town. Back in the small apartment so they could be on call for the rich and famous.

He knew. When it was December 31 and a band decided they wanted a private jet to take them to New York for New Year's Eve, the Britts had to be on call to get the job done. When a band member wandered across the road at three a.m. and wanted Scotch eggs with some Canadian bacon, the Britts had to be on call. More than just a recording studio, Highland Recording was a refuge. A place where every whim — almost every whim — was taken care of.

He stepped up on the wooden deck. A small table, four chairs, and a potted palm looked out over the alley that ran behind the studio. The kids back there were out of control. A gang of fifteen or twenty, they robbed the neighbors, smoked weed most of the day, vandalized nearby homes, and spent most of their time hiding from the police.

The banister was cut from rough-hewn lumber and he lifted his hand, afraid of getting a splinter.

The kids would be blamed. Blamed for any vandalism. They always were. Although, there was a rumor that the Mrs. thought there were spirits. Maybe the spirit of the ghost who died in the fire. If you couldn't prove that the gang of ragamuffin kids were to blame, blame spirits in the building. Spirits who spirited about, doing spiritly things, like smashing guitars, erasing sound tracks, stealing bass guitars, and removing drugs and drug paraphernalia.

Maybe *he* had spiritual connections. He'd often felt like something controlled him. Maybe spirits. Maybe the spirit that he knew and hated. That person, the physical body, was dead and buried, but there was something very strange in the building, as if the spiritual presence still existed.

He inserted the key into the lock, turned it, and opened the door. As soon as the whine of the alarm started he punched in the four-digit code and everything was silent. He waited, just to make sure that no one responded.

Everything was quiet. He'd never gone in this way before. It was always through the front door, the lobby, and he'd memorized the path. This one was strange, and he couldn't risk the chance of using any light source. He stepped inside, quietly closing the door. A dim light shone from a room on the right and he quietly walked toward that light.

Step by step, focusing on the light. One, two three, four—he counted the steps. Five, six, seven, eight. He could make out the far corner of the room. A white, overstuffed chair, a light brown coffee table, and a bookshelf on the far side of the room. Nine, ten, eleven, twelve. He was one step from the room. For a second he stopped. Two seconds, three seconds, four. Anyone who was in the building would have announced themselves by now. He hoped.

He stepped into the room, a nice living area with a flat-screen television and a chair and sofa arrangement. Books crowded the walls on dark oak custom shelves, and a full-figured fig tree overwhelmed the corner. No one sat in the spacious room.

He walked down the hall, every room seeming to run off the hallway. He counted the steps.

Twenty, twenty-one, twenty-two, twenty-three — the kitchen with soft, under-the-cupboard lighting. He quietly stepped in, and pulled open one of the cupboards. He reached up and pulled two china plates from a stack. He stepped back, dropped them on the white tile floor and shuttered as they shattered, the shards skidding across the porcelain. Damn spirits.

Blaming the spirits for the damage done. Maybe it wasn't such a good idea. The spirit who truly haunted this studio may not appreciate his wit. May not appreciate his need to blame the spirit world for the damage he did. But the spirit he despised, the one who haunted this building, that spirit was physically dead. Dead. And how many problems could a spirit, with no physical presence, cause? How many? An Obeah man could tell him, but his guess was the spirit was limited. Limited in his ability to cause any serious damage.

He walked through the kitchen and into the small entranceway. The bedroom. Queen-sized bed, two sets of drawers, an armoire with a television, and a bathroom and closet. Pulling the one drawer open, then the other, he didn't see what he was looking for. He dumped one on the bed. Socks and T-shirts. The second was more interesting. Lacy panties and bras. He held the undergarments between his fingers, picturing Rita wearing the thin material. On an impulse he picked up a lavender thong and shoved it in his pocket. A souvenir. He systematically worked his way through each drawer, dumping them on the bed. He was surprised at the neatness. Everything was folded, compartmentalized, and it made him feel good to destroy that neatness. He took his arm and brushed half the clothes off the bed onto the floor. He kicked them around and walked into the bathroom.

An electric clock sat on the counter, the small hand steadily clicking off each second. He'd been inside for ten minutes and had no idea when someone might come home. With a little more urgency he pulled out drawers, rifling through them faster and faster. Toothpaste and Q-tips, mouthwash and feminine hygiene products, a pack of disposable razors. Shit. This wasn't it at all. The closet. Clothes on hangers, shoes on the floor, and a small hard-shell carry-on bag sat by itself on the top shelf. He reached up and pulled it down. The slight squeak in the bedroom caught him short of breath. Freezing in place, he waited to see if it was repeated. There it was again, maybe the sound of a small child whining. Crying. Spirits? Was it the spirit that he despised? Surely that ghost wouldn't haunt him.

Softly, slowly, he walked into the bedroom. The whining was there again, coming from somewhere on the ground. His eyes darted around the room, looking for the source, and then he felt it brush his leg, and he kicked out. The cat screeched and went running into the kitchen, a blur of gray fur.

Still holding the hard-shelled luggage, he sat on the bed, trying to catch his breath. His heart was racing. Time was running out. Walking back into the bathroom he set the case on the counter and flipped the clasps open. He opened the top and smiled. There it was. Five bags of marijuana. Four bags of fine white powder. He didn't want it all. It was better to take a little, come back and get more, small quantities at a time. One bag of each.

They'd find it missing, questioning why someone wouldn't take the whole stash. They'd wonder if their count was wrong. And maybe the idea of spirits would stay alive. He shoved the bags inside his shirt and set the case back on the shelf. It was then he heard the door open. No alarm. Damn, he'd been so close. He stepped into the kitchen, moving quickly up the hallway toward the studios. Whoever came in was in the apartment. It would probably be a few seconds before they made their way through the rooms.

He stepped out of the hallway into another room, and in the dim light saw a pool table, foosball game, and a series of arcade video games lined up on the far wall. You had to cater to everyone. Every whim. He thought of all the recording artists who had played games in this room. Who had relaxed and chilled out, right here. The room had amazing history.

"Jonah?"

Rita's voice. She might have seen the broken dishes.

"Jonah? Are you here?" Alarm in her voice.

Maybe the clothes scattered around the bedroom. Or the toiletries spilled onto the floor in the bathroom. He had exaggerated his presence. He may have overdone the damage aspect.

"Jonah!"

In just a second she'd either come storming down the hall, checking each room, or she'd call the cops. He didn't need the hassle either way.

Now it was quiet. No voice, and he was aware of the stifling heat in the room. He was sweating, either from the heat and humidity or from the situation. He stuck his head into the hallway. No sign of anyone. He couldn't wait. He'd worn rubber-bottomed shoes, quiet on the white tile, and he started walking, taking long strides. Past the artwork, through the lobby. The quick movement scared him. He grabbed at his stomach where he'd hidden the bags. That damned cat. The gray monster hissed at him from a desk chair. He hissed back, quietly issuing a threat, and with a flick of the lock and a brief glance, he walked out the front door. Just like a paying customer.

CHAPTER TWENTY-THREE

A year ago he could have stayed at the Cove. Or even the Royal Towers, at $25,000 a night. Davis stood under the portico, watching as the fancy cars pulled up, letting out the high rollers, the posers, the tourists, and the opulently rich tenants of Atlantis.

Not too many years ago, the place was a one-trick pony owned by Merv Griffin. A Club Med. Now it was an industry in itself. And he really couldn't afford much of it. Not after the year that Johnny Run had had.

"Sir? Are you waiting for your car?" The uniformed man gave him a puzzled look.

"Uh, no. Just trying to soak the whole place in." He watched the Jaguar convertible pull up and a blonde in a tight sequined dress stepped out. Another attendant escorted her to the entrance as Davis's parking attendant nodded and moved on to three men with outlandish tropical shirts that did little to hide their over-the-belt paunches.

You could have it all in the Bahamas. Davis had smoked a couple of joints and had a couple of Jack Daniel's on the rocks just to steel himself for the experience. Then he'd taken the cab. He had a couple of thousand dollars in hundreds. It was money he could ill afford to lose, but he might need it tonight. It might not be enough but it was going to have to get him through.

The bright night-lights beamed on the gigantic seashells that seemed carved into the exterior, and the lights shone on the monstrous seahorses that paraded around the building and gazed into the artificially green-blue waters. It all made him sad. He wanted back on that horse, the one that crossed the finish line first.

He'd read the story. Teddy Bartholomew was dead. Supposedly strangled. And he'd been by there last night. His memory was foggy, but he knew he'd been there. He couldn't remember why. He'd taken a taxi to and from and maybe somebody could place him at the studio. Maybe somebody like the driver would place him, remembering that he got out, walked the grounds, then got back in. Maybe somebody would remember, but at the moment no one had knocked on the door of his shabby room. There was nothing in the local paper about any suspects.

Just that phone call, congratulating him for causing a buzz. Stirring something up. Someone assuming that he'd killed Teddy Bartholomew. So maybe he quietly needed to take the credit. Because he stood to make some serious money if Johnny Run came roaring back. Serious money. The kind of money that would buy a room at Atlantis. The kind of money that would put him back at the high-roller table.

And the syndicate, this shadowy group of investors, had made it pretty clear that he should do everything in his power to see that Johnny Run came roaring back. Because if the band didn't produce, if this record didn't "hit one out of the park," if the syndicate took another hit, Grant Davis was in some deep shit.

Lights played off the water across the bay and he watched the mega-yachts with their three-story conning towers lined up in front of pastel-colored condos with bleached white balconies and jutting rooflines. It was a fairyland. An overindulgent Disney World, for people with too much money and too much time.

He walked into the building, headed toward the casinos. He knew they hung out here when they weren't working, and tonight they were off. No mourning Teddy Bartholomew. No. This was rock and roll. Stretch and the rest of them would be out partying tonight. They hadn't mourned *his* firing, and Davis doubted there was much of anything that would shut these boys down.

The loud ringing and cacophony of the slot machines hit him with a wall of sound. In the far distance he could see tables of black-jack, Texas Hold'em and other table games. Roulette tables, the dice. What were those lyrics to "Viva Las Vegas"?

A fortune won and lost on every deal.

He could make that fortune happen tonight.

He bumped a little lady who clutched a cup of quarters tightly to her chest as she maneuvered through the row of slots. Each seat in the row was taken, and the men and women pushed buttons as fast as they could, eagerly watching the spinning wheels as they lined up the numbers, the fruits, the bars.

Past the row of noisy machines, flashing lights, working his way back, and then he saw the tall black man. Stretch sat at a table with Sonny, the drummer. Just the two of them, playing blackjack against the dealer. Davis bet that the stakes were pretty high. Even with a record that was a stiff, these guys got some pretty hefty royalties from years gone by. And, they were still a pretty hot act on the circuit. With the current price of concert tickets, Johnny Run made good money. It was just that they could do a whole lot better. And so could the backers.

He walked up to the table, approaching from behind. Davis stood there for several minutes, watching the two men play cautiously, never going too far. They won a hand and lost a hand. The third hand Stretch won a couple hundred bucks. Davis walked over and sat at the end of the table.

Sonny Tatone noticed him first. "Grant? How's it goin' man?" No real surprise in his voice.

"What brings you here?" Stretch looked at him with a frown.

He'd planned how it would go. Filled and fuelled with a little fortification, he stuck out his hand. "Stretch, what brings *you* here?"

Stretch looked at him through squinted eyes, a frown manifesting itself in the furrow on his forehead between his eyes.

Sonny seemed to notice the tension. "Hey, we're doin' another record. Up at Highland."

Davis smiled. "Yeah, I remember those times. I'm here on a little R&R. Needed to get away from New York, you know."

"Yeah. We all need to go away." Stretch looked back to the dealer and motioned to deal another hand.

"You in, Grant?"

"Sure, Sonny." Davis laid out two hundred dollars and the dealer shoved the chips in his direction.

"You heard about Teddy?"

Davis hesitated. He didn't want to seem too eager. "Something. He was in a car and died of an overdose or something like that?"

"He was strangled. Somebody took him out."

"Jesus." He looked at his cards. A ten up, a two down.

"Yeah. No reason so far, at least no reason that we know of."

Stretch took a card. "Funny you show up at the same time Teddy bites the dust."

Davis felt the alcohol in his veins giving him a little rush. Stretch was always giving him a shot. Sarcasm. Cynical zings that showed he didn't trust Grant. "And what the hell is that supposed to mean?"

Stretch was quiet.

Sonny took a card, Davis took a card. An eight.

"Look, I'm sorry about Teddy. I mean, I was sorry when things didn't work out between us. The band and everything. You know, I liked being the manager. I really did. I thought I did a good job, and I liked you guys. I always felt like we clicked. I know, I know, the record tanked, but—" he was blubbering. Probably shouldn't have had that second joint. He needed to just chill. Let it sit here and see what happened. "But, I liked Teddy too. I mean, God, who would murder him?" Davis motioned to a scantily clad waitress. "Jack and Coke."

She nodded.

The dealer showed eighteen, Stretch showed nineteen and

Davis had the twenty. Sonny was over. Davis was starting to think maybe he could actually walk away with some cash tonight. Then he reminded himself why he was still here. "Listen, this may not be the right time to say this, but if there is anything at all I can do —"

Nothing. The two players watched the dealer lay out the winnings.

Finally, Sonny looked up. "We haven't talked about it. I mean it just happened last night." The dealer scooped Sonny's chips.

"We've got to absorb it. How it affects the band, you know?" Stretch spoke without looking at Davis.

Yeah. And obviously you're really broken up about it. Davis kept his mouth shut, waiting to hear what else Stretch would have to say.

The dealer laid out another hand.

Stretch was quiet. He'd never had much to say to Davis. Or anyone else for that matter. Stretch would be the one who would be a problem.

Each looked at his hand.

Finally, he looked at Sonny. "We should talk about it."

"Yeah." He nodded at Davis, his long dreads waving. "We'll talk. You gonna be around?"

Just like that. You gonna be around? He'd worked out an entire presentation and even without delivering it, it sounded like these guys might be interested. At least Sonny was interested. And if the rest of the band listened to Sonny, maybe he had a chance. He'd brought $2,000 and might get away with a couple of hundred more here at the table. Hell, he might even win more than $200. The gods were smiling on him.

He needed to press this. It had gone better than he'd imagined.

"How about if I stop by the studio tomorrow?"

"Sure. We'll be there tomorrow, late afternoon."

Lazy fuckers. Wouldn't even get up until one p.m. "Hey, again, I'm sorry about Teddy."

Stretch didn't look up from his cards. "Yeah. So are we." He looked at the dealer. "Hit me."

CHAPTER TWENTY-FOUR

Eric the cop and his tall, thin partner walked into the bedroom, try-ing not to disturb the already disturbed clothing that was strewn around the room.

"Somebody was looking for something."

"You think?" Sever stood in the kitchen, watching the officers stumble through the investigation.

"Mr. Sever." The short, black officer turned, looked out the doorway, and gave him a grim smile. "Would you like to come down-town with us for some more questions?"

Sever thought about it for a brief moment. It hadn't been a pleasurable experience. "No."

"Then kindly keep your comments to yourself."

Sever took the advice. He leaned against the wall and turned his gaze to the broken plates on the floor. Rita stood over them, looking pale and drawn. She'd realized that the intruder was still in the studio when she walked in. If she'd surprised the person, confronted him, the situation could have turned out quite differently.

"I told you, Mick, something or someone is out to get us. Seriously."

Eric walked back into the kitchen. "Mrs. Britt, do you keep large amounts of cash in the house?"

She laughed nervously. "No. We don't have large amounts of cash. Anywhere."

Jonah came in from the studio. "Something spooked Oliver. He's hiding in the corner of the reception area under a desk and he won't come out."

"Mr. Britt, it seems obvious to me that someone was looking for something special. This wasn't someone just ransacking the place. They were looking for something they knew was in this house. If it's not money, could you venture a guess as to what it might be?"

Sever saw Jonah flinch. Slightly, but a flinch nevertheless.

"No. I've got a collection of guitars in one of the rooms up the hall —"

"Valuable?"

"Yes. And someone broke into that room and smashed one a couple of days ago."

"You didn't call us?"

Britt shook his head.

"Why didn't you call us, Mr. Britt?"

"Look, Eric, there have been some things going on since we opened back up. Nothing too serious, just a handful of events. I'm not positive the guitar didn't just drop from the wall."

Rita frowned and shot him a dirty look.

"There have been a couple of events. Nothing serious."

"Events?" The cop peered from under the brim of his cap, his hands folded on his protruding stomach.

"Things I can't explain. Someone broke in and erased a recording session — a couple of other incidents."

"A recording session?"

"I'd recorded several songs with a band, and the next day the recordings had been erased."

Eric scribbled something on his tablet. "And still you never called us?"

"I couldn't prove it. It might have been electrical. But twice. We called twice. And twice an officer took our report by phone. And about two months ago *you* came out, do you remember? I mean, it's not like we haven't worked together before."

Eric nodded. "Mr. Britt, you even told me you thought maybe

you'd left the door unlocked that time. A small painting was missing if I remember right?"

"Yeah. From the lobby. And just the other day a picture fell from the wall. It's the little stuff. Not much I can put my finger on."

"And this time? Has anything been stolen?"

Britt looked at his wife. "Not tonight, but recently. Maybe."

"What?"

"About a week ago one of our recording acts claims that someone stole his bass guitar. I'm not sure it wasn't just misplaced."

Eric pulled a small pad of paper from his shirt pocket and jotted down some notes.

"It might have been misplaced?"

"I don't see how anyone could have had access to the room where he stored it. Anyway, we're going to cover it so no big deal."

"And nothing else is missing?"

"No." Almost too abrupt.

"You're sure? You've looked around?"

"We will. I mean, once you're done here, we'll check. I'll call you if anything is gone."

"You and your wife have no idea who would cause this disruption? You don't have any suspects or reasons?"

"You know the neighborhood. I blamed some of it on the kids back down the alley. And, Eric?"

"Yes?"

"I know how much time you've spent on our fire, but—"

"But what?"

"To be totally honest with you, the law enforcement here leaves a lot to be desired."

The cop frowned. "Our resources are somewhat limited, Mr. Britt. I'm sorry we don't come up to your expectations. However, we will continue to do the best that we can do."

He spun around, glaring at Sever. "And Mr. Sever was with you the entire evening?"

"Oh, for God's sake. Yes. Mick has nothing to do with this."

He nodded again. "We'll take some fingerprints, but I doubt

that we'll find anything. Shouldn't be more than fifteen minutes. If you think of anything else, please call me at the station." His ending was abrupt and he wrote in his notebook with a final flourish. Don't tell the Nassau Police they aren't doing their job.

Call me at the station or just drop by next door at Etta May's, Sever almost said. The cop was probably more interested in the nutcase next door than he was in the fire and mischief at Highland Studios.

"Thanks, Eric. We'll be outside on the porch if you need us."

Jonah, Rita, and Sever walked outside and sat down on the chairs that surrounded the table on the back patio, looking out at the dark alley.

"Nothing is missing?" Sever watched them both.

They were quiet.

"Well?"

"We'll check later." Rita looked straight ahead.

"Come on, guys. You can tell me."

"We're not sure." Jonah rocked back and forth in his chair.

"Money?"

"No." Rita clasped her hands in front of her.

Jonah drummed his fingers on the tabletop. "We had some drugs, Mick. Some grass, some coke."

"And it's gone?"

"No."

"Jonah, I'm trying to follow this."

"Once again, Mick. This is off the record?"

He took a deep breath and let it out. "Jonah, this record you keep mentioning. It doesn't have much of anything on it at this point."

"I'm sorry, Mick. You want stories? This is the only way I can give them to you. It has to be off the record."

"Yeah. I understand. Although, you've got to admit, it's got the makings of a great story. Producer ripped off. Someone is stealing his stash."

"We think maybe some of it is gone. But whoever took it didn't take much."

"And," Rita gave a slight shudder, "we're not sure any of it is gone. We had some stuff. When some of the bands wanted to unwind —"

"And maybe some of it is gone. We're not sure."

"Maybe?"

"If we had to bet, they took some."

"Why not all of it?"

Britt shrugged his shoulders.

"And you can't tell Eric."

Britt gave Sever a grim smile. "No. But as dense as the little fucker is, I'll guarantee you that he's considered it."

"These drugs?"

"We've got them. Hidden. Don't worry about it."

"Rita, you know a *real* person messed up your home?"

She gave him a hard look. "No one *broke* in, Mick. The house was locked when I came in."

"And Jonah said he set the alarm, Rita. Explain how it was off when you came home. It was off, right?"

"It was and I can't."

"Now you know what we've been going through."

"I watched Jonah lock the door."

"We're changing the locks and the alarm tomorrow. If they still get in, we're calling the Obeah man." Rita didn't smile. She just rocked gently back and forth in her chair.

CHAPTER TWENTY-FIVE

Eric's tall, thin partner left, Eric stayed, and Sever stayed on the porch, watching the stars and listening to a night bird warble. The sound was mournful, and he thought about Ginny. His ex was somewhere back in the States, probably Chicago, maybe L.A., working on a book, a project, some new guy, or her life.

And what about his life? Hustling a twenty-something bartender in the Bahamas, still following rock and roll bands, and trying to wean himself off of the excesses that would be excessive for someone half his age. Sex, drugs, rock and roll. He'd invented the style. And now sex, drugs, rock and roll, and murder.

Somebody was trying to scare him. Maybe run him off this island paradise. The black voodoo doll with pins in its eyes. Was he supposed to leave the island and let the Nassau police finish the investigation? All he wanted was a good story. He wasn't a detective, and he never had any desire to solve a crime. So why target him? Was he on to something? Maybe.

Sever stretched his leg, the strained tendons aching as he stood up. He walked off the porch and took twenty steps down the alley. He could see lights through the windows of the small shacks and houses that lined the narrow stone path. Somewhere he could make out a radio playing a reggae tune. A televised game show sound track drifted in and out from halfway down the block and a loud argument rose above all the sounds, interrupted by long moments of silence.

Then it started again. Man and woman. Sever couldn't make out all the words, but the gist of it was a matter of fidelity. The words "cheating whore" and "fucking bastard" came through more than once.

The alley noise almost covered the rustling from across the way. In the moonlight he thought he saw the bushes by Etta May's house move. No breeze, but the shrubbery moved. Sever froze and watched intently. Someone crouched by her house. A shadow. Slowly it stood up. The shape appeared to be a man, possibly wearing a cap. The person stood for at least a minute, stock-still. Then, started moving slowly toward the alley. Whoever it was tried to blend in with the other shadows, staying close to the trees and bushes that ran behind the house.

Sever took a step, then another, and the figure froze.

"Hey."

Nothing.

"Who are you?"

Again cold silence.

Now he couldn't be sure the figure was still there. The moon was behind a cloud and the thick growth hid the person. If there was still a person there.

"Who's there?" He took another step and still another.

With a burst of speed the person started running, taking Sever by total surprise. Short strides, and hunched over, the figure headed down the alley. Sever spun and followed in pursuit. The pain in his leg nagged at him, but the man or woman seemed hobbled as well, slowing down, favoring the right leg over the left.

Now Sever was closing the gap. His biggest concern was what he'd do if he caught the runner. Was it the burglar? An intruder who'd trashed the apartment?

His breath was giving out, his respiration now ragged and his chest aching. The little exercise he got at the Bayfront Gym in Chicago didn't prepare him for distance running. Not even sprinting. It was a sad state of affairs that he could only last this long.

Now the person turned, heading down a dirt path between two small shacks, and Sever followed in close pursuit. Tommie was going to meet him at three a.m., and she expected a little excitement at that hour. Sorry to disappoint, but he was going to be wrecked by then. One foot after another, he jogged down the moonlit path, seeing the distance close and wondering how much longer his lungs could take it. He was gulping for air, and then the runner was gone. Seconds before, the sprinter had been thirty feet ahead. Now, the path was empty as if the runner had magically disappeared.

Sever ran, ten, twenty, thirty feet, slowing down, his eyes shifting right to left, trying to see where the person may have gone. Maybe the sprinter had collapsed, as Sever thought *he* might do. Maybe turned off and gone another direction. Then, in an instant from the deep shadows of a small blockhouse he saw the shadow hurtle at him. Too late to stop it, too late to stop himself, Sever felt the impact, hard on his side. He went crashing into the dirt and stone. The figure was on him, pounding with fists, striking Sever's body and face as the struggling writer pushed and tried to stand.

The fist landed on Sever's chest and he felt his ribs cave. In desperation he threw out his arm, grabbing the fighter by the neck. There was a guttural growl — definitely a man — and Sever hung on, tightening his grip. Tighter yet so the man couldn't breathe. Now Sever rolled on top, his ribs aching, his lungs crying out for more oxygen. The man's hat had come off and in the pale light Sever could see he had no hair. His black face looked as if he had a mask on and Sever drew back his fist, ready to hit the guy and try for a knockout.

The masked man kicked, coming straight up between Sever's legs. Sever felt the sharp pain before he identified the cause, crying out. His opponent pushed him off, leaped to his feet, and Sever could hear his pounding feet disappear down the alley.

He lay there, feeling the throbbing pain in his groin, the tenderness in his ribs, and still trying to get his breath. Through the agony he made a promise to himself. Either he was going to get in much better shape or he was not going to tackle the bad guys again. Ever. And just as quickly he decided between the two alternatives. Let the bad guys get away.

CHAPTER TWENTY-SIX

Eric wrote down the information in brief, scrawled notes at the kitchen table. Sever rested on a vinyl chair as Rita applied some sort of lotion to the cuts on his face. He drank liberally from the half glass of Scotch Jonah had poured for him.

"Why didn't you yell?" Britt gave him a disgusted look.

"It happened fast, man. It wasn't like I could come up and ask you to join in the chase. By the time I realized there was somebody there, he'd already taken off down the alley."

Britt nodded. "And what the hell did you think you were going to accomplish? It's not even your battle, Mick. Christ, I don't want someone hurt or someone else killed because of what's happening here. Can you understand that? I'm feeling guilty enough about Bartholomew, and the ghost. And I don't even know who that guy is. Two deaths and I don't even know why." Britt buried his head in his hands. Thirty seconds of silence passed, and finally he looked up at Sever. "Man, you should not be involved in this shit. I mean, you go out and about get yourself killed and how am I supposed to react to that? Huh?"

"Yeah." He'd been a fool to chase the guy. What the hell was he thinking? He'd already decided it wasn't going to happen again. "Jonah, it was a dumb thing to do. And you know, it might not have had anything to do with the break-in. Maybe some kid just got spooked or something."

"You know that's not what happened. Hell, it could have been the guy who murdered Teddy. But damn it, you never should have gone after him."

"Jonah, I'm sorry."

The engineer smiled, a tight-lipped smile. "You look sorry. Seen a mirror yet?"

The cop looked up from his tablet. "You said he had no hair and his face appeared to have a mask?"

"I'm not sure what it was. The light was dim, but the brief glimpse of his face looked like it was a patchwork — scars and lines, but I only saw it for a couple of seconds. It wasn't the look of a normal person."

"There are several patrolmen searching the area, but I don't hold out much hope that they will find anything."

The lotion stung, and she'd put some medical tape over a gash just below his ear. He didn't have to see a mirror to know he was a wreck.

"Still up for your hot date tonight, Mick?"

His ribcage was sore to the touch, and when he breathed deeply he could feel the ache deep in his lungs. The sharp, stabbing pain in his leg made him decide never to run again. Unless someone was chasing *him*. The pain between his legs had subsided, but he knew he'd been bruised, and whenever he turned his head or made any facial expressions there was a tightness of skin where the cuts on his face were scabbing over.

"Yeah. I told her I'd be there after she got off. So, I'll be there."

Eric shook his head. "You should be in the hospital. You may have broken a rib. There may be some internal damage."

Sever knew about the Bahamian hospitals. That was the last place he wanted to be. "I don't think so. I'll be fine."

"One last question, Mr. Sever. Were there any words between the two of you? Did you hear him say anything at all?"

"No. I didn't hear anything. A grunt or two. That was about it."

"One further question."

Sever glanced at his watch. He could catch about a half-hour nap before the bartender at the hotel got off work. He could use that nap.

"This person, this man with the mask, he was not by the studio?"

"By the studio?"

"You said he was across the way, am I correct?"

"No, he wasn't by the studio. He was at Etta May's house."

"Mmm. Never once did he set foot on the property here?"

"Not that I saw." Sever winced in pain as she rubbed the lotion into a cut on his arm. "This guy saw me and took off running. He never came over to the studio."

"Could you tell if he'd been watching the studio?"

One more question? This was number three at least. "Couldn't tell, Eric." He was starting to fade.

One more question had started another round. Sever needed sleep. He gingerly picked up the glass of Scotch and took a deep swallow. It burned going down, but it felt good once it got there. His jangled nerves and the assorted pains in his body eased.

"I think Mick needs to lie down for a while." Britt poured more Scotch in the glass. "Eric, if you've got anything else —"

"Could this person have come from inside the house?"

"Look, Eric, I don't know where he came from." One more question? Jesus. This guy couldn't stop.

"But it's possible? That he had just walked out of the house?"

"Etta May's house?"

"Her house."

"Sure." Anything to get rid of the inquisitive man.

Eric jotted something in his book. "And is it possible he was trying to break into that same house?"

"Eric, thanks for coming, but Mick has got to get some rest."

"Of course. Of course. I'll stop by if I have other questions." The officer closed his tablet, shoved it in his pocket and gave Sever a quizzical look. "Do you often involve yourself in other people's problems, Mr. Sever?"

"Are you kidding? It's what I do for a living."

"This is the second time we've questioned you in as many days."

"And your point is?"

"Just an observation, Mr. Sever." Eric glanced at Britt. "I'll stay in touch, Mr. Britt."

You'll be right next door. You could just walk over. Sever almost said it, but held his tongue. The cop was more interested in whether the runner had come from Etta May's house or was going to break into Etta May's house than he was about what had happened at the studio.

Britt walked the policeman to the back door. Sever gingerly stood and watched the short, stout cop walk out. "Thanks, Eric."

"Oh, Jonah, your alarm, your security device? It still has the same code?"

"It does for the moment."

"For the moment?"

"We're going to call the company and change it tomorrow."

"Good."

"Let us know if you find out anything. I'd love to know who's breaking in here. It's driving both of us crazy." He glanced at his wife, sitting at the kitchen table with a bottle of antiseptic lotion, cotton balls, and medical tape.

"Mr. Britt, believe me, we'd like to know as well. We'd like to know who Mr. Sever was chasing, and we'd like to know who killed Mr. Bartholomew. Eventually we'll have an answer."

"Well, thanks again for coming over."

"It's what we do." He glowered at Sever. "For a living." Eric stepped off the porch and in the dim light Sever could see him approach the cinder block house. As Britt started to close the door, the officer shouted back at him. "Mr. Britt, when you have the new security code, make sure you let me know."

"It'll be changed tomorrow. Like I said."

"No. Let me know what it is. I'll need that." And then he was gone.

Sever could vaguely make out the cop, knocking at the next

door neighbor's door. It opened almost immediately and he stepped inside.

Britt turned to Sever and Rita. "Did I get that right?"

"Eric wants your security code?" Rita frowned. "What is that all about?"

"That's what he said, Jonah. He wants your security code."

"Why?"

No one spoke.

"Well, I don't think I'm going to give it to him."

CHAPTER TWENTY-SEVEN

He stumbled, tripping over a rock in the courtyard and going down on one knee. A knee that had been bruised and cut once tonight. Pray to God that they were all in bed. He didn't want to wake up the old ladies and have them find him like this. He'd studied his face in a plate-glass store window half an hour ago and found several shallow cuts and abrasions. No big deal. Not to him. When your face looked like his did, when the quilt-work patching reminded most people of a jigsaw puzzle, what difference would a few more scars make? But the sisters would freak. The blood, the fresh cuts—

Glancing up he could see the old rooms, the bedroom of his youth. Bunk beds, thin sheets, and a worn blanket. A communal shower and the strict rules he'd often broken. Bobby Baron had hated his childhood, but would gladly trade it now for what his life had become.

It was midnight and the moon was behind some dark clouds. A little rain shower in the last twenty minutes meant a lot of water on the streets, and his shoes were soaked. The pain in his legs from running, from walking the long distance back to the convent, just added to his misery.

Baron pulled a joint from his wet shirt pocket and fumbled for a match. He huddled by the building, sheltering his matches from the breeze and the mist that blew by. Strike one. The match briefly flared and faded. Strike two, the damp sulfur on the match tip scraped off.

Strike three, the match flew from his shaking fingers. Shaking his head, part from frustration, part from the chill of the rain and the breeze, he shoved the joint back in his shirt pocket. Even when you had all the ingredients, even when everything was in place, something unforeseen could happen to dampen things.

He slumped against the wall, trying to remember what had gone wrong. He was about to make a breakthrough. He was about to exact revenge. Then this guy came out of nowhere and he panicked. All he had to do was just walk away. Slowly. No one would have said a thing. Instead, he'd run. Like he'd done so many times in his life. Scared of his shadow, scared of the slightest motion. No confidence, no self-image. There wasn't much to be confident about.

But maybe he was being too hard on himself. On one shoulder was the coward, on the other a more confident Bobby Baron. They had each had their moments tonight. There were things he was ashamed of, like running when there was no need to run. But he was proud of how he'd handled himself once he'd been confronted. He'd almost had the guy tonight. Almost took him out. He'd gotten in some good licks, to the face, to the body. And when his attacker got the upper hand, he'd had the thought of kicking him between the legs. He'd found out tonight that he was a scrapper. He was a guy who could get out of a jam!

He needed to stand up for himself. Do it on a regular basis. He flashed back to the coffee shop, where the big guy had suggested that he leave the table. He'd actually been proud of that moment. Baron had been nice, almost gentlemanly. Just taken off the hat and sunglasses and let the goon get a good dose of reality. There were times, very few times, when his looks actually worked in his favor.

He pulled the match pack from his pants pocket just one more time. Just to see if bad luck lasted. He tore a stick from the pack and quickly ran it across the strike pad. The bright spark and flame surprised him and he watched it for only a second before he pulled the joint from his shirt pocket with his left hand, put it in his mouth, and lit the weed.

Although slightly damp, the marijuana cigarette caught fire, and

Baron smiled. Things were turning. He could feel it. Drawing deeply, he inhaled the sweet smoke, immediately sensing the tensions flowing from his soul, the drama in his life easing away, and he slowly stood up, forgetting for the moment the pain in his body. He took another drag, slowly letting it escape from deep inside.

One of the twins next door to the studio had smoked a joint with him. A number of years ago. How many he couldn't remember. The kid was probably sixteen, seventeen, and he'd insisted they sit inside that rusted bucket of bolts that sat on blocks outside the house. And they'd smoked and stared at the stars in the Nassau sky. This kid — he couldn't remember his name — Barney or something, this kid had begged him. Asked him dozens of times if he could just have a hit. And Baron had ignored him. When Baron, the engineer known as Be-Bop, would leave a recording session, he'd light up a joint. By the time he walked to his car he was already starting to mellow out, and the last thing he needed was some young punk kid joining him in a smoke.

But this night, this one time, he'd let the kid have a hit. And as they were sitting in that old junk car, mom had come out, screaming and shouting. Baron remembered hearing the shriek. The hollering, the wailing. And as he sat there in a stoned state he watched her jerk open the car door, grab the joint from her son's mouth, grab *him* by the ear, and pull him from the car. Baron waited until the excitement had died down, then he pulled another joint from his pocket and lit it. Mom and the kid were long gone and he was smoking the second joint of the night. He'd gotten higher than a kite that night. In Elvis's Cadillac.

And the revelation that night stayed with him. He had to dig deep to remember the lesson, and sometimes the lesson was hard to grasp, but it went something like this. In his state of mind that night, in the blissful, contented rapture that he was experiencing, he found himself smiling. The kid would survive, and he, Bobby Baron, had found Nirvana. Nothing was going to disturb his peace. In the midst of this confusion, this chaos, with mother and son experiencing a huge conflict back at the house, with the yelling, the screaming, the major disruption, he realized he could rise above anything. Anything. No problem. He had to go back to that place from time to time to remember, but that lesson had gotten him through a lot. The fire, the major medical rehabilitation, and now, the fight tonight. He could rise above it.

Baron stared into space, not really aware of what he saw. Into the garden, the cornstalks growing tall and proud, and he took another hit. To the dimly lit street where the pack of dogs had congregated. He was above it all. He closed his eyes and saw colors, brilliant colors of red, green, blue, then the pastel colors of the buildings on Bay Street. The pale rose, mellow yellow, faded blue, and mint greens blended into each other.

"Robert?"

He dropped the joint, stomping at it with his right foot.

"Robert? Are you out here?"

Jesus. It was midnight.

"Bobby." The voice was fading. Whoever was looking for him was going in the opposite direction.

"Bobby?"

The voice was fading, going to the other side of the building. He spun around and walked double-time to the front door, carefully opening it and slipping inside. He made his way in the dim light to his room, quickly stripping off his outer clothing and climbing into the small bed. There was no reason for anyone to know.

Tomorrow he could wash the cuts, tend to the scratches and the bruises. Right now it was important to keep the sisters at bay. The less they knew the better. Sister Annie and the clan would have to be kept in the dark. Because when he accomplished what he wanted to accomplish, they needed to be far away from the action and the accusation. Just one more night. Then he'd disappear and they'd never see him again. They'd wonder about him. They'd talk about their disappearing guest for a couple of weeks, then it would all be over. And no one would ever know. No one would ever suspect. He'd disappear from everyone's radar screen, never to be seen or noticed again.

He pulled the pillow under his head, bending his body into the fetal position. With a few deep breaths he found himself drifting into a relaxed state, wondering where things had turned. Maybe it was the night he smoked a joint in Elvis's Cadillac. Maybe it had all started the day he was born.

CHAPTER TWENTY-EIGHT

Atlantis's huge four-hundred-foot aquarium that ran around the sunken restaurant was filled with every kind of saltwater fish imaginable. Thousands of the tropical beauties, parading by the glass wall, drifting in and out of the coral and through the seaweed. Davis had often wondered if the cook staff just reached in and took out that evening's dinner. It would be easy to do. He was hypnotized by the passing fish, the colors, the shapes, the sizes, and the patterns that decorated the creatures. It was a tableau that never failed to impress him. He sat at his table, now focusing on the patrons who spread out through the sizable eating and drinking establishment.

Half the tables were occupied with touristy-looking couples and the occasional high roller who just needed a break from the tables. It was late and he felt relieved. He'd taken care of business. There was no doubt that the boys would give him a shot at coming back. Johnny Run needed him, and he needed that shot. He'd do everything in his power to get Johnny Run's new product to the top of the charts. The recording business was tough. Tougher than it had ever been, and he'd have to use a combination of guerilla street marketing, Internet savvy, networking, and some old-fashioned payola. When all else fails, use cash.

And, of course, he had his ace card already played. The death of Teddy Bartholomew.

How great was this? Stretch and Sonny had pretty much promised him the job. They had nobody else. Teddy was dead and they needed direction. This played right into his hands. It was a slam dunk.

Davis downed his Jack and Coke in one gulp and stood up. The hand on his shoulder surprised him.

"Grant Davis?"

"I am."

"I'm with the hotel. There's a gentleman outside who would like a word with you."

The guy from his apartment who'd punched him the other night. They were going to threaten him again.

"Can you tell me what this is about?"

"Just come with me, Mr. Davis."

This big black man had on a jacket and tie, but he was a bruiser. You didn't want to go up against someone this size. Actually, he didn't want to go up against anyone. "Just tell me what this person wants."

No one else knew he was here. No one except the guy who broke into his room, and Stretch and Sonny. And he'd already talked to them.

"Mr. Davis —"

"All right. I'm coming." Screw the bill. If this guy was with the hotel, he could pick up the tab for Davis's two drinks. Probably twenty-five bucks anyway. Plus tip. He stood up and followed the burly man.

They walked up the steps of the restaurant to the main floor and Davis turned one more time, watching the magnificent aquarium. A waiter was standing at his former table, glancing around. Hell, people probably skipped on their tabs every day. Davis turned around and kept on walking.

Out into the lobby, and through the front door, from the air-conditioning into the parking area under the portico. A short, uniformed officer stood there, the squad car parked against the curb.

"Mr. Grant Davis?"

He wasn't driving, so there couldn't be a traffic ticket. Were they crazy? What the hell could it be?

"Yeah. I'm Davis. What can I do for you?" He shivered. It appeared to have rained, and there was just a slight chill in the air.

"Mr. Davis, how long have you been on the island?"

"About five days."

"And what is your purpose here?" The little cop had folded his arms, resting them on his rounded stomach. He squinted at Davis, with what appeared to be a frown. Davis knew that he could offend this cop and get life, but he detested short, cocky assholes who needed to assert themselves. "I don't have a purpose."

What he did have was a passport, a cheap rented room, and a couple thousand dollars in his pocket. What else did he need to show this cocky cop?

"Mr. Davis, I believe you have a purpose."

"Officer, I'm here to relax. Have a good time. That's my purpose. To drink a little, gamble a little. There's no law against that, is there?"

Davis could sense the parking attendants turning one ear to the conversation. They'd be telling this story tomorrow to all of their friends, with certain embellishments. Right now, there were no embellishments. Davis had no idea what this little prick wanted.

"Mr. Davis, you were the manager for a rock and roll group called Johnny Run, am I correct?"

"Yeah. I *was*." Past tense. He *was* the manager. Not any more. The financial climate had been responsible for that. And maybe he hadn't been on top of the situation. Maybe he could have done just a little better.

More attention from the attendants. Now there were three or four who were staring at him. They were used to celebrity, but still — Johnny Run.

"And you are aware they are recording on our island at this time."

"I am."

"You are aware?"

The guy was irritating. Just say what you wanted and get it over with. "Yes. I was here a bit over a year ago with the band and we —"

Oh, shit. This was about Teddy Bartholomew. He'd just assumed that, when he didn't hear anything that —

"You are also aware that someone killed Johnny Run's current manager, Mr. Theodore Bartholomew?"

Of course he was aware. Hell, yes, he was aware. He'd even been congratulated for pulling it off. That phone call. Davis choked out a "Yes."

The policeman nodded toward his car where a tall, thin officer rested against the fender. "We're asking you to come to our station where we can ask you some questions."

"I can answer anything you want right here. I can answer anything you want to ask with an 'I don't know' because I don't know anything. I know he was killed. That's all I know."

"Mr. Davis, I suppose we can force you to come to the station. With handcuffs, with other restraints, but we don't want to do that."

"And I don't want you to do that. Look, officer, I'm a very low-key, polite guy. I'm simply a visitor here and I would never do anything like kill someone."

"Kill someone? We never insinuated that you killed someone."

"Isn't that what this is about? You suspect I may have had something to do with it?"

The short guy glanced at his partner, who walked around to the passenger side of the car, opening the door.

"Mr. Davis, please get in the car."

"It's late and I don't know why we can't do this tomorrow morning."

"Do you have plans yet this evening?"

Davis glanced at his watch. It was already tomorrow and it still felt like today. "Are you arresting me?"

"No."

"Then I don't have to go?"

Now the short, chubby cop had unfolded his arms and his fingers were tapping on the butt of his gun. "This is not the United States, Mr. Davis. When we ask you to come with us, you don't have a choice but to come with us. Do you understand?"

The guy was pissed off. No reason to push the issue.

"Get in the car, Mr. Davis. There are some questions we'd like to ask you about Mr. Bartholomew and why you are soliciting Johnny Run for the job as their manager."

CHAPTER TWENTY-NINE

"Oh my God."

He nodded. "I know, I know. You see, there was this brawl. Outside."

"What? Why?" She looked shocked, a towel in one hand, a knife in the other.

"It was over you."

She stared at him wide-eyed from behind the bar. "Please, tell me what happened to you. Mick, you look —"

"I know. I checked out a mirror on the way in."

"Over me?"

"Yeah. Guy said you were the second-best bartender on the island."

The look on her face was worth it. The frightened expression, her eyebrows knitted together, and the lines in her forehead, changing to the hint of a smile and disbelief.

"*Second*-best?"

"That's what he said. So of course, I couldn't let him get away with that."

"No." She set the towel and knife down, and picking up a stainless cocktail shaker, Tommie liberally poured Ron Rico rum into it. Then she poured pineapple juice, coconut liquor, and some sort of red mix into the glass, shook it for fifteen seconds and poured it into a tall glass. She shoved it over to Sever.

"So you jumped him?"

Still standing, Sever took a long sip. Whatever the red stuff was, it gave the drink one hell of a kick. "I did." He shoved a twenty across the bar.

"No. The drink is for defending my reputation." She smiled, the frown all gone. "But, tell me, Mick, what really happened to you?"

He took another sip, then pulled out the straw and took a gulp. "I'm all right, seriously."

"This is too bad. I was telling a couple of the girls about this good-looking guy I was meeting later, and now —"

"So it's all superficial with you?"

"It is. Looks are everything. Are you going to tell me how you got this way?"

Sever eased onto a bar stool, feeling the aches and pains in his legs, back, neck, shoulders, wrists.

"Was it really a fight?"

"It was."

She looked down the bar and saw a man holding up an empty Red Stripe bottle. "Just a minute, Mick."

Gingerly, Sever looked around the bar. It had thinned out, and only a handful of customers sat at the scattered tables. Just two at the bar. She walked back and leaned on the bar.

"Tell me."

"I asked you what you saw across the way, and you told me that it appeared there was an orange glow moving across the windshield of the old car."

"I remember."

"I think that may have been the beginning of some strange things that have been happening on that side of the road. First there was Teddy Bartholomew —"

"And now?"

"Tonight, after Jonah and I left you, we found his apartment had been broken into and someone threw a lot of stuff around. Apparently looking for something."

"Mick."

"We called the police, and they came out and filed a report. I walked outside and saw some stranger crouching in the shrubs by the little block house up there. He took off running and I chased him."

"You chased him?"

"I did."

"The cops were there?"

"Yeah."

"Mick, why didn't you walk inside and tell the cops that the possible intruder was running away?"

"Well, I probably should—"

"How old are you?"

"Why does that—"

"Mick, I happen to go for older guys. But guys who know their limits. So what about your face?"

He was quiet as he sipped on his drink. Being chastised by someone young enough to be his daughter hurt. He'd visited this situation often. He was just plain too old for this shit. "I ran into the guy."

"Ran into him?"

"He ran into me. Knocked me down. We had a fist fight, a kick fight, and he got away."

She shook her head. "You are something else, aren't you?"

"I am. Something else. I'm not sure what."

"Is this the time you say 'you should see the other guy?'"

He laughed. "I think I got the raw end of the deal."

"You're in pain."

"No. Not much." He was sure she could tell.

Tommie smiled softly. Her dark skin, dark eyes, dark hair mysterious in the dim light of the bar. He was looking forward to her getting off work. And he was dreading it at the same time. Any sane man of his age would have gone home, taken a hot bath, and climbed into bed. Any sane man of his age would never have chased the guy and gotten the shit kicked out of him.

But no one had ever accused Mick Sever of being sane. Doing what he did required a certain amount of insanity.

"You think that the orange glow that I saw from all the way over here has something to do with this break-in and your chase scene tonight?"

"Something is going on over there."

"What could I have seen?"

"I don't know, but I'm guessing that Teddy Bartholomew and somebody else were smoking a joint. Possibly you saw them pass the cigarette back and forth."

"Maybe. I still think it was just a reflection from a light or a star."

"I don't think so. Bartholomew was found dead, in the car, with a joint shoved in his mouth."

"And you think whoever killed this Bartholomew might have been sharing the cigarette with him?"

"Possibly."

"So I saw the sign of this man just before he died."

"But you didn't see anything else."

"No. Nothing. I didn't even know what I was seeing in the first place."

They were quiet for a moment.

"Tonight, you take me to the spot where you stood, okay?"

She nodded.

"Maybe you'll remember something else."

"Mick?"

"What?"

"Why is this important to you? Is this part of your story?"

"It wasn't. But it is now."

The two men walked in and heads turned. One medium-sized white guy with dreadlocks, and one really tall black guy, ducking as he walked through the doorway.

Sever looked up and recognized them. Along with half the customers in the bar.

"Hey, Mick." Sonny raised his hand.

"Stretch. Sonny."

They walked up to the bar. "What the hell happened to you? To your face?"

"As Tommie said, you should see the other guy."

Sonny laughed.

"What brings you guys out tonight?"

"We were at Atlantis. The tables turned on us so we left." Sonny nodded at Tommie. "Hey, girl."

"Sonny." She reached for Ron Rico rum and poured a full shot. A table erupted in laughter and the brief burst of noise drowned out his response.

Sever smiled, the physical action pulling at the cuts on his face. Tommie knew them all.

She presented them with two highball glasses, dark-colored rum with a concoction of fruit juices. "Boys, you've got about forty-five minutes to drink up."

They picked up the drinks, dropped money on the bar, and drifted off, a group of young rowdies coming together, surrounding them.

"To be young again, Tommie. Like you, like Sonny, like Stretch."

"Bullshit, Mr. Sever. You haven't matured much beyond about eighteen. And it's the age of your mind, isn't it? Not your physical age."

"Tonight I feel about ninety."

She looked into his eyes, studying him for a moment. "Natalie is closing, so I'll be off in thirty minutes, Mick." She walked to the other end of the bar, pulling bottles off the shelf and pouring another tropical delight for a customer. When she came back, she reached across the bar and took his hand. "After all you've been through tonight, are you sure you still want to get together?"

"I'm sure."

He wasn't at all.

CHAPTER THIRTY

He couldn't sleep. His nerves were raw, and the pain too strong. Bobby Baron lay quietly, thinking about the island. His island. The wealth and the poverty, the haves and the have-nots. If you were determined, if you wanted to reach for the golden ring, this was probably the best place to do it. Take Atlantis for instance. Talk about making things happen. This tropical, opulent resort rivaled anyplace in the world. Right on Paradise Island.

But everyone seemed to have a short, short memory. It seemed to even the locals that the place had always been glitz and glamour, but if you grew up here, if this was your home, you knew the truth. Paradise Island had been far from glitz and glamour. The place had been used to breed livestock not so many years ago. It was called Hog Island, and pigs and cows were the mainstay of the small piece of land. In 1960 some heir to the A&P grocery chain had purchased it for eleven million dollars and now celebrities showed off their expensive twelve-million-dollar homes. Celebrities like Oprah Winfrey, Michael Jordan, and others. Hog Island was now Paradise Island with its towers and casinos and yachts. What was the saying? *You couldn't make a silk purse out of a pig's ear?* The hell you couldn't. You could have it any way you wanted it in the Bahamas.

Then there was Blackbeard the pirate, who ruled Nassau and looted the villages and passing ships, raped the women, and terrorized the population. The locals built forts with some serious firepower to try and stop him, and it took the British Navy and five musket balls to fell the big man and his flaming beard. But from 1713 to 1718 Edward Teach a.k.a. Blackbeard had it his way. You could have it any way you wanted it in the Bahamas.

And in recent history, a presidential candidate named Gary Hart left Nassau for Bimini with his blonde mistress, posing for a picture that ended up in every newspaper in the United States. Hart's wife quickly dropped him from the position of favorite husband, and the voting population quickly dropped Hart from their list of favorite politicians. But for that brief moment, Gary Hart left Washington behind, got on a ship called the *Monkey Business* and sailed with some blonde sweetheart to Bimini. Pretty cool. He went out doing it his way.

And in Nassau, stately homes looked out onto an idyllic sea, homes built with drug money, by former owners who now lived in hiding or in her majesty's prisons. These drug lords who hid on small islands like Andros, Harbor, Cat, and others became modern-day pirates, living in tropical luxury and avoiding the Bahamian law authorities.

Opulent luxury, abject poverty, a strict belief in tradition and the observance of ancient laws, and at the same time total disregard for authority, it was all part of the Bahamas. There was everything and there was nothing. You could have it your way.

Bobby Baron had been here long enough to know. You could believe in anything, become anyone, and still be an integral part of the culture. It was the greatest part of being Bahamian. It was the worst part of being Bahamian.

He sat up, stiff and sore, the muscles in his legs and arms cramping. Gingerly swinging his legs off the bed, he stood and walked to the chair where he'd thrown his damp clothes. Carefully bending over, he pulled on the pants, eased the T-shirt over his aching shoulders, stepped into his canvas slip-on shoes, and quietly walked down the hall and out the door. He couldn't be put off by the man who chased him down the alley. There was work to be done. Atonement.

Retribution. Paybacks. Words he'd never even considered two years ago. Now they filled his mind.

He was in Nassau, where you could achieve anything. Or, nothing at all. And Bobby Baron had nothing to lose. Like the tourists who gambled at Atlantis, at the Wyndham Crystal Casino, the one-time wonders who put it all on the line. Like those optimistic gamblers, and the pathetic losers, it was time to go for broke. He really did have nothing else to lose.

Barely an hour had passed since he'd huddled beside the sisters' convent, taking a drag off the joint. Now he reached in his pocket and pulled out his final rolled cigarette. The matches seemed drier and he lit it with the second strike. Two drags, three, he felt the calm, and some of the pain subsided.

Baron needed to go back. He couldn't afford a taxi, and this time the walk would kill him. He'd planned it out ahead of time, and he'd pocketed the key from the keyboard in the kitchen. The sisters had an old Chevy van parked in the circular driveway and he had the key. License to steal, or at least to borrow.

The commotion would have died down by now, and no one would be suspecting anything. You never returned to the scene of the crime. Almost never. But, this was Nassau in the Bahamas and anything was possible. The best and the worst. You could have it all in the Bahamas.

Baron turned the key, hoping the engine wouldn't wake the sisters. It coughed once and he turned it again. Twice. Finally the spark caught and he heaved a sigh of relief. Slowly he drove around the curve, nervously looking at the building in the dark, half expecting to see lights coming on. There was nothing. No sign of the sisters. They'd never even know he was gone. He planned on being back long before the sun came up and no one would be the wiser. If everything worked out, there would be a big commotion on the island tomorrow morning.

Bobby Baron pulled onto the street and turned on the headlights. He was going back to see if he could finish the job. It was about time.

CHAPTER THIRTY-ONE

The short, stout, uniformed cop dropped Davis off at his room, one hour to the minute after they'd picked him up at the casino. The little guy, Eric, opened the back door to let him out and stopped him for just a moment with his raised hand. "Before you go, I need to know, have you ever been inside the house next door to the studio? The concrete-block home?"

"No."

"Do you have a key or a security code for the recording studio?"

Davis felt the headache kicking in. He'd lost the glow of the Jack Daniel's and he needed to get a drink. And this asshole was still asking questions. He thought he'd answered just about everything at the station.

"Well, do you?"

"No. No key, no security code."

"Did you have a key or security clearance when you were working there?"

Davis shook his head. "I've never asked for one, never received one."

"One more question. Have you ever been in the old Cadillac that sits on blocks outside that home?"

Well, that was a different story. When he worked on the last album, the one that tanked, he'd been in that car several times. Smoking a joint with the kid next door, late at night, after a long recording session. The kid seemed to know when those sessions were going to end. He'd be waiting outside, and a couple of times Davis and the kid lit up in that bucket of rust. Got toasted. He could use a hit right now.

"No."

"Never?"

To get nailed for doing dope with the guy next door? He wasn't going to admit to that.

"Never been in the car."

"One other thing. Would it be okay if I came up to your room and went through your articles? Sort of see for myself?"

"No. It wouldn't be okay. Look, I told you I had nothing to do with the break-ins or the murder of Teddy Barholomew. Can we please just drop it?"

Eric nodded. "If you get ready to leave Nassau, I want you to contact me. Understood? I may have a couple more questions for you."

The questions down at the station had been pointless. How well did he know Bartholomew? Barely at all. Was his trip to Nassau in any way tied to the Johnny Run recording session? Duh. He wasn't going to admit to that. When was the last time he'd visited the studio? He certainly wasn't going to admit he'd taken a taxi there that night, the night of the murder, and the cops didn't seem to have any records to show he *had* been there.

The fact was they had no facts. It was a fishing expedition, and the only reason they'd picked him up had to be that Stretch and Sonny had told someone he was conveniently hanging around trying to get his old job back.

Were they really interested, or had they just wanted to report on him to the authorities?

He should be pissed. These two jackasses, Stretch and Sonny, telling him they'd look into having him back, then calling the cops. It must have been them. Who else would have done it?

He had money in his pocket and a taxi could get him to Compass Point. The band was staying at the hotel, and wouldn't they be surprised to see him at this hour of the morning.

Back in his room, Davis poured himself a Jack and sipped it straight, letting it burn on the way down. Making up for the third one he probably would have had at Atlantis. The cops had destroyed that enjoyment. He'd have to be careful. He could use the gig with Johnny Run, and maybe they hadn't turned him in. Maybe there was another set of circumstances. But if he had to bet on it, if he had to make an educated guess, he figured it had to be Sonny and Stretch.

After another pour of Jack Daniel's, he wasn't so sure. The cops finding him at Atlantis. How would they know? And then, after one more short pour, he decided that these boys *had* called the authorities.

But he had to be diplomatic. Couldn't blow up at them. Couldn't let them know he was pissed off. Davis just needed to set the band straight. He had to convince them he would never kill their manager just so he could get back in control. Come on, he was smarter than that.

He had to convince them he had the vision to get this new record on the charts and keep it there. He alone knew how to rocket Johnny Run to the top.

Davis looked at the Jack bottle with watery eyes and poured one more very short shot, barely covering the bottom of the glass. He threw it back and stood up, a little wobbly as he held onto the bed for support. A moment of dizziness passed and he walked out of the shabby apartment, down the steps to the street. Where the hell he was going to get a cab at this time in the early morning he wasn't sure, but he had to get to the hotel.

He had to talk to the band. His future depended on it. His income depended on it. And, he reminded himself, his life depended on it. The backers had let him know that if he didn't pull this one out of the fire, if he didn't put this album at the top of the charts, they'd blame him and him alone.

Davis started walking, trudging up the street. Somewhere there was a taxi, and he hoped it came along soon. His walk was more of a stagger and he couldn't keep that up very much longer.

CHAPTER THIRTY-TWO

They'd arrived at the hotel about two a.m. and Sonny had convinced him to have a quick drink. Tomorrow was a workday. Tonight was theirs. They'd just about broken even at the casino and wasn't that a reason to celebrate? Wasn't that a reason to have another drink?

"Hey, it's Sever, the reporter." Stretch pointed to him.

Sonny nodded. "Hey, Mick." As he walked closer he noticed the reporter's face. What a mess. Sever told him the other guy looked worse.

They talked briefly, and Tommie, the bartender, mixed them a rum concoction that was curiously strong.

Several female patrons gave them a look, and a heavyset drunk with a pink flowered silk shirt shouted at them from his table. "You guys think you're musicians. Hell, when I play with myself, I play better than you."

"Fucking drunks. We can drink these outside, man." Stretch motioned to Sonny and the two men walked out to the beach. The sound of small waves hitting the beach kept the din of music and voices at bay. They stood still, watching the moon play on the restless water, as if hypnotized by the majesty of the scene in front of them.

"If it wasn't for the fans and the record companies, this could be a good business." Stretch frowned and took a sip of his drink.

"Nothing would be left, but I suppose you're right."

"Is it just this band, or does every group have its share of ass-holes?" He rubbed his forehead with his thumb and index finger. "Christ, they give me a headache. I needed this drink." He tilted the glass and drained it by half.

"Assholes? The fans?"

"The fans, and the ones who work for us."

"Speaking of that, what do we do about Davis?" Sonny asked.

"We don't." Stretch looked down at the five-foot-eight drum-mer with the long dreadlocks. "We don't do Davis. That's the point."

"Cops were going to pick him up for questioning. Chances are he'll know we ratted him out."

"Fuck him. He's a weasel. With Bartholomew out of the way, Davis had a great opportunity to come back as manager. Seeing him tonight, listening to him, I think there's a good chance he may have had something to do with Teddy's murder. Think about it. It just seems a little too convenient."

Sonny pulled a cigar from his shirt pocket. Biting off the end, he lit it with a cheap plastic lighter and sucked in a mouthful of smoke. He let it drift from his mouth in a thin stream. "Davis? Come on, Stretch. The guy was with us for five years and for five years—"

"And for five years we weren't sure what the hell he did. You know that. We discussed it at band meetings. He took one hell of a salary, but I never was sure what he accomplished."

"He did take care of the business side of things. At least we didn't have to do that. And he seemed like a nice guy." Sonny shook his dreadlocks from his face and swallowed some rum. "You know, Stretch, I didn't get into this business expecting murder. That's more for the rap acts isn't it? I mean Tupac Shakur, Biggie Smalls—"

Stretch eased onto a lounge chair in the sand and looked up at the sky. "I don't want to come back here, man. Nassau sucks. I'm not doin' this again, I don't care how good Jonah Britt may be. No suit is going to tell me where the hell to record next time, I don't care how well this CD does."

"It's not all bad, Stretch." Sonny sat in the chair next to him. "We got some sun, some eighty degrees, and the Bahama chicks ain't all bad. It's a lot worse back in the States. Snow, freezing temperatures, rain—"

"Tired of it already, Sonny. Somebody steals my guitar, fucking Jonah doesn't have any kind of security, and now somebody kills Bartholomew."

Sonny tapped the ash. "You didn't like him anyway."

"Didn't give a damn. Don't. These managers are bottom-feeders. Suckin' the blood from us. When we do well, they take too much. When things are slow, they still take too much. Still, I don't wish anyone death. Especially if it was on account of us. That just doesn't go down well."

"Do you think it was?"

"Was?"

"On account of us?"

"I think the band had something to do with it. Especially if Grant Davis was involved. I'm tellin' you, Sonny, I don't trust the scumbag. Do I think he could be behind it? Yes, I do."

"Jeez. I can't wrap my mind around the idea that we'd be responsible for someone's murder."

"I'm just saying it could be."

Sonny took a drink, swishing it in his mouth. "So we don't want Davis back?"

They both looked ahead, focusing on a distant ship that passed on the dark horizon.

"*I* don't want Davis back. In fact, I'm not sure we need a manager."

Sonny turned his head, looking at his tall, black friend. "Somebody's got to keep things together."

"You pay a bookkeeper. You pay an accountant. You pay a lawyer. You pay an agent and a P.R. firm. You pay a producer and engineer. You pay back the record company for all the crap they do for you and you pay a road crew, and Ticketmaster—" Stretch took a drink and set the glass in the sand. "Don't you get it, Sonny? Everyone is on the take, and we're the only ones who do the work."

"Still—"

"There's no still, man. And then there's the bank."

"The bank?"

"The guys who put up the money. Sponser the tour, pay for all that shit. And they expect a cut."

"So you think —"

"I think there's way too many people on our payroll. And I'm tired of it. You tell me what the hell we need a manager for? An extra cut is all. On top of all the others. Hell, it never seems to end."

"Stretch, we're not doing bad."

"No. But I'm tired of picking up the tab."

The air was damp, with a slight chill. Not the tropical night that you hoped for when you were in the tropics. It had rained earlier and the night sky was still spotty with clouds. Sonny shivered, waiting for the drink to warm him.

"It's like the harder we work, the more people depend on us. Screw it. I didn't get into this to make other people rich, Sonny. I'm the one who's responsible for the product. I'm the one who sells the music every night. Do you understand what I'm saying?"

The drummer ran a hand through his hair, pushing the dreads out of his face. "Maybe that's where we're different. I like having it all taken care of. If we have to pay a little more —"

"I'm tired of the hangers-on. I'm not into an entourage, Sonny. That's an ego thing, and I don't care about the ego. What I want is the money. Show me the money. Just show me the jack, Jack."

The two young girls, maybe early twenties, stood just a few feet away. Each had a napkin and a pen in her hands. Stretch caught them from the corner of his eye and slowly stood up. "Do you ladies want something?"

"An autograph maybe?"

He studied them. Two best friends from maybe Ohio, who came down for some fun, but their plain looks and shy demeanor kept them from having the time of their lives. "We're a little busy here. Maybe some other time."

The girls stood there, apparently not sure they'd heard him.

They were *fans* for God's sake. And right now he didn't need fans. He didn't need anybody.

"Here. Let me sign those." Sonny stood up, gave Stretch a dirty look, took the proffered napkins and signed them both. "I'm sorry for my friend. He's a little distracted at the moment."

The women glanced at each other, thanked Sonny, and walked away.

"Still got to please the fans, Stretch."

"Fuck 'em." Stretch stood up and watched the two women walk back to the bar. Signing autographs, playing the celebrity role. It was all bullshit.

Stretch and Sonny both remained standing, sipping their rum concoctions, Sonny mixing a mouthful of alcohol with a mouthful of smoke.

"So we tell Davis that we're not interested?"

"*We* don't tell him that. I'm simply voicing my opinion, man. Come on. This is a band, a democracy. It's a vote. Anthony and Child still have a say. I'm not trying to run the band, Sonny. You guys do what you want. Me, I say forget about Davis. That's my vote, pure and simple. I don't want the son of a bitch back. First of all the guy may be a killer. Huh? May have killed Bartholomew. Jesus, think about *that* for a minute. Second of all, he has our last album written all over him, and that was a disaster. I'm lobbying for never having that jack-ass in our group again."

"We can all take some blame for the last album."

"No. If we didn't have a manager we could take some blame for that. It would then be our fault. But we did have a manager. Grant Davis." He'd raised his voice, pushing every word. "We *did* have a manager and he made the arrangements for the last CD. That was his idea. I lay that at Grant Davis's feet. Another point for taking control of our destiny." Stretch gave him a cold, hard stare. "I'm tired of fuckers like Grant Davis getting rich because of my sweat."

"Hey, did I hear my name being mentioned?" Grant Davis walked onto the beach, a yellow-something drink in his hand. He approached them, slightly weaving in the sand. Either drunk or stoned. With Davis it could be both.

Stretch spun around, immediately trying to decide how much Davis could have heard. "Yeah. We were talking about you. We were talking about the manager thing. We'll probably put it to the band tomorrow as to what we want to do about that position."

"Guys, I had nothing to do with Teddy Bartholomew's death."

"Teddy's death?" Sonny fumbled with the question.

"Come on guys, it's obvious you think I was involved. I worked together with you guys for five years. You know me better than that. Do you really think I'd kill someone to get back with this band?"

Stretch looked at him, staring into his eyes in the dim light. Shooting daggers through them, letting him know there was suspicion. Letting him know the bass player wasn't giving Davis a free ride.

"Look, I know you guys talked to the cops. It had to be you. Hey, it's okay. But I didn't come over here, to Nassau, to fuck with you guys. It's a coincidence. And I certainly didn't come over to get rid of Teddy. Come on, guys, that's not me and you know it! That's all I wanted to say."

"Yeah. The cop, Eric, he looked us up and asked some questions. Wanted to know if we could shed any light on the murder. We just mentioned, you know, mentioned that our old manager was on the island. We didn't mean to get you in any trouble. Nothing personal, Grant. It's just that things are a little bit strange right now." Sonny shot a look at Stretch, as if he wanted the big bass player to agree. He raised his glass and clinked it with Davis's. "Here's to rock and roll, man."

"Yeah. Here's to rock and roll."

Stretch kept his glass by his side. He glowered at his partner, then spun and walked back toward the bar.

"Did I say something wrong?" Davis's eyes followed the tall black man.

"Probably."

They both watched Stretch enter the bar and disappear from view.

"What? What did I say?"

Sonny's lip curled with disgust. "You were with us for five years, Grant. You should know by now anything you say to Stretch could be the wrong thing."

Davis kept his eyes on the bar, searching for Stretch. "Oh yeah. I forgot."

CHAPTER THIRTY-THREE

Sever stood outside the hotel by the pool, looking at the ocean. He never tired of the hypnotic sight of that vast body of water. His rum went down smooth, and he savored the fermented fruit juice mixer. He normally stayed away from sweet drinks, but this one was special. Tommie had made it just for him. She never had told him what the name was. Maybe she'd invented it. Tangy, a little sweet and sour, and he could feel it working its magic already. The soreness, the aches and the pains faded into the background, and he took another swallow.

Several couples lined a pier that stretched into the water leading to a thatched-roof hut at the end. He watched the duos holding hands and staring off into the water. The dream of a future with someone was beyond him. He'd had his chance. That was in the past. There wasn't anyone to grow old with now. He could prove it. He was growing old, fast. And there was no one. Tommie was a godsend, but at best a one-, two-, or three-night stand.

"Hey, Mick."

He turned and saw Jonah coming toward him with a glass of Scotch in his hand. "I thought I left you behind."

"I know. I thought you did too. I decided to get some early sleep tonight, but my hours get so screwed up."

"I was waiting for Tommie to get off." He thought about the cloth doll in his room. Tommie was close by. And, she had access. And

Jonah, right across the street. But what reason could either one have? Pins in the eyes. Maybe the "ghost" had left it.

"Yeah. Look, I just thought you might want to know. Eric stopped by. It's one reason I'm still up."

"You're kidding? More questions?" This cop must be the only law enforcement on the island. "Does that guy ever sleep?"

"I figured he was stopping by Etta May's and decided to pay me a visit. Anyway, he had some questions, but he had some answers, too."

"Answers?"

"They got some fingerprints off a dish that the intruder dropped in the kitchen. Since we'd washed that dish, it was clean and there were only two sets of prints on it. They weren't mine, but one set appears to be Rita's. She probably put the dish in the cupboard. The other set of prints they're looking into."

"The Bahama police worked that fast?"

"They got fingerprints, Mick. It doesn't take that long. We have a real chance of finding out who this guy is. Eric said it was pretty simple. He took *our* fingerprints, and visually they compared the prints on the plate."

"So not everything is *CSI Miami* with the fancy labs and DNA?"

"Pretty elementary over here, Mick." He smirked. "This is Nassau in the Bahamas, remember?"

"So when is he going to figure out who your ghost is?"

"Depends. Could be hours, days, weeks."

"Or years?"

"Yeah. But they found the prints and he's working on it."

"Guy is a regular Sherlock Holmes. You know, he may be sharper than I thought he was."

"Don't bet on it. When I left I saw the cop car in front of Etta May's house. I question his intelligence when it comes to his choice in women."

Sever smiled. "Not my type."

"Etta May?"

"Yeah."

"Not mine either, but I guess there's someone for everyone, Mick. As strange as that relationship seems, I do believe that. Look at some of the couples out there today. Jesus. Total mismatches. You know, you see the beautiful babe and the slob of a guy but man, they hook up and it ends up working."

"Describing your own relationship?"

Britt smiled and took a drink of Scotch. He looked away from Sever staring into the black, endless sea. The moon came out from behind a bank of clouds and reflected off the surface with a golden trail that disappeared in the distance. "It's funny, Mick. We've been together twenty-five years. Even when we got married, I gave it ten years tops. Now we're friends, lovers, business partners."

Sever nodded.

"Mick, he wants you to stop down to the station."

"Been there, done that, buddy. No thanks."

"I didn't get the impression you had a choice. He wants your fingerprints."

"What?"

"Look, he's getting all the bands that are still here. Anybody who's been in the studio for the past several weeks. It's no big deal."

"For the record, Jonah, I didn't break Rita's dishes."

"I'm sorry, man. Just passing the word. And speaking of relationships, where is Ginny now?"

Sever watched that same trail of gold, twisting and turning on the water. "I don't know. Haven't talked to her in almost six months. I screwed that up, Jonah. But it's nice to know some people can make a relationship work. Especially when you're involved in this business."

Sever saw her walking out to them, drinks in both hands. Red wine. Her shorts showed off her long brown legs, and she gently swayed as she approached him.

"Hey, Mick. Jonah."

Sever glanced at Britt. "Some people are attracted to Etta May's matronly style, but this is more my type." Sever put his arm around Tommie as she set the drinks on a small table.

"What do you want tonight, Mick? Do you want a romantic walk on the beach, or do you want to go around to the other side and watch the old car?" She gave him a coy smile, and the lights by the pool reflected in her eyes.

Jonah glanced at him. "Watch the car? What? Elvis's Cadillac?"

"I wanted to look across the street and see how much was visible from the hotel. Tommie may have seen two people passing a joint in the car the night Teddy Bartholomew was killed."

"From?"

"The other side of the hotel."

"Two people? Do you have an idea who the other person might have been?"

Tommie shook her head. "I told Mick, it might just have been a reflection on the windshield."

"We know *somebody* was smoking in that car."

"And if somebody besides Teddy was in there maybe Eric could get his fingerprints. It could be the same guy who ransacked your apartment."

"I assume they dusted the Cadillac for prints."

"Did Eric mention that they'd checked the Cadillac for fingerprints?"

"No. Just told me they found prints on the plate."

"They may never have checked the car. Remember, Jonah, it's Eric we're talking about."

"Good point. Well, if they found anything they haven't shared it with me."

"How many people do you think have been in that Caddy, Jonah? How many? Over the years?"

Britt shook his head. "Dozens. Hundreds."

"Then there are probably hundreds of fingerprints. I doubt that Etta May or Bernard go out and clean the steering wheel every day."

Tommie watched them with an amused smile on her face. "Are you two boys playing detective?"

Jonah pointed to Sever. "Actually, Mick's had a hand in solving a couple of murders during his career."

"Oh, really? Well then, I'm even more impressed. I knew you were a famous journalist, but it seems there's more to explore."

"For the most part, it was dumb luck."

They were quiet for a moment and Sever could hear a Bob Marley tune coming from the bar. Right across the street was a studio struggling to survive and a car where a man had been brutally murdered. There was an apartment that had been vandalized not more than three hours ago and the scene of a chase and a fight where Sever had been taken down. You could have it all in the Bahamas.

Jonah laughed. "All the people who sat in that car? If this was *CSI Miami*, they'd check the DNA. In one hour, they'd know the name of everyone who ever came in contact with that heap."

Sever downed the last swallow of the rum concoction. "I wonder if all that DNA crap is actually true. Could someone really sweep that junk heap and come up with the DNA of someone who sat in it?"

"Who? Our ghost? The guy who killed Teddy? Is that really possible?"

"I don't know. I wonder if you can get traces — skin cells, hair."

"Yeah, but there's thirty, forty years of traces in that car. I imagine you'd be hard pressed to separate all those skin cells and hairs."

"Just imagine if you could. I mean, what if you could figure out somebody who sat in that car thirty years ago. Actually know who the person was."

Tommie, a smile playing on her lips, looked confused. "What happened thirty years ago?"

"Thirty years ago? How could you find traces of somebody from thirty years ago? And why would you want to?" Britt was puzzled.

Sever picked up his wine and tasted it. Full-bodied, a little dry, but a nice change from Tommie's fruit-laced rum drink. "It's just a question, Jonah. I really don't understand DNA. But if you could find something —"

"Find what?" Britt seemed confused "I doubt that there's anything left after thirty years, Mick. What the hell do you expect to find after thirty years in the old junker?"

"Etta May says that it was Elvis's Cadillac."

"What? Oh, come on. You've got to be kidding. You can't be serious."

"Mick," Tommie put her hand on his arm. "You think that Elvis really owned that car?"

"I've heard the story, my friend. A dozen times." Britt shook his head vigorously. "The lady is delusional. If I was a doctor I'd have her," he hestiated, "her *and* her kid committed."

"Regardless, I just wondered if there would be any prints or DNA left from the King."

"You're crazy. You know that?" Britt laughed.

"You've got to admit, it would be pretty cool."

"I asked you, Mick. Do you believe that Elvis really owned that car?" Tommie sipped her wine. She obviously thought he was out of his mind as well.

"I believe that Etta May thinks he did."

"She's crazy. Etta May is a nutcase, and the same goes for that kid, Bernard." Britt spread his arms. "Do you realize what you're suggesting? Just because a crazy broad — no offense, Tommie — just be cause a crazy broad concocts some story, you can't buy into it. Jesus, Mick. You're a reporter. You of all people should be able to tell a lie from the truth."

"But Jonah, she's passionate about it. She really is. I think she really believes that Elvis gave her that car. Can you imagine? If she is right?"

Sever was caught up in the possibility. The lady had certainly sounded convincing. Elvis had passed away in 1977. Over thirty years ago. The date worked, the timing was there. What if he had actually given her the car? If the DVD was accurate, he'd given away over two hundred automobiles.

"Did you hear what I said?" Jonah broke into his reverie.

"*I* heard what you said. Crazy broad, no offense, Tommie. Do you think I'm a crazy broad, Jonah?" Tommie put the glass to her lips and sipped some of her ruby red beverage.

"No. My God, no. I simply apologize for the word broad."

"I heard what you said, Jonah." Sever took a deep breath. "You said I should be able to tell the difference between good and evil, lies and truths, good judgment and bad judgment."

"Well, I'm not sure I put it quite like that but—"

"My friend, it's not as easy as that. Some people are born liars, and they are the second hardest to crack. And some people live a lie so long that they believe that lie. That lie has become ingrained in them. There is no question to them that the lie is a truth. It's crystal clear to them. Those people are the hardest to crack. And until I interview them, I can't possibly know what the truth is. Even after I interview them, half the time I'm wrong. Half the time, Jonah."

The three were quiet, letting the argument and confusion die down. Either a band or jukebox was playing a version of "Stir It Up." Sever mentally sang the words a fraction of a second before the vocalist. Trying to think things through, letting the music calm him.

Stir it up, little darlin'

A Bob Marley tune. What a feel. He'd had that good-time feel when he heard Elvis's music, too. The early stuff especially. "Jailhouse Rock" came to mind. The song still gave him a jolt.

He'd dreamed of interviewing the King. A serious interview, not the fluff pieces that were coming out in the sixties. Early in his career, he'd wanted to interview the singer and get to the real soul of the man. Elvis Presley. For God's sake, the man was the king of rock and roll.

He'd actually made several calls to Presley's management. He was turned down every time. Sever was a nobody, and the King didn't have time for some teenage freelance writer who was trying to make a name for himself. So on August 13, 1977, he'd driven to Memphis from Chicago. On a whim. Thinking during the entire drive of how he would approach the man. Drive up to gate? Sit there in his car until Presley drove out. "Hey, Elvis, just a couple of questions." And he had pages of questions.

He'd camped out at a motel just down the street from Graceland. For three days he'd waited. The singer was starting a tour the following day in Portland, Maine, and Sever knew that would end his chance.

On the third day, he'd just stationed himself outside the gate when he saw the cars start pulling in, one after another. Dozens of them. And then, an ambulance. And he'd had a sinking feeling on that hot, muggy August morning that his chance for an interview, anyone's chance for an interview, had just vanished.

"If that car really did belong to Elvis it would be worth a fortune."

"I know what this is all about, Mick." Britt was grinning. "With all the crap you've got to work with over here, with my studio, with Teddy's murder, you're still looking for the next story aren't you? You've got all this to work with, and what do you do? Try to set up the next big scoop."

"Jonah, how can you accuse me of that. Come on. I'm just saying—"

"No, my friend. Be honest with me. If it was possible to prove it, I mean if someone could prove it was Elvis's car, you'd have one hell of a story, wouldn't you?"

Sever grinned, the skin tightening around his cuts and bruises. "Well, it might be a good story, yeah. I've got to be vigilant. You never know where the next paycheck is coming from, Jonah."

CHAPTER THIRTY-FOUR

He pulled the van into the dimly lit Compass Point Hotel parking lot, stepping out with a small satchel. A security guard nodded to him as he headed for the bar, his cap pulled low over his face. He looked over his shoulder, noticing that the guard now had focused his attention on a carload of young men.

Baron ducked low, hiding behind two automobiles, and reversed course, walking quickly down to the road. All he had to do was cross the street and with just a little bit of luck he would take care of his business in just a few short minutes. It would all be handled.

He could make out the studio, the block house next door, the Cadillac up on cement blocks, and the cop car next to it. The cop car. It had been there earlier tonight and the last time he'd come by, in a taxi. Maybe it was a fixture. Maybe it was another purchase by the crazy lady and her drug-addled kid. Maybe in a week or two they'd have that cop car up on blocks as well.

Baron stared at the scene. He'd been dreaming of the moment, and barring someone chasing him down the alley, or stumbling on him in the midst of this act, it would all come together.

He looked both ways, lifting the brim of the cap. Couldn't afford to get hit by a car at this stage of the game. He walked quickly across the street, the muscles in his legs feeling tight, like he'd run a race. Just a few hours ago he had.

Once on the other side, he looked back. No one seemed to have noticed. The weight of the satchel in his right hand reminded him of what was at stake. He hefted the fifteen-pound case, recalling from memory the contents.

The cop car, up the rise. What if there was a cop there? Maybe it wasn't a collected vehicle. Maybe there really was a cop. And what if they were waiting for him? Guns drawn, knowing exactly what he was about to do. Oh, Jesus. Maybe he'd given them some indication earlier in the evening. How could the guy who chased him have a clue what he was up to? Had they ID'd him? Did they know his true motivation?

Baron fell to the ground, suddenly aware of his own physical presence. Who could see him? Were there cameras that recorded his movement from the hotel across the street? Or maybe the recording studio straight ahead? There were cameras everywhere, at traffic stops, stores, on streets, and you never knew when one could do you in.

Someone was watching. He was convinced of it. Bobby Baron hugged the ground, trying to blend in, become as one with the earth. Over a year ago, the fireball had burned his flesh. The chance of being discovered tonight burned at his soul. He'd never felt this kind of fear before.

He clutched the satchel in his hand and slowly raised his head, looking left, right, and straight ahead. Inhaling a deep breath, Baron slowly regained his composure, his heart rate slowing down one beat at a time.

Get the panic attack under control. Think positive thoughts. Try to remember that his one true purpose lay just ahead. His life, his imminent death, all depended upon what happened tonight, and if he were successful, he would celebrate his vengeance. If he failed, there was always another day. There was no other way to look at the situation. If you were successful in all your ventures, then God be praised. If you failed, there was always another day. You could have it all in the Bahamas.

CHAPTER THIRTY-FIVE

Grant Davis bobbed his head to the rhythm of the music. He didn't recognize the song, but the lyrics seemed appropriate.

Somebody sold you, she sold you out
Somebody told you, there is no doubt
All of your troubles, all of your lies
They got you in trouble, you should have been wise
But you tell your stories
Without regret
You'll pay the price, yeah
They're not done with you yet

He had told some stories. But to the best of his recollection, he'd never killed anyone. He'd been out of his mind the night of Teddy Bartholomew's death, but Davis knew it hadn't been him.

It wasn't as if he wasn't capable. Hell, his rage had been over the top for years, but he would have remembered — wouldn't he? If you killed someone. Crushed his larynx? You'd remember that.

The cab bounced, hitting one of the thousands of potholes in the street. Davis looked out the window and recognized the neighborhood.

"Hey. It's right here, man." Damned drivers take you around the block four or five times, jacking up the rate before they drop you off. He knew where his place was.

The taxi driver stopped, the brakes grinding. Guy would have to get a job done on the brakes, and soon.

Davis flipped the driver the fare, adding a buck tip. Fuck 'em. He scooted out before the man could count it and jogged up the path to his room. Job done. Screw the cop who'd taken him in for questioning. Screw Stretch. He'd talked long and hard to Sonny after the bass player had left and he just had a feeling. A feeling that the drummer was on his side. And if he could swing a three-out-of-four vote, he'd be back, making a living managing Johnny Run. Back in charge.

Stretch was on the other side, that was obvious. But right now, all Davis needed was Sonny, Lee Anthony, and Jimmy Child. The rest of the band. Their votes would put him back in the driver's seat. Back where he could control the destiny of Johnny Run. And that destiny was a hit album from Highland Studios in the Bahamas.

His cell phone buzzed and he put his hand on it, feeling the vibration. No one called him on this phone. Hell, no one ever called period.

"Hello?"

"Grant?"

"Of course." Who did they expect?

"You and I met in your room several nights ago."

Of course he remembered. He still had pain in his ribs.

"Grant, there's something we need you to look into."

Christ, another *thing*.

"The local cop, Eric Evans, is digging a little too deep."

"Too deep? You said the Teddy Bartholomew killing was a good thing. I thought everyone was happy about the murder. It would help the cause."

The voice on the other end was muffled, talking to someone off line while he held his hand over the mouthpiece.

"Am I right?"

"Yeah. It could help sell records. Bring a lot of attention to the project. There's no question about that."

"And this cop, he's part of the buzz. Am I right?"

"He is."

"Then what's the problem?"

"Did *you* kill Teddy Bartholomew?"

They thought he did. They'd called and congratulated him for the act, and he hadn't denied it. They figured that he'd killed Teddy so he could create a commotion and take back his old job. "Does it matter who killed him?"

"It might."

"Look, the cops took me in for questioning. They let me go, so I'm pretty sure they don't think I did it."

"Did you kill Bartholomew?"

Relentless. What was the point? The manager was dead. The publicity machine had already been cranked up.

Holding the phone between his shoulder and his chin, Davis grabbed the bottle of Jack Daniel's from the dresser, twisted off the top, and poured a plastic cup half full. He poured it down his throat, barely noting the charcoal flavor of the Tennessee sipping whiskey. Sipping, hell. He needed a long drink. Not just a sip. He filled the cup to the top, noting that the bottle was nearly empty.

"Davis, I'm waiting for an answer."

"No."

"No? No, you didn't kill him? Or no, because this is a cell phone and the call might be picked up by someone else?"

Trick question. They thought he'd killed Bartholomew. Thought he was doing everything possible to draw attention to the new album. If he admitted he'd killed the new manager, it could come back and bite him. If he told them he hadn't killed the manager, they'd think he wasn't doing his job. Damn. What to say? What to do? Davis studied the wall, cracked, pitted, and in need of at least a thick coat of paint.

"Look, I think I'm in a good position to take the band back. I can control this thing, and we can get our investment back. I think we can make some serious money."

"Well, think again, Grant."

"You don't agree?" Now what?

"Eric Evans, the cop who questioned you tonight? He's got what appears to be your fingerprints from inside that Cadillac."

Oh, shit. Inside the damned car. Were things unraveling? Davis took a deep breath and a deep drink.

"That same car where they found Bartholomew. And they've just found a taxi driver who can put you at Highland Studios the night of the murder."

His heart rate was up. He could feel it racing. And his skin was clammy, sweat breaking out on his face and arms.

"What do you think?"

What did he think? He thought he should have stayed Stateside. He thought he'd like to fly out from this godforsaken island in the next hour and never come back. He closed his eyes, trying to put something together. "Look, it's all a guess. They're just taking a wild stab. Honest, man, that's all there is. I didn't do it."

"Grant, we'd like to see you get back with the band, too. But if that cop thinks that you're a good suspect, you're going to spend some time in jail, and the band isn't going to hire you back."

"You're sure about this? The fingerprints?" Damn. How could they possibly have found those prints? After all this time? He should have just admitted it. Hell, the cops weren't looking for a dope smoker. They wouldn't have blinked if he'd just admitted it. But he hadn't. And now, how would it look?

"We got it on pretty good authority."

"The taxi driver?"

"Claims he picked you up where you're staying and dropped you off at Highland. Late that night."

His hands a little shaky, Davis took a long drink. The brown beverage spilled over the edge, staining the cheap carpet at his feet. "Is there anyone else they're questioning? I mean, there's got to be somebody else. Come on, man. Got to be. I'm telling you, I didn't do it." There was a sharp pain right behind his eyes. All of a sudden, a sharp pain.

A long silence followed on the other end. Finally the person spoke. "Grant?"

"Yeah, what? What?"

"From our previous conversation you led us to believe that you *had* killed him. That you were responsible for Bartholomew's death."

"No, Christ, no. I mean, I knew it would help sales, getting all that press. But no. I never meant to —"

"Never meant to what?"

"Damn. Stop it. I never meant to infer — never meant to say that I killed him. You never heard me admit to that." He reached up and wiped his forehead with his hand. It came away damp with perspiration.

"I don't remember you denying it."

"Oh, come on!" Take his chances with the dumb cops? Or with this group? Two options and neither one sounded good.

"Who else would want him dead?"

Who? Maybe the guy on the phone. There was that possibility. They were setting him up. Making it look like he was the murderer. Maybe this guy was the one who called the cops on him. Damn, you couldn't trust anybody. "Maybe somebody in the band."

"Why?"

"Teddy Bartholomew was useless. He was simply a fill-in, until they got a real manager. They knew that. He was a drain on the payroll, a doper, a toker. Maybe he pissed off somebody in the band. I don't know."

"Think about it, Grant. You've got more reason to kill him than anyone else. You could get your job back."

Davis was quiet. He did have more to gain than anyone. And now, he had more to lose. God, no. Not a murder rap in Nassau. Not anywhere, but especially here, in the Bahamas.

"Grant, from what we've heard, it's early in the process. This cop, this Eric Evans is just starting to put it together. That's probably why you were let off tonight."

"I'll call him. I can explain those prints. I smoked dope with the kid next door. Hell, last year. In that car. I'm sure I touched shit. The door handle, the steering wheel, the dashboard. I don't know. The whole thing just slipped my mind, you know. Last year. A long time ago, you know? So, I mean, I'll talk to him. Right now. I mean, I can't let this go any further. God, that's all I need. To get arrested in a foreign country. Not here, man. Not here."

"Take care of it, Grant. Because there's a lot at stake."

This son of a bitch. Telling *him* there was a lot at stake? Only his ass! Only the chance to be hung on this Caribbean Island. A murder charge? Damned right there was a lot at stake.

"I will. I'll take care of it."

"We won't talk again. Got it?"

"Yes." He got it. These guys would salivate at the thought of Grant Davis getting arrested. It would just add fuel to the fire. The press would gang up on him, and the story of Johnny Run and the new album would be even hotter. At his expense, the album would sell millions of copies.

He flipped his phone, his hand shaking. Call the station. Hell, the officer would be off by now. Too late at night, too early in the morning. So what do you do? Wait until the sun comes up? Wait until this asshole goes back on duty? What if he gets up early and starts putting all the pieces together? No. Tackle it now. Find this son of a bitch and have it out.

Davis downed the last of the Jack in his glass and poured just a short one. This time he walked to the bathroom sink and put just a little water in the cup. Didn't want to get too wired. He should have explained it all to the cop. But no, he had to couch the response. Couldn't just be open about it. Damn. Damn, damn, damn.

Think. Stop shaking and think. Where to go, what to do. Every minute that he let the suspicion grow, every second, it would get stronger. Fingerprints, a cab ride, the timing of his visit to Nassau. Damn.

He couldn't believe this was happening to him.

He poured back the Jack, a Johnny Run song pounding in his head. It just popped into his brain and now was clear and loud, screaming at a high volume.

Tellin' me lies and makin' up stories
I couldn't live on yesterday's glories
Got to find somethin' new to do with your life . . .
Hold it all in or let it all out
No matter what you do there can't be any doubt
The truth is the truth and that's all there is when you reach the end . . .

He'd seen the cop's car. Right across from the Compass Point Hotel. Right next to Highland Studios, and parked right next to the Cadillac. The rusted-out pile of shit that sat on blocks in front of the block house. That piece-of-crap former automobile where he'd shared a joint with the kid next door. Over a year ago. And if that cop, Eric Evans, was there, he'd confront him right now. By God, right now.

Taxis ran all night, or the jitney bus. The one-dollar bus ran twenty-four hours. He was sure it did. Or, hell, he'd hitchhike back to the studio. To that block house and the cop car. He didn't care how late it was, this festering problem had to be put to rest immediately.

A murder charge. In a foreign country. He'd read stories about that. You never heard from those people again. Now that was scary. He couldn't let that happen. Davis missed New York like he'd never missed it before. He drank the last drop and tossed the cup at the trash can, missing by two feet. Walking to the doorway, he glanced back at the shabby room, wondering how he'd gotten into this situation in the first place.

CHAPTER THIRTY-SIX

Markus James, a.k.a. Stretch, moved with a swagger. Out to the parking lot, looking for his rental car. He needed to take a drive, open the windows and clear his head. He took long measured strides, moving to the rhythm of a song in his brain. An AC/DC tune. "It's a Long Way to the Top if You Want to Rock 'n' Roll." Good walking music.

Glancing across the road, he saw the studio in the moonlight. Like the house in *Psycho*, its shadowy relief rose from the ground at the top of the rise. Two cars were parked next to the building, and the tiny cinder-block home next door looked like a very small guesthouse.

His gaze swung back, looking for his car. Where the hell had he parked it? Then back to the studio. Someone was rising up from the ground, right in front of the building.

The shadow of some person, a person who apparently had been lying on the ground and, like Lazarus, was now rising from the dead.

Stretch watched as the figure crouched, then sprinted up the small hill. Someone at this early hour of the morning, heading for Highland Studios. Maybe the same person who had broken into the studio and stolen his guitar. Maybe.

The bass player measured the distance. He was two minutes walking distance from the studio. He strode across the parking lot, down to the road, and looking both ways, he quickly crossed over. He searched the landscape with his eyes, hoping to see movement. There was nothing.

He thought about using stealth as he approached the building, but when you were six foot five with a smooth, shiny, black head, there was no way you could hide. He strode toward Highland Studios, the music still playing inside his skull. *Gettin' had, gettin' took . . .*

Up the slight rise, long, smooth strides, as he approached the front porch. Someone had left a drink and a half-smoked cigar in an ashtray on the table. Stretch gazed across the lawn, next door, and down to the street. Across the way he could make out the dark, shadowy cottages of the Compass Point Hotel, the daylit pastel colors now a murky gray in the dim light. No sign of anyone. He tugged on the door handle. It was locked.

Around back, the Britts's apartment. There was a patio back there as well, where he'd done a line of coke or two. Or maybe more. He walked around the white building, keeping an eye out for a sign of anyone who might be lurking in the shadows. The thought struck him that he might be considered a stalker himself. Trespassing, looking very sinister at three in the morning.

There was no one. He eased himself into a lounge chair on the rear porch and pulled a joint from his shirt pocket. Fumbling with the matches in his pocket, he finally freed one from the small box and lit the cigarette, inhaling deeply. He held it inside for as long as he could, then exhaled, feeling his body melt. There'd been a lot of stress. Now, maybe not so much.

He took another hit, thinking about managers and engineers, producers and record companies. They could all go to hell as far as he was concerned. Maybe this would be his last stint with the band. With royalties, with all the money that rolled in every year, every month, every week, every day, maybe he'd just get out of the business. It wasn't about the music anymore. It was about feeding an army of hungry vultures, and he was just tired of that.

If he downsized, he could probably live on that income and savings for the rest of his life. And never again have to worry about assholes like Grant Davis. It wasn't about the fame. It wasn't about the adoring fans or the women who threw themselves at you, thrusting their phone numbers and underwear into your hands. It was about the music. And the music had pretty much become an afterthought.

Another hit, letting the smoke do its magic. Maybe he'd do a line of coke back in his cottage at Compass Point. He had a fresh supply of smoke and coke. But for now, he just relaxed and let the mellowness wash over him. There was plenty of time tomorrow to decide his future. Right now he just wanted to relax. And try to figure out who stole his guitar. He started naming the people he knew. There was Jonah and Rita Britt, the guys in the band, Mick Sever, Bartholomew —

CHAPTER THIRTY-SEVEN

The cop car sat next to the Cadillac. Davis said a silent thank you to whatever spirit could hear him. Yes, it was very early in the morning, and he could just wait for the cop to come out of the house. Or, maybe he could just knock on the door, ask for Eric Evans, and explain that he had nothing at all to do with Teddy Bartholomew's death. Nothing. It was a coincidence that he was here the night of the murder, and even a stranger coincidence that his fingerprints were in the car. Surely the kid would back him up. They'd smoked a joint sitting in the rusty Cadillac. Of course he'd put his hands on the steering wheel, and maybe on the dash. Certainly he'd put his hand on the door handle. It just wasn't a big deal.

And as he stumbled out of the cab, handing the driver a wad of bills, it hit him that maybe, just maybe, Sonny and Stretch were messing with him. He'd been sent home from the police station hadn't he? Eric the cop had finished with his questions. What if the two members of the band were messing with him. What if there really was no cab driver who reported taking him to the studio that night? And what if the police really hadn't found any fingerprints? For crying out loud, how long did fingerprints last? Surely someone would have wiped them off after a year.

Davis stood by the side of the road as the cab drove off. The rise of land was dark, and the studio and the little block house stood out, shadowed in black relief by the faint light of the moon. As he walked up to the studio, he caught the whiff of marijuana. He could use a joint right about now. Somebody was smoking. Maybe that kid. The one who'd shared a joint with him last year. Davis checked the Cadillac, but no one seemed to be in the car. Damn that kid. Damn the fingerprints. Damn the taxi driver who'd ratted on him.

Maybe the smoke came from the kids who lived in the slum alley behind the studio. If he remembered right, Jonah had told him a couple of those kids made a living selling drugs. Probably the kids, smoking up some of the profit. Young punks who stole anything they could get their hands on just to buy drugs. And their buddies who sold them those drugs and pocketed their money. Alleys like that were a vicious cycle.

He'd brought one joint with him. To help the time pass. What to do, what to do. Go up and knock on the door at three thirty in the morning? Or maybe sit in the car and wait until daylight? Maybe smoke the joint, close his eyes, get a little rest before he talked to the fat cop. That was probably the best idea.

He lit the weed, sucking it into his lungs. The Jack had made him just a little lightheaded. This sent him over the edge. His eyes rolled back in his head, and he felt like jelly. There wasn't a bone in his body. Where was the other smoke coming from?

Davis leaned against the front porch column for a minute, staring at the old car and the cop car next to it. The moon was behind a cloud and the faint light from across the street filtered through two palm trees, causing eerie shadows to play on the automobiles. It was as if they were caressing each other, the shadows moving seductively over the auto bodies.

Taking a deep breath, he eased around the studio, still following the trail of smoke. He took another hit of his own, then saw the silhouette of a big man, sprawled in a chair on the back porch. The orange glow of a cigarette was in his hand. Couldn't be the cop. The cop was short and round. And he was too tall to be Jonah.

He approached the figure, watching carefully. He could smell the marijuana, and then the strong acrid odor of gasoline. Gas, maybe coming from the cop's car.

"Hey, Stretch, is that you?"

"Who the fuck?"

"Stretch, it's me."

"Who's me?"

Davis laughed. Giggled, then laughed again. Then started giggling, a high-pitched titter that he couldn't control. "Who's me? Me, that's who's me." He took a breath, breaking the laughing jag.

"Who the fuck are you?"

"Stretch, Stretch. It's your old buddy, Grant."

"Buddy? I was never buddies with anybody named Grant."

"It's me, big guy. Grant Davis."

"Did you steal my guitar?"

"What?"

"Did you steal my guitar? Come back to steal some more?"

"What are you talking about?" His mind was foggy. He was being questioned about a murder, not a stolen guitar.

"Stretch?" He approached the porch, leaning against the building for support.

"Yes or no, Davis."

"No."

"Did you kill Teddy Bartholomew?"

"No."

"Then why are you here?"

"Here? Here, here?"

"On the island. What, you got shit for brains? I'm asking you. If you didn't come here to kill Teddy Bartholomew, then why are you on the island the same time we are?"

Davis studied the big man. He couldn't make out the expression on his face, but he certainly didn't sound like he was just passing time. "Stretch, do you smell like gas?"

Quiet for a moment. Finally, "No. It's not me."

"Somebody smells like gas."

"Maybe you?"

Davis raised his arm, sniffing to see if the odor came from him. "Shouldn't be smokin' if we smell like gas."

"You don't seem to want to answer my question. What the hell are you doing here?"

"Stretch, I am here to help you guys. To be a good manager once again. And you are messing with me. Trying to get me in trouble."

The big man closed his eyes. "You got yourself into this trouble. Nothin' we ever did got you there. You got there yourself."

"Stretch, I didn't kill—" He couldn't remember the name. The name of the manager who'd been killed in the Caddy.

"Did you steal my guitar and sell it to the Hard Rock Cafe?"

More shit. Being questioned for murder, for stealing.

"Tell me the truth, man. Somebody stole my bass guitar." Eyes still closed, like a sleeping giant.

Davis sat down on the edge of the porch, sitting before falling. He took a hit on the cigarette, holding it deep, then he blew the sweet smoke out, wondering again where the strong gasoline odor was coming from. "The truth is, I don't remember stealing anything from you. I told you. I'm sure I didn't steal your guitar, man. Why?"

"You were here. Eric the cop told us you took a taxi to the studio. He's got the driver admitting that he brought you here."

Davis raised his voice, shouting at Stretch. "Fuck Eric the cop. I'll deal with him myself, okay?" He would. He'd talk to him and convince him he was not involved in this crap. "I came by." Why didn't anyone understand? He hadn't killed the manager. He hadn't stolen anyone's guitar. Christ, he was just here to try to get his job back. "I was here to see the place. I'd like to be making a hit record with you guys again. It's the only reason I'm on the island, man."

Stretch's eyes snapped open. "That's just the point, man. You *didn't* make a hit record. And even if that record had been a hit, you didn't have shit to do with it. You want to be a part of the process but you've got no talent. You've got zip. You're a useless motherfucker, just plain useless. Tits on a boar hog. You took your salary, your cut, your bonuses, and you amounted to nothing." Stretch watched as Davis pushed himself from a sprawl into a sitting position. "You're a leech, man."

"Watch what you say." Davis took another toke, his head revolving.

Stretch laughed, long and loud. "Watch what I say? I say you're a piece of garbage. Whale shit. No good to anybody. That's what I say."

They both heard the loud scream, a wailing sound coming from next door. It exploded from the tiny block house with a high-pitched shriek that split the dark and reverberated in the air.

"Jesus." Davis's head spun around again and he climbed to his feet, feeling weak and wobbly. "We maybe should go over and see if everybody is okay. Should we go over and—"

Stretch moved quickly for a big guy, pushing himself from the chair and stepping down off the porch. He hesitated. "No. It's none of our business. None of my business. I don't know those people."

"Jesus, Stretch, somebody sounded like they were in pain."

"You go. Make yourself useful. I don't do other people's problems. Not theirs, and definitely not yours. Understand?"

Davis nodded. He didn't understand at all. Too many drinks, too many drugs. He didn't understand why he couldn't just have his job back and get back on the gravy train. It made no sense to him at all. He drew one more lungful of smoke and flipped the cigarette into the air. The home-rolled joint spun through the air, toward the block house. He watched it ark, the orange spark, spinning end over end as it landed two feet from the house.

With a whoosh, then a huge roar, the ground was engulfed in hot orange flames. Davis screamed, his eyes blinded by the bright flash, and his skin absorbing the scorching heat. He slowly opened his eyes and in a blur he saw Stretch, on his feet, dumbstruck. The bald black man looked stunned, then backed up, finally turning and running down the deserted alley. When Davis regained his focus, the little house was surrounded by a raging ring of fire, engulfing the bushes and small trees and climbing the white walls of the house. He screamed again, inhaling the black smoke from the gasoline fire, the raw chemical fumes burning his nostrils and his mouth as he ran. Ran as hard as he could, trying to get a fresh breath of air, anything but the heavy gas fumes that permeated the air.

Davis blindly ran toward the alley. He didn't know where Stretch had gone, didn't really care. He just knew he had to get away from this horrific fire. He pulled his shirt up as he ran, covering his face, trying to filter out the smoke. Somewhere up ahead he could get some air. Somewhere up ahead he could slow down, find Stretch, and make him see that he was making a mistake. Davis really was a good manager. He could really help the band get back on top.

Just a little farther. Somewhere up ahead.

The sky lit up again as flames engulfed another tree or bush. For a brief moment, Davis could see all the way down the alley. Shadows of houses and scrub trees, broken down fences, and trash cans. And he could make out someone about one hundred yards down the path. Maybe it was Stretch.

Davis pushed it just a little harder, his lungs burning from the smoke and the run. He needed to catch up with Stretch. Christ, he had to clear himself with someone tonight, and it didn't look like it would be Eric the cop. With this house on fire he'd have enough to deal with.

CHAPTER THIRTY-EIGHT

The three of them finished their drinks, Britt giving Sever a knowing nod. "Well, partner, it's time I headed back to the ranch. Hell, Rita probably thinks I fell in the water. Leave you two alone."

Sever smiled. "Come on, we'll walk you to the road."

Tommie touched his forehead gently, running her finger over a bandage. "Are you sure you want to stay out with me? You've been through a lot tonight, Mick."

He had. And the thought of going back to his cottage on stilts, his home away from home with its batik fabrics from West Africa, beaded Zulu bottles and hand-painted ceramic vases from Morocco played in his mind. Just to lie in his bed and have the ceiling fan cool him. The idea appealed to his tired, bruised body.

He also wondered if he had anymore gifts waiting for him. Like the cloth doll with the colorful, coarse cloth dress and kerchief. The doll with the pins in her eyes, and the message that he should butt out of the death of Teddy Bartholomew.

And the reason for staying up? He wanted to explore the Bahamian girl. She was a nice divergence from the way things were going. Or maybe she was more in tune *with* the way things were going. And more like an accomplice. Ginny had been his accomplice. His lover, wife, friend, and accomplice and every time he found someone, maybe someone like Tommie, he was reminded of Ginny. Bright, intuitive, funny, and just good to be around.

"Let's walk Jonah home and we'll discuss our options. Okay?"

"Sure. I just get worried about old men who think they can go the distance." She laughed out loud.

"A challenge has been issued." Britt smiled as they walked through the bar, empty now but for a handful of patrons who nursed almost empty drinks.

"Everyone's left." Sever motioned to the tables. "When the best bartender on the island is off her shift, they all go home."

They heard the growing noise as they neared the exit. Customers crowded outside the doorway, looking up the hill.

"What is it?" Britt brought up the rear, shouting to Sever.

"Something happening on your side of the road, Jonah." He let go of Tommie's hand and pushed his way through the crowd. Ten deep, they lined up, standing outside the bar and in front of the cottages, pointing and talking in hushed voices.

The horizon glowed a bright orange and as smoke drifted back across the road, Sever could tell it was a new fire. The crackling of burning live trees and shrubbery could be heard all the way to the Compass Point Hotel, and, pushing his way to the front, Sever could finally see the blaze. The house, made of concrete block, was engulfed in flames, the ground surrounding it scorched, and he watched it lick at the taller trees, bushes, and greenery. Cement walls on fire? Obviously an accelerant. The fire had been deliberately set. Thank God it wasn't the studio. Still, it would be a problem. Sever wondered if Rita was okay. Then he thought about Etta May and Bernard. Would they have had the common sense to vacate? Or were they trapped inside?

The flames shot into the air, and he felt Britt brush against him.

"Shit. Man, I hope Etta May and the boy are okay."

Sever nodded. They could hear sirens in the distance, maybe two or three. Their shrill, piercing wail cut through the noise of the crowd.

"Damn it, Mick. There's something evil over there. I swear there is."

"Rita?"

"I just called her on the cell. She's safe."

"Was she sleeping?"

"Was. She said somebody was smoking dope outside the studio. She could smell it. There were loud voices, so she looked out the window to see what was happening and the next thing she knew the place next door just blew up."

"So she thinks —"

"Doesn't think. She knows. She looked out the window just before the place caught fire and saw Grant Davis, Johnny Run's former manager. Davis was apparently upset about being accused of Teddy Bartholomew's death."

"Grant Davis? She heard this conversation?"

"She didn't get it all, but the gist of the conversation was that Davis thought he was going to be hung out to dry, or die may be a better word. He apparently was here the night of the murder, and let's face it, the guy has the perfect reason to kill Batholomew. If Teddy is dead, Grant Davis has a chance to move back in, right?"

"What a devious plot."

"He was Johnny Run's manager for the last five years. And I suppose he got used to the idea. I mean, I know he liked the money, the fame, the girls."

"And Rita says he started this fire?"

"It appeared that way. From where she stood."

"Unbelievable. All you're trying to do is produce a hit record and this band and its management are creating havoc. Teddy Bartholomew, their current manager, gets murdered in the car next door. Grant Davis, their previous manager, starts a fire next door. I can't get ahold of this, Jonah."

"I didn't say I understood it, Mick. But Rita is all right and that's what really concerned me. She's actually very calm."

Sever watched the house, black smoke rising high above the flames. The people inside. The cop, the kid, the mom.

The wail of sirens was closer, splitting the early morning air, and Sever could see the glow of the flashing lights from the fire engines, still quite a way from the site, but moving fast. Through the flames and smoke Sever could make out the two cars, sitting side by side. Like sentinels guarding the burning fort, Elvis's Cadillac and the cop car, watching as all hell broke loose.

CHAPTER THIRTY-NINE

His head snapped up, and in a fleeting second, he knew what had happened. He didn't know how it happened, but it had happened. The gas had somehow ignited, and he wasn't even ready. Damn. He flung the empty red plastic container as far as he could into the fire as the orange flames licked at the house. What the hell had happened? He held his satchel in his right hand, wondering if he should toss it as well. Something had gone dreadfully wrong. Baron hesitated, then flung the satchel into the raging inferno. Let everything be destroyed in the fire. No evidence, no proof that he'd been involved at all. No sign that he'd spent the last six months of his life figuring out how to dole out his revenge.

The extreme heat was almost unbearable. Baron put his arm over his face, his memory flashing back to the studio fire. The brilliant flash that exploded around him, searing his body and blistering his skin. He'd tried to put that memory away, but it was back with a vengeance.

Baron wasn't ready for this. Not at all. Where the hell had it come from? Even after he'd poured the gasoline, he still had time to decide. Decide if he was going to go through with the ignition. But someone or something had sparked the fire. Someone had taken his decision away from him.

He jogged to the porch. He'd just finished pouring the gas on the far side of the house, and now these people would be roasted alive. He knew what that was like. Not much fun. He never would have started the fire without a warning. But someone else had.

He pounded on the door, beating it with his scarred hands, in a burst of compassion hoping they heard him and would escape. There wasn't any more time. Baron leaped from the tiny porch and ran toward the alley, the hot gusts of wind stealing the oxygen from the air. For the second time in twenty-four hours, he was running down the dark, deserted dirt and cinder road where the lowlifes lived. Shuttered windows and boarded-up doorways on the lonely houses stood as a reminder of the poverty across from the opulent hotel, restaurant, and lounge. The super rich, the super poor. You could have it all in the Bahamas.

Damn. He'd made the decision to pour the gas, but always gave himself the out. He wasn't sure he could ever have struck the match. And now, someone or something had started the fire. Baron glanced over his shoulder and saw the flames had reached the roof, climbing into the palm trees that circled the building.

He gasped, his lungs aching as he pushed on, stretching as far as his legs would allow. He needed to put as much distance between himself and the fire as possible. His mind was troubled, jumbled with the thought of what had just happened. It was some little consolation that at least he'd given them a chance. When they answered the door, someone would see the fire and vacate the premises. It was more than they'd done for him.

The fire was never meant to take lives, but simply to send a message. Let them know that he knew. He'd painstakingly put it together in his head. As he ran, he put the pieces together, gulping in air for his oxygen-starved brain. For over a year he'd worked on it, let it simmer in his mind. He'd thought it over. Over and over, and now he was certain. Etta May and maybe her twin boys had started the fire in the studio. There was no question.

Oh, he didn't take it personally. The bitch may or may not have known that he was in the building. She probably didn't even know he was the one who smoked dope with her brain-addled kid. But he was sure of one thing. The lady or the kids had started the fire. She'd wanted the problem to go away for years, and finally took matters into her own hands. She'd wanted the den of iniquity to disappear from the face of the earth. There was no other explanation. Etta May wanted the studio to evaporate into a fiery hell.

His feet pounded the dirt and cinders as he ran down the path. The dry heat from the flames faded as he distanced himself from the flames.

The drug-addled musicians, the loud music, the evil people who Etta May saw destroying Bernard's life, Samuel's life, she wanted them all gone. She wanted an end to the evil that permeated her surroundings. And finally, she'd decided to make that dream come true.

He was torn about the personal attack. Maybe she *did* know that Bobby Baron had given her kid drugs. And maybe, just maybe, she'd decided to take him out when she started the fire. Maybe she had decided to send a message and burn him alive in the inferno. If there was personal intent to her attack, so be it. But he was still alive. Someone else had paid the ultimate price, and Baron had a pretty good idea of who that was. But his plan was to get even, regardless.

He gasped, slowing his speed until he was barely jogging. Even at his peak condition he couldn't have continued this run, and he was far from peak condition.

Baron had planned his revenge for the last six months, deciding that he'd have to take what should have been the Lord's work into his own hands. And now this. It had been stripped from him, the opportunity, or the choice, to actually burn the home. How the hell had it happened? Damn. Damn. Damn.

He jogged with a limp, his breath coming in shallow gulps now. Just get away from the fire. Distance himself from the raging blaze and get back to the convent. It never should have happened like this.

And then, from out of the blue, the man hit him, a full-body smack down. From nowhere the body came out of the dark, smashing into him. Baron crashed to the ground, the vision of the giant shadow attacking him still in his mind. He struggled to get up, but the big man was holding him from above, his hand tight on his throat.

Déjà vu. He'd been in this same alley, in this same situation earlier in the evening and he'd come out of it victorious.

The big black man held him down, pushing him into the dirt and cinders that covered the alley. Baron relaxed, sucking in deep breaths, filling his lungs with as much oxygen as possible, and, as his muscles relaxed, the man's hand slowly did as well.

Baron took another breath, and another. One more and the man removed his hand.

"You poured the gasoline? You tried to burn down the block house?"

Baron knew that voice. Who? Very familiar.

"I'm asking you."

He'd met the man. Who the hell was it? That voice, the strength of the man. Of course. Stretch Cunningham, the bass player for Johnny Run. The bald-headed black giant with the attitude. A giant pain in the ass in the studio. Stretch gave him crap at every turn, every measure, every note. Stretch had never wanted Baron on the last project. The two men detested each other.

The big man hadn't figured it out yet. He had no idea who Baron was. Baron turned his head, peering through the darkness, trying to make out the man's features. It was now obvious. It *was* Stretch. That's who it was.

"One more time."

"Stretch. It's me." His voice was little more than a croak. He had to let him know who he was and maybe he'd let up. Surprise him. Stretch would surely never recognize Baron. There was nothing left to recognize.

The bass player looked closer. He leaned in, then recoiled in disgust. "My God, man, who are you?"

Baron saw him back up, getting to his feet and stepping back. He knew the effect he had on people. There was no question that his looks were repulsive. He lived with it daily, weekly, monthly, and would for years to come. God willing. And all he'd wanted was to exact revenge on the people who had started his descent into hell.

Because that's what it was. His own climb into the bowels of the earth. He was a monster from the depths of hell.

Stretch was still retreating, and Baron pushed himself up from the dirt and cinders.

"Did you steal my guitar?" Stretch had stopped now. Holding ground.

"Your guitar?"

"Tell me who you are." The tall man was speaking in hushed tones, taking tentative steps forward now, slowly walking toward Baron.

Baron stepped back, stumbling on a large stone behind him. The big man was moving faster now, was going to grab him. Maybe try to strangle him again.

"I asked you a question, freak. Who the hell are you? The ghost? Is that who you are? Some supernatural freak of nature?"

There was no place to hide. The man with the long legs could outrun him. The man with the long arms could outhit him. But Bobby Baron had a private place. When the kid next door to the studio got hauled inside by his mom, when the beating started and the screaming kid and mom were battling, Baron remembered closing his eyes, smoking his joint and drifting away in Elvis's Cadillac. He could survive anything.

Now the man was six feet away, and his hands were stretched out. Even in the dark, Baron could see his eyes, wide and wild. Stretch had been drinking, smoking, or something that ratcheted up his anxiety level.

"Be-Bop? It's you? You son of a bitch." He froze for just a moment, the recognition registering. "You tried to destroy our career, you stole my guitar, and now you try to burn down the house next door? What the hell is wrong with you, you miserable bastard. It is you, isn't it? Did you burn the studio? Was it you who burned down Highland Studios?"

Baron reached down and picked up the heavy boulder, the same stone he'd stumbled on.

Stretch took a step and another and another.

Baron held the boulder tight. To some people that stone would be an obstacle. But to some it would be the stone that David used to slay Goliath. With a strength he didn't know he possessed, Baron swung the boulder around, hard, smashing it into the big man's face, and Stretch went down. Silently the big man collapsed and lay perfectly still. In a second the deed was done.

Baron dropped the stone and walked away. He had to get back to the convent. The sisters would miss him, and he didn't want them to take away his dessert.

CHAPTER FORTY

Davis crouched, sobbing and taking in large lungfuls of air. The bright orange glow lit up the alley and he could see the shadows of people on their back porches and out in the postage-stamp yards, watching the fire as it devoured the scenery. The sirens were loud and he hoped that they would find the people in the house alive and well.

Slowly, ever so slowly, he stood up, feeling the tight pain in his legs, the burning in his lungs, the sweat dripping from his face, and he said a prayer to whatever gods would listen, thanking them for letting him escape with his life. It had been one hell of a night.

He was shaking, partly from fear, partly from the moment, and partly from the sweat on his body as it chilled in the cool night air. Slowly, still breathing deeply, he walked down the alley, away from the studio and the burning building. He had no desire to go back and see up close the damage the fire had caused.

He saw the figure walking in front of him, maybe one hundred yards ahead. Stretch. Then he realized the stature wasn't right. Whoever it was walked slowly, hunched over as if the weight of the world was on his shoulders. He was a smaller man, but that was all Davis could tell in the dark. Once in a while a burst of flame from the house would throw more light down the road and he could see the man up ahead with his head buried in his chest.

Davis turned once more to see the fire, the majestic orange and yellow flames now graceful against the black sky. When he looked back down the road the walker was gone. As if he'd vanished without a trace.

Davis continued to walk. Now he was the lone hiker, scuffling his feet, trying to figure out how he could get to the main road and find a taxi back home. His breathing was returning to normal and his heart rate was slowing down. He wiped at his face with his shirt sleeve and licked his lips, tasting the bitter flavor of soot and sweat on his skin.

This trip had not gone according to plan. Come to think of it, there was no plan. He simply wanted his job back, and after his conversation with Stretch tonight it was obvious the bass player would lobby very strongly not to hire him back. The man made it clear he wanted nothing to do with Davis again. In fact, he'd told him — his foot hit an immovable object and he stumbled, catching himself before he fell in the dirt.

Davis bent down, surprised by a bloodied body. He touched the figure on his face. He pulled his hand away quickly, rubbing his fingers together and feeling the sticky substance that covered his skin. He gently touched the face again, feeling for the mouth, the nose, anything that would let him know if the figure was breathing, alive or dead.

Leaning in he could see the nose. Bent, broken, and no sign of any breathing. Beside the body lay a large boulder, and he lifted it, his bloody sticky fingers smearing the smooth surface. Davis dropped the boulder, and stood up. It was Stretch. He'd fallen, and hit his head on a rock. The big guy who'd always given him a rough time. The guy who was going back to the band to try to ban him forever from their midst.

He turned again, gazing at the fire as cascading water from the hoses rained down on the hot building and foliage, causing a hissing sound even this far away. Clouds of steam and smoke soared to the sky.

The syndicate, that group of investors who wanted untold millions for their financial participation, had called him and said go to the island. Once here they'd told him his mission was to get involved, at whatever level, get involved with the current project. Get involved and make it a hit. Like it was the easiest thing in the world to do. Then why the hell didn't everyone do it?

And then Teddy Bartholomew was killed. Convenient. If you wanted to take over as manager, it made sense to have the present manager vacate his post. Permanently. Then Stretch let it be known that he didn't want Davis back. Well, if you want to become manager of a group, it helped to have your lone detractor *leave* the group. And from the brief examination of Stretch's body, Davis was pretty sure Stretch had left the group. For good.

Davis now considered himself either the luckiest guy in the business — or the unluckiest. He remembered his mission tonight. Eric the cop considered Davis a person of interest in the death of Teddy Bartholomew. Davis's taxi trip to the studio in an inebriated state the night of the killing and his fingerprints in the Cadillac pointed right to Teddy's death, and since there were no other viable suspects, Eric the cop was pointing his finger. At Davis. So, Davis's mission was to talk to Eric. One on one.

He needed to tell him that he could explain everything. There was no reason to even think that he was capable of killing another human being. He assumed, considering that the block house was up in flames, that Eric wouldn't be in a frame of mind to talk to him at this very moment. He should probably find a better time to stop by or maybe make an appointment.

Still, things seemed to be working out. Stretch no longer posed a threat. Davis wiped his hands on his pants and walked down the path. Sooner or later it would lead to a road and he'd flag down a taxi to take him back to the rooming house. He'd see Sonny and the rest of the band tomorrow, or in a couple of days. Tell them how sorry he was about Stretch, suggest an audition for a new member of the band, and he'd be back in the manager's seat quicker than you could say *hit record*.

Actually, things were working out all right. Now if he could just get Eric off his case.

CHAPTER FORTY-ONE

Sever ran across the street, feeling the strain in his knee as his feet hit the hard pavement. Sometimes walking wasn't even easy, and now he'd tried running on his bad leg twice tonight. Once down the alley behind Highland Studios and now running toward the fire. He must be crazy. What was it that Tommie said? She liked older men, but ones who knew their limits?

He glanced over his shoulder and saw Britt close behind. Up the hill, ahead of the fire engines. An eerie orange glow bathed the buildings and the trees, and the ebb and flow of the orange and yellow flames cast enormous shadows on the ground that moved like the wind. The whole scene was surrealistic.

Sever stood for a moment, feeling the heat penetrate his clothes and his skin. Each cut on his face felt like it was on fire, and he considered his options. He could watch until the fire engines arrived. Or he could see if anyone needed his help. And at that very second, he heard the scream from inside the house. Above the whoosh and roar of the fire, he could make out the scream of someone.

Looking back, he saw Britt was twenty yards behind, and looking forward, he could see the fire was concentrated on the side of the house facing the studio. The front of the small white structure was the only part of the house that wasn't engulfed in flames. Smoke poured from the open door, and Sever guessed that most of the fire damage was on the outside. Smoke was choking whoever was still inside the home. Taking a deep breath he charged up the two steps to the concrete porch and stepped into the doorway. His eyes stung, the acrid smoke thick with the odor of gasoline. He could make out a figure standing against the wall on the far side of the room and he crossed the floor in ten quick steps. Sever released the breath, slowly, and tentatively took another. This one was filled with smoke and he coughed it back out.

"Please, help me."

Etta May, coughing, choking. She stood flat against the wall and he grabbed her around the waist and lifted her up. Sever's knee buckled and he tried to lock it, slowly adjusting to the weight of the short, stout woman. She screamed again as he retraced his ten steps, getting outside the door with his cargo and moving away from the building. The sharp pain in his knee told him he couldn't walk much farther. He knelt, depositing the woman on the ground, and grabbed a breath. It wasn't fresh, but it was better than inside the house. He breathed deeply, then coughing, hacking as if he was going to cough his lungs out.

"Who else is inside the house?" He shouted over the roar of the flames.

She looked up at him with wide eyes, petrified, as if she'd seen a ghost, smoke swirling around her.

"Etta May, who else is inside the house?" He coughed again. She wasn't making this easy. "Is Bernard inside? You've got to tell me."

She shook her head, her wide eyes filled with tears. "Samuel. He's not here."

"Mick." Britt was beside him. "What the hell, man. You never should have gone in there. Are you crazy?"

He thought she whispered something, but the roaring fire drowned it out. "Talk to me, Etta May."

She was in shock. A little louder this time. "Samuel."

The fire engines screamed down the road, the red flashing lights adding to the bright orange glow of the fire.

"Etta May, for God's sake, tell me, where's Bernard?" He was shouting, and he could feel his eyes starting to tear up from the smoke. Was there a Samuel still inside? Wasn't he the twin?

She reached out with both hands from her seated position on the ground, almost pleading. Her eyes searched his and finally she said it softly, then louder and louder. "Eric is inside. Eric is inside. Eric is inside the house."

"Where? Tell me where?" His voice was strained.

"In the kitchen, in the back."

"Mick, you're out of your mind. Please, man, don't—"

Sever spun around and raced back to the block building, surprised at how his leg didn't really hurt that much after all. It still made sense to go in the front. He wasn't even sure there was a back door. He'd made it once, and as small as the house was, the kitchen couldn't be more than another four or five steps farther.

He walked up the two steps to the tiny porch and stepped inside the house. Smoke swirled and the place felt like a brick oven. The heat was almost unbearable and the place was cooking. Ten steps to the back wall and he looked for some sort of an entrance to take him into the kitchen. He let out a breath of air and prayed that he'd find the entrance fast because he couldn't get enough air to make this work unless everything happened in the next minute.

Finally he saw it, over to the left. A small archway from the living room and he stooped over and moved through it, struggling to see through the thick gray smoke. Sever saw the man, seated on a wooden chair by a tiny table. He was hunched over, obviously passed out. Deadweight. This wasn't going to be easy. He stepped to the body, tugging at the man's arms, trying to get a hold on him. Under the arms. Sever lifted, trying to take some of the polluted air into his lungs at the same time. He managed to get the short, heavyset cop up and out of the chair. Coughing and choking, he dragged the man across the wooden floor, the heels on Eric's shoes scraping against the boards. He moved backward, looking over his shoulder. Didn't want to run into a chair, a sofa, or a lamp.

Out the front door, the cop's head nestled under his chin. Holding him under the arms, the legs sprawling out, he backed down the steps, gasping for some air, and there was Britt.

Britt moved in quickly, taking the cop from him and Sever walked ten steps and collapsed on the ground. He lay there for thirty seconds, sucking in air and feeling the tremendous burn in his lungs.

A fireman ran up to him, helping him to his feet.

"You've got lots of blood on your neck. Are you all right?"

Blood? Sever ran his hand over his neck. It came away red and sticky. His neck was the last place that hurt. What could he have done?

"We'll take you to the hospital and have it checked. There's an ambulance at the foot of the hill. I'll get a stretcher."

Sever felt his neck again. No cut, no damage, no pain. Maybe he'd spit up the blood from all the coughing. Then it hit him.

"Wait, hold on."

The fireman turned around. "What? I'll send someone with a stretcher."

"No." Sever searched the hillside, looking for Britt. He finally spotted the man, down the hill, crouched beside the cop. "Down there." He pointed.

"What's down there?"

"The man on the ground. Eric Evans. He's the one I pulled out of the house."

"And?"

"It's his blood. He'll need the stretcher and the ambulance."

CHAPTER FORTY-TWO

He'd stumbled down to the main road, and even at that early hour of the morning, he'd found a taxi. Good thing, too, because he certainly couldn't have found his little rented room by himself.

Davis fumbled around with the lock, finally getting the key to fit, and he took five steps and fell on top of the tangled sheets and blankets of the unmade bed. What a night. He'd fought with Stretch, schmoozed with Sonny, gone over to talk with the cop, fought with Stretch, started a fire, then found Stretch either passed out or dead in the alley behind Highland Studios. Then again, it could all be a dream. Just a figment of his imagination. He'd had quite a bit to drink, and he'd smoked a lot of marijuana. From past experience he knew that his judgment could be impaired under those circumstances.

Davis took a deep breath, then another. After about five minutes he crawled across the bed, reached for the dresser, and pulled the bottle of Jack Daniel's off, holding it tightly. God, the worst thing that could happen would be that he would drop the bottle. Now where was the Coke? He remembered there wasn't any Coke. Davis twisted the cap and put the neck of the bottle to his mouth. He took a long swallow, letting the amber fluid burn all the way to his stomach.

He wondered if there was a flight out tomorrow. Maybe go back to the States, wait a week or so, then call Sonny and see if he could schedule a meeting. Things would probably be a little up in the air for the next couple of days.

Davis stood up, went to the small sink in the bathroom, and splashed some water on his face. He thought he might be sick and he waited until the feeling passed. Another pull on the almost empty bottle and he started to feel a little better. Maybe he'd take a little walk. Clear some of that smoke from his head. He was aware that he reeked from the smell of the fire.

Down the stairs and outside, his bottle of Jack in his hand. Just a short walk, then a couple hours of sleep. He had to get the hell off this island. As soon as humanly possible.

His cell phone chirped, and he pulled it from his pocket with his spare hand. Davis stared at it, considering whether to answer it at all. Every time he did, there was bad news on the other end. "Yeah?"

"What the hell happened?"

"I thought we weren't talking anymore."

"Davis, are you aware someone was killed in the fire?"

Had they found Stretch's body? Wait a minute. Stretch was far away from the fire. They couldn't mean the big bass player. "How did you find out about the fire so soon?" It couldn't have been more than an hour ago. Who was this guy and where did he get his information?

Silence on the other end.

"Hello?"

"Grant. You've caused a lot of trouble."

"No. I haven't. I haven't caused any trouble at all. I haven't done anything. I tried to explain that to you the last time we talked. You're not listening, man. I'm only here because you asked me to get involved and—"

"Jesus, Grant. Not to this level. The group is *not* happy. All we ever asked you to do was to make something happen so the new record takes off. And now that you've got started, you don't seem to stop."

"The fire. It wasn't me. I mean, it was accidental. You've got to believe me." The smell of his clothes and the smoke on his skin and hair nauseated him. He poured the last of the whiskey down his throat and tossed the bottle as far as he could into some brush by the side of the road.

"We want nothing to do with this, Grant. Nothing to do with you. None of what's happened tonight can come back on us. So whatever you did, you did on your own. We'll deny we ever talked."

"I didn't do anything. Really. And aren't there cell phone records. I mean, if anyone ever looks into it, they'll know you guys were calling me."

Silence again.

"Grant, the cop who was investigating Bartholomew's murder — Eric somebody?"

"Eric Evans?"

"Yeah. He died in the fire tonight."

"Whoa!"

"Yeah. You've got problems, my friend. Big problems. And you're threatening me with cell phone records? *You've* got the problems, Grant."

Eric the cop was dead? Now in a perfect world, that would be a good thing. The cop who thought Davis was involved in Bartholomew's murder was dead. But the really bad side was, somebody — this syndicate in particular — thought Davis had started the fire. And they thought he'd killed Eric the cop. This was not good. How could everything have gone so terribly wrong?

"There's not a threat implied. I'm telling you I didn't start the fire, and I didn't kill anyone. Look, I don't even know your name, but I may need some serious help. You guys wanted me over here. It wasn't even my idea to come over here. I didn't kill Teddy, I didn't start the fire, and I didn't kill a cop. Do you hear me? Do you hear me? You've got to believe me."

There was silence on the other end.

"Honest to God, I haven't done any of these things." He was shouting into the phone and getting no response at all.

Silence.

"Hello. Hello?"

There was no one on the other end.

Davis stood there for a moment, ten feet from his rented room. Several miles from Highland Recording Studios where this all began a little over a year ago, and one thousand miles from New York City.

The wail of a police siren cut through the early morning silence and he could see the flashing lights as they approached. Grant Davis raised his arm and heaved the phone after the bottle of Jack. Then he took off on a run, not knowing where he was going, just knowing he had to go somewhere. Anywhere but here.

CHAPTER FORTY-THREE

Sever took a bite of the special, seafood en papillote. It had been a long time since he'd been to Graycliff. The five-star restaurant, hotel, wine cellar, and cigar factory on Hill Street had matured well. It already had almost 250 years on it, so the four or five since he had been here hadn't done much damage.

"The dinner is to your liking?" the waiter asked.

"It is. The pastry is superb, the fish is flaky and tender. Very tasty."

"The grouper is perfect." Britt nodded.

"Excellent." Rita smiled.

"These are a gift from our manager." He laid two freshly wrapped Graycliff cigars on the table by the two men, smiled, and walked away.

"What? They assume a woman doesn't smoke?" Rita made a face.

"Well, you don't. These are great cigars, Mick." Britt picked his up and smelled the wraper. "Damn, this is fine tobacco."

Sever nodded. "We've been avoiding the situation, Jonah. What happened to Eric?"

"What happened? I only know what Etta May said."

Rita took a sip of her wine. "She said that she wasn't in the house when his head got bashed in. She found him like that just before the place blew up."

"That was it. And the police seemed to take her at her word."

"I risked my life to save him."

"And if he'd still been alive, I'm sure he would have appreciated it."

"She knew."

"I'm sure she did. But there was a lot of commotion and a lot of fire and smoke." Britt was defending the woman.

"The bitch let me go back in there, Jonah. *With* the smoke and the fire."

"Mick. It happened. She was in shock and he was —"

"Dead."

"Yeah. Dead."

The waiter stood by the table. It was the second time tonight, as if he'd just appeared out of nowhere. He cocked his head, as if he wondered about the discussion of the dead. Then the uniformed man picked up the bottle of Charton et Trebuchet Montrachet Grand Cru with its poached pear essence from the ice bucket and refilled the three glasses.

"Three hundred thousand bottles of wine in the cellar, Mick."

Sever nodded. "The famous Graycliff wine cellar. It was a prison at one time. I've had the tour."

"Could be. I just know that every time I'm here, it's the best damned wine I've ever had."

The three of them were quiet for a moment. Sever stared out the window, watching cars drive by in a steady stream. No cop cars.

Britt sipped the white nectar. "Damn, this is good. I was at a party a couple of months ago. Sean Connery rented the cellar dining room and there were about twenty of us. We had some fine wine that night too. But not any better than this."

"Jonah," Rita put her hand on his. "We can't ignore the issue. I know you don't want to talk about it, but there was another fire and another dead body. And it happened next door. And we were right there. It happened. And I don't think it was just coincidental."

"So where does that lead us? Back to the ghost? The Obeah man?"

She stared off into space, not responding to his chiding remark.

"Rita, I'm not denying it happened. I'm not denying there may be a connection. The first thing I thought was let's move. Get the hell off this island. Another fire, another dead body, but we don't know what happened. Not yet."

"And I'm not suggesting that a ghost was involved. But to have the same set of circumstances, a fire and a dead body, right next door, it's just too weird."

Sever sipped his wine. "You've got a better handle on this one?"

"Mick, I know this much. I watched Grant Davis argue with Stretch. On our back porch. They were both obviously stoned, but they were shouting at each other. I didn't hear everything, but enough to know that it was about Davis coming back with the band."

"And you told the cops."

She shook her head. "I did. Adam. Eric's partner."

"Adam Cary. The quiet guy." Britt looked into her face. "And you said that Grant started the fire."

"Jonah, I'm not sure. It looked like he did. I was watching the two of them from the window. It was dark, and like I told Adam, it appeared that Davis tossed a cigarette — his joint, at the house. The next moment the fire exploded."

"And Adam said?" Sever took another swallow of the expensive wine, wanting to appreciate it, but more caught up in the story.

"He said he'd follow up with Grant. He told me the police had questioned him about Teddy Bartholomew's death, and knew where he lived."

Silence again, each of them caught up in the fire and the death.

Sever took another bite of the fish. He chewed it thoughtfully, listening to the talk going on around him. He could pick up strains of conversations, all of it very benign. Nobody else was talking about murder, arson, and the killing of a cop. This was a restaurant for benign conversation. A place to savor the food and the atmosphere. Wasn't happening at this table.

Britt finally broke the silence. "Grant Davis wouldn't hurt a fly. I can't believe that they really think he would kill Teddy Bartholomew."

"Jonah, I saw him throw the cigarette."

"Rita, there's got to be another explanation. I mean, Davis is a goof. He's a little fucked up, but he's harmless. I just don't think he's capable of killing someone."

"What about the argument, between Stretch and Grant Davis?" Sever wanted to push her just a little further. "Davis wanted to come back to the band?"

"And Stretch didn't want him. That was the gist of it."

"You must have heard some of the conversation. You know what it was about."

"When it got loud, I couldn't ignore it. And they were getting loud. Hell, Mick, what I really wanted to do was go back to bed."

Jonah smiled. "But the argument was too good to miss."

"Well—"

"What did you hear? What sticks out in the conversation?"

Rita averted her eyes. She glanced around the room, watching the mixture of tourists and locals enjoying the five-star surroundings. The sound of silver on china, the hushed tones of intimate dialogue.

"Rita, come on."

"Look. I don't know if Grant Davis started the fire. It appeared he did. He tossed the cigarette and the place exploded."

"Hey, it's up to Adam. It's up to the cops to decide that. You just told them what you saw. You had to do that." Sever wanted to keep the interview going.

"Yeah. But—"

He waited. Finally he asked the question. "But what?"

"I told them what I saw. I didn't tell them everything I *heard*."

"Rita," Jonah raised his voice, "quit stalling and tell us. What did you hear that's so mysterious?"

"Grant Davis."

"Davis said something?" Sever could sense it. Something big.

She buried her head in her hands, elbows on the fine white linen table cloth. "Mick, it may not have meant anything. And if I tell the cops this, it could get him in a lot of trouble. Do you know the penalty for murder down here?"

He did. A rope around the neck. "What did he say, Rita?"

"They were arguing, and Grant Davis got really loud and said 'Fuck Eric the cop. I'll deal with him myself.' "

Sever sat back in his chair and reached for his wine. "He said that?"

"What do you think? I'm making it up?" He'd irritated her.

"And it was Grant Davis, not Stretch?"

"I'm positive, Mick. It's the one thing that came across quite clear."

"Say it again."

"He said 'Fuck Eric the cop. I'll deal with him myself.' "

She'd repeated it exactly the same. She was positive.

Jonah hadn't touched another bite. "Jesus, babe, you've got to tell Adam. You've got to tell somebody."

She looked pleadingly at Sever. "Mick, what if it meant nothing?"

"I'm not an attorney, Rita. I don't know what anyone would think. It doesn't convict him, but it sounds like a threat. When somebody refers to a cop saying 'I'll deal with him,' and the cop ends up with his head bashed in, I'm with your husband on this. I think you've got to tell the police."

"I like Grant, Mick. The last time he was here with Johnny Run, we'd sit out on the porch and have some really interesting talks. I mean, when he's not stoned or drunk, he's a pretty nice guy."

Sever gave her a weak smile. "Maybe when he is stoned and drunk, he's not a nice guy."

"Mick," Jonah's hands were balled into tight fists. "Maybe Davis really wanted his job back. He wanted to be the manager of Johnny Run."

"I don't doubt that he did."

"And the one way to get that job back was to get rid of Bartholomew."

"It would help."

"And when the cops got suspicious, he had to get rid of one of the cops."

Sever threw up his hands. "It's as plausible as any other explanation. But you just said that Grant Davis couldn't kill anyone."

"I still don't think that he could. But I think it's important to at least tell Adam what we know. What Rita heard. Agreed?"

"Agreed."

"Boys," Rita was watching the lobby where a cigar maker handrolled Graycliff cigars and placed the prestigious label on each of them, "now might be a good time."

Sever looked at her across the table. "A good time for what?"

"To tell Adam."

Sever turned his head and watched the tall, skinny officer walking quickly toward their table, a very determined look on his face.

CHAPTER FORTY-FOUR

"No one was killed in the fire." Britt pointed at the house.

"No one was killed *because* of the fire. But the cop may have been killed while the fire was burning."

"True. But Etta May and the kid—" Britt let the comment hang.

Standing on Britt's front porch, Sever studied the small block house. Following an after-dinner interview at the station, they had a little more information about the fire. And the apparent murder of a police officer. And, a story that shook even Sever, who often thought he was unshakeable. The supposed murder of Stretch Cunningham. All in one night. Even the cops seemed somewhat overwhelmed.

"And the inside is supposedly not too bad. Smoke, but no fire damage." Britt had seen what fire damage could do to a structure. To his structure. Burn it to the ground.

At the station Adam had told them it was the gas and the shrubs and trees that caused the smoke and flames. The house didn't suffer much damage. And that made sense. The structure was made of cement with a tile roof. Not exactly the kind of materials that burst into flame.

"You saved her life, Mick." Rita stood beside them, surveying the damage. The trees were nothing more than charred stumps, the bushes, flowers, and crotons were ashes, burned to the ground. The blackened earth that surrounded the house seemed to follow the pattern of the poured fuel.

"I think Etta May is too tough to die." Sever reached down with his hand and put pressure on his bad knee. The pain was real. He'd put that leg through hell in the last twenty-four hours.

"God, I hope I didn't get Grant in trouble."

"Rita, he said what he said. And you saw the fire start from his cigarette."

"I know, I know. But I keep thinking there's another explanation."

A night bird called, insects were chirping, and up the road the Wyndham Crystal Palace Casino was bustling, he was sure. Howie Mandel, the comedian and game-show host was putting on a show, and the tourists had packed the theater. The event was sold out. And only a handful of people cared that a cop had been killed early this morning. A musician had been killed in the alley, just a couple hundred yards from here. Other than that, things were back to normal. Human life was expendable. A friend of Sever's, Bobby Vane, a big guy who managed bands, used to say humans were *expandable*. Of course Bobby Vane weighed about four hundred pounds.

A lone figure walked up the hill, long dreadlocks swinging around his head. He gave the group a wave. In the fading light, Sever recognized Sonny, the drummer. He walked up to the porch and joined them in their viewing.

"Thank God it didn't happen here. At the studio."

Everyone nodded.

He was quiet. Finally, "The thing with Stretch. What's that all about?"

Sever the reporter turned his attention from the little house. He had a story to write. It was time to ask questions, not answer them. "What exactly did you hear?"

"Somebody killed him on that path, that alley back there." Sonny pointed behind the studio.

"Who told you?"

"I don't know. I was having breakfast across the street and somebody mentioned it. It really freaked me out."

"We didn't learn until dinner when a cop came in and told us," Rita said.

"They called me and the guys into the station about an hour after I heard. Questioned us for another hour. Did you guys deal with the tall, skinny dude?"

"Yeah. Adam. He was Eric's partner, the cop who died in the house." Britt frowned. "You know we've had three deaths in three days. I can't wrap my mind around it."

Sonny tugged on the thick braids. "Well anyway, I told them what I knew."

"And what was that?" Sever, mentally writing it all down.

"We had a talk with Grant Davis last night — early this morning."

"We?"

"Stretch and me."

"At Compass Point?"

"Yeah."

"About what?"

"It was no secret. He wanted to manage us again. And Stretch and I both knew that the cops were looking at him as possibly being involved in the death of Teddy Bartholomew."

Sever pressed on. "So that's what your conversation was about?"

"It was."

"And what was the result of your talk."

"Stretch and I had told the cops that he was sniffing around for his job. We told them that Grant wanted to be our manager again, and was almost begging for the position. And they let us in on a little piece of information. They found his fingerprints in the old Cadillac."

Sever shifted his gaze to the junk heap. The fire hadn't done any damage to it, not that anyone would ever notice. Hell, *his* fingerprints were in the car. Everyone's fingerprints were in that bucket of bolts. Maybe the King's. "So that's all you talked about?"

Sonny took a deep breath and held if for a moment. Then he slowly let it out, buying time while he framed the answer. "I don't know if I'm supposed to tell anyone this. But what the hell. First of all, Grant wanted to talk with the cops. He wanted to come over here and talk to Eric, and convince him that he had nothing to do with Teddy's murder. And, I mean, he wanted to come over at three a.m., wake him up, and tell him. The guy was frantic. He was afraid they were going to arrest him and no one would ever hear from him again. He kept saying he had to get it straight with the cops."

Rita's eyes were wide. "So he did want to take care of Eric. That's what he meant. He wanted to make his case and clear himself?"

"Yeah. Exactly." Sonny gave her a quizzical look.

The four of them stood on the porch as the light faded, the smell of dirty smoke and soot still in the air. Sever tried to sort the players in his mind. It wasn't easy.

"Davis was afraid of being charged for murder. He kept telling me that he didn't trust the Bahama legal system," Sonny said.

"So that was the extent of your conversation?" Sever knew there had to be more.

"No. He was really upset with Stretch. He felt that Stretch had never given him a break, and he was afraid that Stretch was going to lobby to keep him out of the band. Stretch left, walked out on the conversation. Grant stuck around and kept pushing me to talk to Stretch and get him to change his mind."

"Was Stretch out to get him?"

"Yeah. He really was. Didn't like Grant at all. Truth is, Mr. Sever, we weren't going to hire Grant back. He didn't have a prayer. It wasn't just Stretch, because Stretch never liked anything. He was sour on the band, on our staff — on life in general."

"You don't sound like you're too broken up about Stretch Cunningham's death."

Sonny Tatone closed his eyes for a moment and massaged his temples with his index fingers. "I'm not. I mean, I'll miss him in the band, but I think he was going to leave anyway. And to be perfectly honest, Stretch was a pain in the ass. I'm not going to really miss him, and that bothers me."

Sever knew the story. Just because four guys got together for music and a career didn't mean they bonded like brothers. And even brothers didn't get along all the time. It was strictly business.

The police car eased into the parking lot, surprising them. Adam and a new black partner stepped out and approached the porch.

"Evening, officer." Britt stuck out his hand.

They'd seen the man earlier in the evening when he'd approached them in the restaurant. Walked right up to them and told them that the body of Marcus Cunningham had been found behind the studio. Wanted to know if they knew anything about his death. Wanted to know who wanted him dead, because they'd reached their conclusion. Marcus "Stretch" Cunningham had been bludgeoned to death. A clear case of murder, and Adam let them know he was getting a little tired of the murders that were happening in and around the studio.

The officer had said it point blank, in the restaurant, before he asked them to come down to the station. "Mr. Britt, we have an unidentified body from the original fire at your studio. We have the murder of Theodore Bartholomew just three days ago. We have the suspected murder of officer Eric Evans and the murder of an American musician, Marcus Cunningham. We need some answers, and we need them fast."

Britt and the assembled had not been able to give them any answers. Rita had told him that it appeared Grant Davis set the fire. That was the only thing she shared.

"Evening, Mr. Britt." The officer shook his hand and took off his hat. "A couple of new things we need to talk to you about."

Britt motioned him to have a seat, and the officer and his associate sat down. Rita and Sonny stood at a distance while Sever pulled up a chair. He invited himself to the party. It was the only way to get the full story, and the story just got better and better. *Newsweek* was going to be so glad they'd hired him for this assignment.

Sever, Rita, and Jonah had all gone to the station, and Sever had been fingerprinted. They'd been questioned and then dismissed. Now, there was new information and that had to be good for the story. Bad for the cops. Bad for Britt and Rita, but this was going to make one hell of a read.

Britt sat down next to Adam the cop. "What's the problem now? More dead bodies?"

"No. Thank God." He folded his hands in front of him and stared hard at Britt. "What do you know about Grant Davis?"

"Davis? You probably know what I do. He was the manager for a band that's recording here." Even though the police had interviewed the band, Britt was sure this local cop had no idea who Johnny Run was, "and—"

"'Pullin Out The Stops,' 'Rip It Up,' I know the band well, Mr. Britt." He nodded briefly at Sonny. "And we've had the band in the station already today."

Britt was surprised. The guy knew his music.

"But I'm more interested in what Mr. Davis was doing here. On the island. Mr. Tatone has already told me that Davis was making overtures to get his job back. Had you talked to him at all?"

"No."

"So you can't verify why he was here? He never approached you about a job, the band, or anything else?"

"I have not said one word to the man since he's been on the island."

Sever spoke up. "What's Grant Davis got to do with the death of Stretch Cunningham?"

Adam glanced at his partner. "Can we tell them?"

"Sure. Why not? Maybe they know his whereabouts."

"What can you tell us?"

Adam frowned. "We need to find Mr. Davis. Quickly. Do you have any idea where he is?"

"No idea."

"We checked his room, and he's not there. We have to find him. It's imperative."

"You still think he may have killed Teddy Bartholomew?" Britt looked puzzled.

"We do. We also think he may have had something to do with the death of my partner and friend, Eric Evans."

Sever took the mental note. Technology on the island may lack something, but it didn't take the cops long to start putting pieces to-gether. Rita had given Adam the information on the fire, so they must have been working on Davis as their lead suspect.

"And we have his fingerprints on the weapon that was used to kill Marcus Cunningham."

"What?" Britt was taken back.

"The weapon used to kill Marcus Cunningham."

"You're saying that Grant Davis murdered Stretch Cunning-ham? He hasn't got it in him."

"We believe otherwise, Mr. Britt."

"Fingerprints on a weapon?" Sever questioned the officer.

"There's no question, Mr. Sever. Mr. Cunningham was killed with a rock. A boulder, and Grant Davis's fingerprints are on the boulder. In blood."

Sever shuddered. In blood. As gruesome as the image was, it was going to be a must-read story. The kind of story that won awards.

"With the possibilities of three murder charges on Grant Davis, I sincerely hope none of you is giving us erroneous information. And I hope that none of you is keeping his location a secret. Harboring a fugitive is a very serious crime in the Bahamas. Especially if that fugi-tive is a murderer."

They looked at each other, the reporter, the drummer, the pro-ducer, and his wife. Finally Rita spoke up.

"None of us knows where Grant is. We've shared everything we know with you. It's just a very strange situation. As you know, we're just trying to recover from the fire that destroyed our old studio. The fire and the dead body they found in the ruins. And now we have three murders and another fire next door. With all of this going against us, do you really think we would, as you put it, harbor a fugi-tive?"

"Mrs. Britt."

"Don't 'Mrs. Britt' me, Mr. Cary." The bitterness rolled off her tongue. "This is extremely unnerving and for you to sit there and basically threaten us is something I won't stand for."

"I'm not suggesting—"

"Yes you are. From the time our studio burned to the ground, you and your friend have given us a rough time. You act as if we planned these fires and deaths as a way to keep you busy."

Sever pushed his chair back a little in case the fireworks exploded in his direction.

"Rita," Britt put his hand over hers, "it's okay. It's been a rough day for everybody."

Sever could see a tremor in her arm. She restrained herself, and the tall cop stood up.

"I thank you for your time. Please understand that this has not been an easy time for me, either. Eric and I were good friends, and we have been partners for a long time. I was to be best man at his wedding."

"His wedding?" Sever and Britt said it at the same time, looking at each other with surprise.

"Yes. He was going to announce his engagement to Etta May Albertson in just a few days."

CHAPTER FORTY-FIVE

Over a double Jack and Coke he tried to remember the name of the club. Sitting in the dingy little bar, knocking back his bourbon and cola, he tried to retrace his steps. What the hell was the name of that place?

The gangster with the sleeveless tee behind the bar ignored him as he lifted the glass to his lips. Davis concentrated. Some girl had invited him to the place, just a couple of days ago. And it was this big room with couches and a cement floor, but for the life of him he couldn't remember the name. And it could be the life of him. What he remembered was the bartender. The guy had tried to sell him a gun, and right now that sounded like a good idea. Having a gun.

Some kind of security. The cops were after him, and he had a hunch that the syndicate was after him, too, and he still wasn't sure why.

Davis concentrated harder, then swallowed a slug of the dark beverage. Sometimes when he drank he remembered everything quite clearly. Sometimes he didn't. What the hell was the name of the club?

He still had almost $2,000 in cash stuffed in his jeans, and a gun, even an under-the-counter weapon, couldn't cost more than four or five hundred bucks. And he had a return ticket to New York. And speaking of return tickets, he figured the authorities probably had the word out at the airport. He'd never be able to leave under his own name. It just seemed important to get a gun. He was in a foreign country, and the cops were looking for him. They had evidence on two crimes that he'd never committed. He was in a foreign country, and there was a syndicate that was trying to distance themselves from him. And in the process, they may decide to blow him away.

What was that club?

This had all started when he brought Johnny Run to Highland Studios over a year ago. When he'd agreed to let some washed-up hack producer engineer the session. It had all started when he smoked a joint with some idiot kid in an old, beat-up Cadillac and left his fingerprints on the car. Maybe you had to start at the beginning. Maybe that was where he should go. Go back to the studio. Get that kid to admit he had been in the car over a year ago. Get Jonah Britt to stand up for him, and convince the cops that he didn't need to be arrested and locked up. Start at the beginning. Then get on the first plane out of here and never, never, ever come back. This god-forsaken island and everything on it could burn to the ground and it wouldn't bother him at all.

He pushed five bucks across the bar and the muscular man with graffiti tattooed up and down his arms poured two fingers of Jack with a splash of Coke into a new glass. He never once looked at Davis, and there wasn't another soul in the entire bar.

"Hey."

The man had moved to the other end of the counter and was washing glasses.

"Hey, do you know the club in town where the young people go? Couches, cement floor, really popular?" Unlike this hole in the wall.

"Why?"

This guy would probably understand. "Because the bartender offered to sell me a gun."

"You can't buy a gun on this island."

Oh, shit. Never should have mentioned it.

"Never mind."

The thug walked down the length of the bar, now staring directly at Davis. More trouble. More bad news.

"You want a gun?"

He nodded, afraid for his safety, afraid for his life.

The big man reached behind him, yanking something from the waistband of his pants. "Here. You want to buy a gun, give me five hundred dollars. And don't say nothin' to nobody. Got it?"

"Yes, sir. I've got it." He pulled five one hundred dollar bills from his pocket and put them on the stained bar top.

The bartender pushed the gun to him and Davis picked it up, surprised at its weight. Solid. "Got bullets?"

"How many you gonna need?"

He didn't know and he shrugged his shoulders.

"There's eight in the clip. You need any more than that you're on your own."

Davis nodded. He never wanted to look like a rookie, so he jammed the pistol in his waistband and pulled his shirt over it. Taking another mouthful of whiskey, he decided to get a cab. Confront the situation head on. Meet with the kid, meet with Jonah Britt. Damn, it was time to clear the air and put some distance between him and these problems. He gulped the last of the drink, feeling it race through his veins, and walked to the door, a little wobbly, a little lightheaded. That would pass.

"Fluid." The bartender directed it at him.

"I'm sorry? What did you say?"

"Fluid. Name of the bar where the guy tried to sell you a gun."

CHAPTER FORTY-SIX

Samuel Albertson searched through the drawers. He'd helped Mom all he could. All he would. And somewhere in her dresser was a pistol. He'd seen Eric Evans give it to her. Told her it was for her own safety, to keep those musicians and their drugs away.

He'd given her a gun, and Samuel wanted it. He wanted a little safety of his own. The cops were digging again, and he was afraid that this time, they just might stumble on the truth. God, he hoped she hadn't put it in her purse.

He pulled out a second drawer, and a third. Everything smelled like creosote, like burned rubber or tar.

Was the ghost hanging around? Laughing at him? Or was that son of a bitch twin, Bernard, watching him? His charred spirit, back from the fire, envious of Samuel's role in all of this?

Was the ghost of Bernard aware that he'd been setup? Was he aware that mother and brother had decided to take care of two problems at once? Destroy the den of iniquity and the crazy twin at the same time. He probably knew. Samuel believed that from the grave there came an ability to see everything clearly for the first time. But this was Bernard. Bernard the burnout, and even in death, even as a ghost he was probably over at the studio, lounging in Rita Britt's bedroom, waiting for her to come in and take off her clothes. Bernard was better off as the ghost, because as a living, breathing human being, he had been a waste.

Samuel walked to the small closet in his mother's bedroom and ran his hand up on the high shelf. Feeling something heavy and metallic he jumped, catching it with his fingers. It was the gun. Why the hell she'd put it up there he had no idea. Hell, she couldn't reach it up there. And as he pulled it down, the piles of cash came tumbling down with it.

There must have been fifty stacks of hundreds. $50,000? He couldn't take his eyes off of it. Enough to move out of this cracker box and get the hell off the island. Get away from his mother's insecurities, her crazy stories about the car, and get away from the ghost. He stared at the money spilled onto the floor. When had his crazy old lady put away fifty grand? The bills were old, musty, and smelled like smoke. He bet they still spent. Merchants would still take those bills in exchange for products and services. Old money was still money.

He shook his head, unable to fathom his good fortune. He'd managed to squirrel away just over fifteen hundred bucks. Five hundred bucks just from the guitar that he stole from Highland Studios. The one he forged the signature on. Hard Rock thought that was a steal. He'd thought it would tide him over until he could get off the island and find work. But now, this windfall put a whole new spin on things.

For the moment, the cops were looking for Grant Davis. They were blaming the murder of Theodore Bartholomew on Davis. And Samuel knew better. They were blaming the murder of Eric Evans on Davis. And Samuel had been standing not ten feet from his mother when Eric the cop accused her of stealing his keys and breaking and entering the studio next door. He'd turned to Samuel, his mouth hanging open in surprise. He'd finally figured it out, but never figured out that Etta May could do that much damage to his skull with the flat side of a hammer.

And finally, they were even blaming the death of the bass player back in the alley on Grant Davis. And the funny thing was, Samuel had no idea who Grant Davis was. He'd never met him. And this guy was taking all the heat. Thank you, Grant Davis.

But now, he had to get off the island. Before they figured out that Davis *hadn't* killed Teddy Bartholomew. Before they figured out that Davis *hadn't* bashed in Eric Evans's head. Before they realized who started the fire next door, and before they realized that the ghost was really who Samuel *pretended* to be. The evil, sick, twisted twin. The crazy motherfucker who drove him nuts. Drove his mother nuts. And sooner or later, they *would* figure it out. They'd understand that Samuel was really Samuel and that lives and property had been destroyed by his mother and him. He didn't want to sit around and wait for that to happen.

Samuel grabbed a shoe box from the floor of his mother's closet, dumped the scuffed flat shoes from the container, and stuffed the money inside. A gun and fifty grand. He could take a mail boat, escape to one of the islands until things calmed down, then fly to the States on a small charter plane. It should be easy. With $50,000, anything was possible. Sorry, Mom.

He threw the shoebox into his small suitcase, stuck the small pistol in his pocket, and walked out of the bedroom. She wouldn't be back for an hour or so and he could put plenty of distance between them. Get a taxi, take a mail boat from Potter's Cay Dock and go to Norman's Cay. He had a friend there who would hide him for a while. The nice thing about the Bahamas was you could have it anyway you wanted. Plenty of places to disappear.

He heard the footsteps as someone walked up the steps. Damn. Mom was home. He tossed the suitcase into the closet and walked into the tiny living area. Someone was pounding on the door. That wasn't Mom. He walked to the door, hesitated, then opened it.

"Hey, man. You are exactly the person I came to see."

Samuel looked at him, into his face and up and down. "Do I know you?"

"Man, I hope you do. I've been in some deep shit because of you."

Guy was crazy. Samuel started to close the door, but the little guy pushed right past him.

"We've got to talk."

"No, we don't."

"Bernard, I smoked a joint with you about fifteen months ago. In the old car out there. Now the cops have my fingerprints from that piece of junk, and they think I've been involved in a couple of murders. I need you to stand up for me, man. Tell them that you and I shared a joint way back when."

Christ. It was Grant Davis.

"Look, I've got an important appointment and I've got to —"

"No." Davis grabbed him by the shoulders. "You're the first person I'm coming to, and you're not going to ignore me. My life is on the line here, and I need you to deal with the cops. Do you understand?" The man's eyes were bloodshot and dilated. He was either high or drunk. Samuel guessed both.

Samuel felt the fingers digging into his skin. "Let go of me. I don't have time for you right now." He pushed at Davis, but the wiry guy held on tight.

"I'm not begging, I'm telling you. You and I need to go to the cops right now. Without your testimony, I'm in a lot of trouble."

"Mr. Davis —"

"You *do* know who I am." He grinned and let go of Samuel.

"And I don't —"

Davis reached behind his back and pulled out the gun. In less than a second, the grin went to a leer and the barrel was three inches from Samuel's face. "Bernard, you're coming with me."

Samuel put his hands in the air. "Okay, okay. You can put the gun down."

Davis lowered the pistol as Samuel yanked his own from his pocket. God, he thought, if you really are watching out for me, let there be a bullet in the chamber. He pulled the trigger and the explosion and recoil surprised him, kicking him back into the lone chair in the room. When he looked up, Davis was standing there, his gun hanging from his hand.

"You didn't have to do that." The eyes glazed over and blood mottled on the man's shirt, quickly soaking the fabric. Grant Davis collapsed on the spot. Somebody was watching out for Samuel. Thank God.

CHAPTER FORTY-SEVEN

"Someone got to him before we did." Adam Cary watched the medics cover the body with a thin sheet.

Etta May sobbed in the corner, wiping at her eyes that had to see the blood spattered carpet where the body had rested.

"Davis had a gun in his hand." Sever wasn't aware if it had been fired or not.

"You saw it, Mr. Sever."

He had seen it. He'd been the first one in, and whoever killed Grant Davis had already left. If it had been the kid, he must have pulled the trigger and run, because there was no sign of anyone. "So if Bernard shot him, it was self-defense."

"We're not there yet, sir. There is a lot of investigating to be done."

Sever nodded. And it would probably be much like the investigation of the fire next door. They'd never get to the bottom of it. Britt stood by his side inside the tiny living room, clenching his hands.

"Jesus, Mick. What kind of a story are you going to write now? This thing is so far out of whack, I mean, I'd be surprised if another artist would ever come over here to record."

"You're a wizard, Jonah. They'll come because you're damned good at what you do. That alone will sell the studio. And, that's the angle I'm going to take."

They walked out of the tiny house, forty steps to the front porch of the studio. "I have to admit, this has been the most intense week I've ever spent on a story." Sever lowered himself into a chair.

"That's not exactly reassuring."

"Grant Davis. What a disaster."

Britt ran his hands through his shaggy hair. "A one-man wrecking crew. I never would have guessed it. Apparently he caught Bartholomew smoking in the Caddy and decided to kill him. He thought he'd get his job back by eliminating the competition."

"Apparently."

"And apparently he knew enough about the ghost theory that he dug out the eyes. Trying to reinforce the idea that the ghost was trying to eliminate sound and vision."

Sever grimaced. It hurt his eyes to think about it.

"He freaked out when he heard that the cops found his fingerprints in the car and decided to kill Eric Evans."

"Any chance we could get a drink?" Sever needed one. The scenario just didn't seem to work.

"Sure. Scotch?"

Britt walked into the building, and Sever took a deep breath and stared at the sky. The stars were just starting to punch their way through the encroaching darkness. "Starlight, star bright, first star I've seen tonight." What to wish for? Get off this island, away from the smoke and the blood. Get this story written and move on with his life. No. Wish for a successful comeback for the Britts. There was a good wish. Although the events of the last four days weren't going to help.

"Here you go, man." Britt walked back out, handed Sever a Scotch and water, and put a rum drink in front of himself.

"Jonah, you haven't mentioned the keys. The ones they found on her nightstand. Those were your keys and your passcode?"

Britt shrugged. "We were stupid."

"What do you mean?"

"I talked to Rita and we finally remembered who had a duplicate."

"You said no one had a duplicate."

Britt buried his chin in his chest and looked at the ground. "Mick, I feel dumber than shit. I clearly gave the keys and security code to someone else."

"Who?"

"Eric Evans. The cop."

"You're kidding?"

"No."

"Why?"

"Because he asked. And because when you are in the Bahamas, you do what you're told. If the authorities tell you they need something, you do it."

"Why the hell would he need your keys?"

"He was over here a lot, Mick. I'd be back in the studio with the headphones on, and it was just easier for Evans to let himself in. When he needed to talk to me, he'd just unlock the door and come in. Once in a while he'd check up on the studio for us. I never thought about it at the time. But now — listen, I know it doesn't make any sense, but the fact remains he had the keys and code."

"But why would you give your keys to anyone at all?" Sever grew up in a bad part of Chicago. And even in the good part where he now lived, you didn't pass out keys or security codes.

"Because we used to give them to *everyone*. Open-door policy. It used to be one big happy family, Mick. An endless party. And it *was* a party, my friend. Oftentimes twenty-four seven." Britt raised his head, and looked at Sever through his tired, bloodshot eyes. "So when a cop, a cop for God's sake, asked for the keys, I guess we thought that was a pretty safe bet."

Safe? With drugs in the building and a cop with the keys, it didn't sound safe to Sever. And the Britts had totally forgotten they'd given the keys to Eric Evans. "Yeah. The party days are over, Jonah."

"The truth be told, I'm getting too old for that shit, Mick. These last few days have worn me out."

"You don't believe that Eric broke into your studio and did all that damage?"

"Why would a cop mess with us? It could have been Etta May or Bernard 'borrowing' the keys."

"Good point. Etta May was trying to run you out, Jonah. Someone was constantly messing with your studio and maybe that was supposed to intimidate you."

"You think Etta May borrowed Eric's keys?"

"I do. Or one of the kids. I'd bet on it. They'd come over here, break a guitar, steal some drugs, erase a recording session. It was a subtle attempt to drive you away."

"And it almost worked."

"And what if," he was jumping to conclusions, but the situation seemed to call for it, "what if Eric found out that Etta May and the boys were borrowing the keys?"

Jonah picked it up. "He'd be pissed. And he'd figure out that they were the ones terrorizing us."

"So to save herself and her kid —"

"She beat Eric over the head?"

"Hey. While we're busy solving crime, we may as well solve them all."

"Mick, she hated us. Accused us of fucking up Bernard. She blamed us for the kid's mental state. As you know, she's not the sanest person on the island. And regarding her kids, you know, I saw that Bernard everyday, him and his brother, and I would swear that he was pretty much normal for the last year or so. So I don't know why she was so adamant about the damage we were supposedly doing. The kid was a whole lot better this last year than he ever had been."

They were quiet, watching as another cop car pulled into the lot. Maybe forensics. But Sever questioned whether they had a forensic squad in Nassau. "I don't think Davis killed Teddy Bartholomew either."

"No?"

"He had a reason. Get rid of the manager so he could take over. But Tommie saw what appeared to be two people smoking joints in the car, and my bet is that one of them was Bernard."

"And if it was Bernard?"

"I sincerely think Etta May could have come out and strangled Bartholomew."

Britt threw up his hands. "Jesus, Mick, I can't keep it straight. I doubt if we'll ever know who killed him."

The two men sipped their drinks and Sever thought about the plan to put Highland out of business. "So, if you had to guess, who started the fire?"

"Which one?"

"Let's start with yours."

"It would be a guess."

"Guess."

"Etta May. Or Bernard. Or Samuel."

"And if it was Etta May, if she tried to burn you out, she had access to the entire investigation."

"Hell yes, she was sleeping with the investigator. That crossed my mind. She was glued to Eric every day he was over here. I believe that's one reason she got so close to him. The reason she started dating him."

"And the ghost? The dead body?"

"We'll never know, Mick. I was sure it was the person who started the fire and got caught in their own inferno. But now, I don't know."

"Who started the fire over there?" He pointed at the scorched little house.

"The official line is Grant Davis. Because if the cops are right and Davis killed Eric Evans, he was trying to destroy the cop's body in the fire."

"God, it gets confusing. The cops will eventually sort it out." Sever slid lower in his chair, wondering when it would all end.

"They'll never get it right, Mick. Never."

"Here's to better times, Jonah. Here's to a new life for Highland Studios." They touched glasses and took another drink.

CHAPTER FORTY-EIGHT

He stepped onto the mailboat, pulling his cap down low. Maybe fifteen people got on with him and he avoided eye contact with all of
them. Hiding behind the big sunglasses, he eased himself down on a
hard wooden bench and closed his eyes. He could get a short nap in
on the ride to Norman's Cay.

Someone would find the van down at Compass Point. The
sisters would know he'd taken it, but you couldn't really steal a car in
Nassau. It had to turn up somewhere on the island. He felt somewhat
guilty, just walking out, but his entire mission, his entire plan had
fallen apart at the end, and he needed to walk away from it.

There were no future plans. For six months, ever since he
worked out the logical conclusion that the lady and her children had
been behind the horrific fire, his entire life had been consumed with
seeking revenge on the house of Etta May, and now —

"Excuse me."

The young man with the small suitcase brushed against him as
he sat down on the bench. Baron moved to the right, giving the man
more room. He peered at him from under the brim of his hat. Peered
a second time, then a third. Bernard. Or Samuel. One of the Albertson twins. There was absolutely no question. Going to Norman's Cay.
Miracle of miracles. Another chance for revenge had just been
dropped in his lap. A golden opportunity. Baron hoped the kid had
some cash with him, because he was seriously low on funds.

CHAPTER FORTY-NINE

"We could have driven you to the airport, Mick."

"You've got a session. And Rita has to feed the band."

"Yeah. Don't even know who these guys are, but we'll do our best."

"It's going to happen, Jonah. You're going to bounce back." He tossed his suitcase into the trunk of the cab and got into the backseat. "Thanks for everything."

"When are we going to read about ourselves?"

"I'm guessing it will be four or five weeks for the feature." He'd been filing almost daily on the breaking news surrounding the band, the studio, and the murders.

The driver backed out, easing onto the road. Sever glanced at the small soot-covered house with Elvis's Cadillac prominently displayed outside. Etta May stepped out onto her tiny porch, and Sever blinked. She had a colorful dress on, made of what appeared to be a course fabric. The identical pattern of the voodoo doll dress. The voodoo doll with the pins in her eyes.